A SHIFT
IN THE
AIR

PATRICIA D. EDDY

If you love sexy romantic suspense, I'd love to send you a short story set in Dublin, Ireland. Castles & Kings isn't available anywhere except for readers who sign up for my mailing list! Sign up for my newsletter on my website and tell me where to send your free book!
http://patriciadeddy.com.

PROLOGUE

Seventeen Years Ago

Caitlin

*W*aves crashed against the jutting rocks below, but Caitlin didn't mind. A bit of spray tickled her calves, and the water sparkled like diamonds in the summer sun.

"Come see!" she yelled, tossing a glance over her shoulder at her best friend. The boy she'd fallen in love with—not that she knew what love was at only seventeen—gave her a shy smile as he sauntered over.

Two years older, with a hint of stubble lining his jaw, Fergus always snuck off with Caitlin after her daily lessons and chores were through. They'd steal moments among the ruins of the old castle outside of town or at the edge of the cliffs, laughing and practicing their charms—he with earth and she with air.

When he sat next to her and linked their fingers, she pecked his cheek, then pulled away quickly. Her mother was too close to risk anything more.

From a hillside overlooking the bluffs, Caitlin's mum worked the land, occasionally using her air charms to help her move piles of rocks or bits of dirt as she dug the hoe into the soil.

The winds had a life of their own not far from the Cliffs of Moher, swirling and snapping like an animal caught in a snare, and Caitlin wove a charm of her own to protect her and her teenage crush from the onslaught.

Mum's lips tightened, a hint of disapproval pinching her features, and Caitlin sat up a little straighter. She knew she wasn't supposed to work her charms out in the open. Elementals were rare, and her mum had told her story after story of those with earth, air, fire, or water being targeted, hunted even.

But whenever Caitlin mentioned those tales to Fergus, he laughed them off and told her they were just stories parents used to keep their children from showing off.

Hadn't she earned the right to make her own decisions by now? She was seventeen. Almost an adult. Almost ready to set out on her own, maybe somewhere far from Doolin. Maybe somewhere with the handsome boy at her side.

"Ye're the prettiest girl in all of Ireland," Fergus whispered in her ear.

Caitlin blushed and met his gaze. His jaw had strengthened in the two years he'd been away in Scotland, and he was no longer a boy. No. Not at all. He'd grown into a man, and yet he was still here. Still interested in the likes of her.

"I'm not," Caitlin said as a blush warmed her cheeks. She was too thin, though her mum insisted she'd soon grow into her body. Her sky blue eyes and full lips were passable, but she hated the freckles across her nose and cheeks.

Fergus squeezed her hand. "I can't live without ya', Caitie. I didn't want to move to Scotland. I thought about ya' every day. Waitin' for yer letters was torture. But I learned so much studyin' there. I want to share all of it with ya'."

"Really?" A wide smile curved her lips, and Caitlin hid it in her cupped hands, hoping Fergus wouldn't think her foolish for being so...girly. "I missed ya' so much. No one else understands me."

"Not even yer mum?"

Caitlin shook her head, her reddish-brown curls bouncing in the wind. "She wants me to stay in Doolin forever. There's a whole world out there," she said, flinging her arms out to sweep over the restless waters. "We could go anywhere, yeah?"

"Anywhere." His hazel eyes danced as he chuckled. "London's nice. So is Glasgow. What do ya' think?"

"I want to go somewhere new. Exciting. Somewhere I can use my charms and not have to worry all the time."

Fergus beamed. "There are so many places we could go. I'll take ya' to London. Paris too. Barcelona. Even America."

"But...how will you fly?" she asked. Earth elementals were tied to the land, and her mum had told her few—if any—ever left the place of their birth. It was too hard for them to be on a plane.

"I have a secret," he said as he brought her hand to his lips and brushed a kiss to her knuckles. "A way we can be together anywhere. A way I can fly and not have to worry."

The tethers that bound Caitlin to Ireland, to Doolin, and to her mother started to unravel, and she felt so free. Outside of this place, she'd be able to soar, her element unchecked by the harsh restrictions the local community imposed: no charms in view of humans and no fraternization with werewolves, fae, or practitioners—witches.

"When can we leave?" Caitlin asked.

"Soon." Fergus's warm breath tickled her cheek. "I learned a special charm in Scotland. One very few people have ever been strong enough to try. It requires two elementals who love each other very much, and trust completely. Ya' trust me, yeah, Caitie?" At her nod, he continued. "We could make it work. We'd each hold a piece of the other forever, and yer air would strengthen me. Let me do...so much."

Caitlin chewed on her lip and cast a quick glance back at her mother, finding her distracted. She took Fergus's hands and held on tight. "Yer sure it's safe?"

Eyes dark, despite the bright summer sun, Fergus nodded. "I'm sure. We'd be bound together, and nothing could ever tear us apart."

"I want that," Caitlin said as a strange warmth filled her belly. "Forever."

She felt so safe with Fergus. He was different. His earth element thrummed with power, and he always used his charms to make her laugh and keep her safe. She didn't fear being at the edge of the cliff. Between his earth and her air, she'd never fall.

"Then let's do it," he said. "I'll have a part of yer element. The charm will keep us closer than two people have ever been. I'd be stronger than any other elemental in the world, and I'll protect ya' forever."

"Would I have part of your element too?" Caitlin asked.

A shadow passed across Fergus's face as a bird soared over-head. Caitlin tracked the flight, waiting for the boy she loved to answer her. But he leaned in, cupping her cheeks and kissing her, and she forgot she'd even asked the question.

Eleven Years Ago

Liam

CAITLIN STEPPED OFF THE CURB, brown hair blowing in the breeze. Liam's arm snaked around her waist, and he pulled her against him.

"Careful, luv. Dublin's a bit busy at rush hour, yeah?"

A bus rumbled by, the double-decker yellow and blue

monstrosity careening through the space Caitlin had occupied only seconds before.

"Feckin' buses." She relaxed against him, but Liam could feel her heart pounding. "Though this is nice."

Liam frowned. Her voice held a hint of pain, desperation. Was it the near miss? Or something else?

His wolf stirred inside of him, begging to stake his claim on the slight woman in his arms. She smelled like spring rain and fig blossoms, and Liam could lose himself in her scent. She was his mate. His wolf knew it, but the man? The man understood humans didn't think in those terms. And his Caitlin was no wolf. The full moon was less than a week away, and he had to figure out how to tell her.

Despite his confidence, his love for her, and the intense need that pulsed through him whenever they were close, he still balked at saying the words.

The ache of the mating call stiffened his muscles, settling deep within his bones. Mating was as much physical as emotional, and his parents had once described the experience as a pull so strong, you felt it with every breath. Until now, he hadn't believed them.

Caitlin turned in his arms, and Liam pressed a kiss to her temple. "It's gettin' cold. Would ya' like a coffee? Or we could go to the pub?"

"I'm peckish," she said. "Let's find a pub." They'd scarcely taken two steps when Caitlin shuddered. "No. Not now. Not again." The horror in her voice riled his wolf, and when she stumbled, bracing her hand on a postal box, Liam tried to help her up, but she flinched and pulled away.

"What is it, luv?"

Her blue eyes clouded over, silver flecks flaring to life, and she took two steps back. "I can't go with ya', Liam. I have to get out of here. Right now. Run. As far and as fast as I can."

"What? We've had such a time of it these past two weeks. I thought ya' were plannin' on stayin' with me. I want ya' to stay."

The previous night, they'd kissed on Ha'penny Bridge as the stars glittered on water as still as glass. The gentle caress of her fingers along his cheek and the raw desire churning in her eyes... had he mistaken it?

"I can't. I'm sorry. This was a mistake."

Liam's eyes narrowed. "A mistake?" Frustration set his wolf on edge. A visceral need to claim her and keep her safe had him clenching his hands into fists.

Caitlin cringed as a growl rasped from Liam's throat. She left the scent of fig blossoms in her wake as she darted back.

"Please, Liam. Don't be angry with me. I can explain. Quickly. And then I have to go." She kept a foot of distance between them even as he stepped forward, and Liam froze.

"Luv, are ya' scared of me?" He towered over her. Liam worked construction in Bellingham—had done so ever since he'd left Ireland to find himself before he'd be called to lead his father's pack, and the work had only enhanced what nature—and his werewolf lineage—had given him naturally.

Despite his position as foreman, Liam didn't hold with making his men do everything. Add in the sparring he did with some of the members of his pack on off-days, and he could easily be mistaken for a prizefighter in a dark alley.

"Caitlin, I'll ask ya' again. Are ya' scared of me?"

A shake of her head didn't match the tremble in her hands. "Not of you."

"That's no answer. Not a proper one. Ye're scared of somethin'. Scared enough to throw away what we have without even tellin' me why. Ya' don't do that to someone ya'..." Liam caught himself before "love" slipped from his throat, "...care about."

Caitlin glanced up and down the street, shivering in the frigid winter air. "Not here."

"Bewley's?"

She nodded and allowed him to take her arm, walking her to a quiet coffee shop a few blocks off the main road. While Liam ordered cappuccinos, Caitlin slipped into a chair at a corner table facing the street. Her gaze darted between him and the door.

What had happened to her?

She was terrified, and with how she held herself stiffly, how sure she was of her plan to run, he didn't think this was the first time she'd had to do so.

Coffees in hand, he slid one cup in front of her and took his seat. "I'm listenin'."

"Ya' won't believe me."

"Try me," Liam said.

"Do ya know what an elemental is?" Caitlin took a sip of coffee, hiding behind the mug.

"I've heard of 'em. Never met one."

She ripped into a sugar packet and dumped the granules into her palm. Holding his gaze, she took a deep breath. A tiny tornado swirled over her hand, lifting the sugar in a delicate spiral before depositing it into her cup.

Shock tightened his throat, and he scanned the small space, hoping no one had noticed. His voice, when he found it again, was rough and strained. "Can all elementals do that?"

Caitlin flattened her hands on the table. "No. My element is air, so I can call the wind. Sometimes I can even influence thoughts. Compel actions. Ya' can only have one element—" she took a shuddering breath, "—except in rare cases."

"Rare cases?" Liam leaned forward, desperate for any shred of logic he could hold onto that might keep Caitlin with him.

"There's a group of practitioners—witches—in Scotland. The Thirteen. They've been huntin' elementals for years, and when I was a girl, they found an earth elemental who'd do their bidding."

"Why?" Liam asked. He took a sip of his cappuccino and licked the foam from his upper lip as he waited for her answer.

Caitlin squeezed her eyes shut, and a gentle breeze ruffled Liam's long, untamed reddish locks.

"The more I tell ya', the more ye're at risk," Caitlin whispered. "But they want all the elements. To bring them together all in one person."

After glancing at the door again, Caitlin set down her cup and started fiddling with her purse strap. "They can take an element. By force. Steal it away from a person and..." Her voice faded, and she swallowed hard.

Liam's wolf begged to be let loose. His mate was terrified, ashamed even, and he couldn't understand why. He didn't move, didn't look away. If he had any hope of salvaging what they had—what he'd thought they'd had—he'd find it. If she let him.

"How is that even possible? It's part of who ya' are, yeah?"

Caitlin twisted the leather strap around her fingers, and her breath hitched. "Bollocks. I'm makin' a feckin' mess of this, and I don't have the time to explain. The past two weeks with ya'... they've been perfect. Truly. I'd stay with ya' forever...if I could." Caitlin eased his hand from his mug.

Tracing the lines on his palm, all the way to his wrist, she sighed. "I love yer hands, Liam. I won't forget ya'. Ever."

"Ye're talkin' like I'm never goin' to see ya' again." He tightened his grip on her fingers as his wolf raged inside.

"I'm..." She refused to meet his gaze, and tried to pull away. "I'm bound to another."

Liam's vision went red as he pulled back and sat up straight. He wasn't an arse—he'd never have pursued another man's woman. "Fuck me."

"Luv—"

"Am I? Yer love? Ya' had another man this whole time? Why would ya' do that to me?"

"I didn't. Not the way ya' think... I hoped—" She swayed in her seat, the blue depths of her eyes turning an odd color—almost hazel—before she clutched the table with a groan. "I don't have much time left. To be...me. I don't love him, Liam. I thought...I thought he'd disappeared. I hoped he'd *died*. That his...his work had led to his end somehow..."

A tear tumbled down her cheek, and Liam ached to comfort her. Man and beast fought for control—his wolf desperate to steal her away and protect her, but the man slain by her betrayal.

"Yer eyes. They're glowing." Caution widened her gaze. "Ye're not goin' to shift, are ya'?"

Liam sucked in a sharp breath. "Ya' knew." He forced the words out, gripping the table hard enough he worried it would crack.

At her nod, he leaned forward, inhaling her unique scent and dropping his voice so only she could hear. "No. I won't shift. How long have ya' known?"

"Since I met ya'. Yer wolf is so much a part of ya', Liam. I saw him in yer eyes that first night—that's what drew me to ya'. Were-wolves and elementals, we've a long history." Her eyelids fluttered, and she leaned back in her chair. "I should have told ya' from the start. But I can't change the past. If I could... Please forgive me."

"I can't—not without knowin' why. I'll be alpha one day. We don't do casual relationships, luv. We mate for life. So when ya' tell me ye're bound to another, that there's a man out there with a claim to ya'..."

"He has no claim on my heart. He might've—many years ago —but he twisted and destroyed whatever kindness, whatever love I once felt for him and now I hate him." Caitlin dashed a second tear from her eyes. "When I said bound, I meant by a spell, a charm. By magic, not by love. We're linked by our elements. Or by mine anyway. I can't escape him. Ever. He can find me no matter where I go, and he needs me to finish what he started. At least that's what he thinks, and he's not one to be reasoned with."

"If ya' want to leave him, ya' can," Liam growled. "No man's that powerful. And I'd protect ya'." His wolf asserted his claim, the overwhelming need to touch her forcing him closer, his fingers covering hers.

She clutched his hand with such strength, and her short nails dug into his palm. "Ya' don't know Fergus. He's dangerous. Has magic on his side. I couldn't live with myself if ya' got hurt."

His anger threatened to suffocate him, and the ache in his chest from his wolf clawing his way to the surface... No. No one would hurt the woman he loved.

"Where is this fuckin' tosser?"

"Close." Caitlin scanned the street before returning her gaze to Liam. "It's not important now. He's in Dublin somewhere, and he's called to me. If I don't go to him, he'll hurt me." Her voice was so small he had to strain to hear her.

"That will never happen," Liam spat.

By Caitlin's sharp inhale, she'd probably seen the wolf in his eyes again. He'd certainly felt the beast rear up. But Liam didn't care. The strength of a pureblood werewolf could match any creature on earth—even a vampire. Liam tossed back the last of his cappuccino.

"I'll drive ya' to him myself. One of the advantages of bein' what I am, luv. Only a proper idiot'll stand up to a werewolf."

"Fergus will," she said quietly. "And he'll beat ya'. End ya' for even touchin' me. Every time I've tried to leave him, he's found me. He won't stop. Whatever luck allowed me these past three years, it's gone now. I have to accept my fate. I'm his, and I always will be."

"Ye're not makin' any sense. Why did he leave ya' alone for so long? I'm tryin' to understand, Caitlin. Help me." With every word, he felt her pulling further away from him.

"He's mental. Not...all the time. When he's sane, he's sweet and respectful and...almost the boy I once cared for. It's why I let him take my element in the first place. There was good in him once. Until the Thirteen took it and left a monster in its place." She shook her head, and her eyes hardened. "It doesn't matter now. Can't ya' see that? Ya' need to forget about me. These past two weeks—they've been the best of my life. I thought I was free, but I was wrong. I can't keep pretendin' that I can do what I want. Fergus always finds me.

"The last time I ran, I got all the way to Glasgow before—" Caitlin choked back a sob. "Ya' can't protect me. Not against him."

Shoving her chair back, she lurched to her feet and slammed her hip against the table in her haste to flee.

Liam grabbed her wrist. Desperation roughened his voice until his words escaped in a growl. "I can. I will. I won't lose ya'."

Another tear raced down her cheek and plopped onto the stained wooden table. "Ya' made me happy, Liam O'Sullivan. I haven't been happy in a long time. And when he takes me again... I'll cherish the memories we made."

Caitlin leaned down, stealing a quick, desperate kiss that roused his wolf into a frenzy.

A gentle caress of air surrounded him with her scent and ruffled his napkin before it faded, leaving Liam with only the memory of her touch lingering on his skin.

The deep sense of peace held him still and soothed him. Until the shop door slammed and shattered the moment, and when he turned towards the sound, the sight of Caitlin's tear-stained face shimmering through the glass brought him back to the present.

With one last glance, she turned and ran.

———

FOR THE NEXT TWO WEEKS, he scoured the small towns in western Ireland. Ennis, Galway...all the way to Doolin. He must have asked a thousand people if they knew Caitlin Brannigan, and each refusal twisted the knife deeper into his heart.

Brannigan was a common name. Too common.

One woman shook her head at his question, crossing herself

and recounting the tragic death of Kionah Brannigan in a land-slide years ago.

"She had a daughter, and the wee lass disappeared not long after. She might have been yer Caitlin, but I canna be sure."

At a local pub in Doolin, a wizened old man gave him a hard stare and mumbled something about love, loss, and pain as he rapped spoons together against his thigh. Then, the man's hazy gray eyes cleared, and he uttered one final phrase. "Hidden in darkness, under the sky, yer fate is tied to the one who does not lie."

The man's cryptic words brought no comfort, and he moved on to the bartender, hoping for the smallest scrap of information to help him find his mate.

"Worked in the woolen shop, I think," the bartender said as he swiped a rag over the weathered wood. "Slung pints for a time. Always with a smile that never reached her eyes. She disappeared years ago now. Off to Dublin she was, I think. Old Paddy would know."

Liam glanced back at the old man and shook his head. "That one's as daft as a brush. He told me nothin'."

Every conversation, every lead that didn't pan out, every night without his mate drove Liam deeper into despair. He barely ate, slept, or shifted.

His parents' frantic phone calls went unanswered, but despite Liam's sorrow, he couldn't ignore a call from his alpha, Mike.

"Get back here, Liam. You're needed. Nathan's moving to Albany to join his mate's pack. I need a beta, and it's going to be you."

"No," Liam spat into the phone. He wanted nothing to do with his pack at the moment. Or perhaps ever again.

"I won't live forever," Mike said quietly. "You could be the pack's alpha one day, if you don't take over your father's pack, and you need to start stepping up."

The vote of confidence would have meant everything to him any other time, but without Caitlin, the words rang hollow.

"I can't give up on her, Mike. Not yet." Liam held his breath, hoping his alpha would understand.

"One week. No more. Consider that an order."

As the call disconnected, Liam hung his head. He couldn't disobey an order. Especially not from Mike. The alpha gave so few.

The Bellingham pack offered him an independence he'd never have found with his father's wolves. He loved the life he'd carved out in Washington, and he couldn't risk losing it. Not when his hope of finding Caitlin was fading every single day.

The moon waned, and when it disappeared from the sky, the mating call receded to a dull thrum in his heart. He had to go home.

His last day, Liam headed to the airport in Shannon. But before he got on the plane, he met with the alpha of a small pack his da' had told him about. Over a pint, Liam confessed everything. His pain, how desperate he was to get Caitlin back, how lost he was without her.

They switched to whiskey when the alpha wolf bristled at the name Fergus. "That man is as mental as a three-headed bear. Ye'll never best him. That is if ya' even find 'im. He disappeared years ago after killin' a lass with fire in her blood. The elemental community fled these parts not long after, and Fergus left with 'em. You'd best give up on yer Caitlin. Yer life—and yer pack—come before a pretty young thing ya' never made yer own."

In the end, Liam's loyalty to the man who'd given him a home won out over the dying hope Caitlin would return to him. Though Liam would have bet his life she wanted him, she'd made her choice.

When he boarded the plane back to the States, he left his heart scattered in pieces over the Irish countryside.

CHAPTER ONE

December

Bella

*D*ead. Katerina and Jeremy were dead. Eviscerated and mauled by the werewolf pack Katerina had been hunting for years.

The stench of blood, burnt clothing, and earth—so much earth—filled her nose, and Bella retched as she stumbled into the hotel room. She barely made it to the toilet before she heaved up what little was still in her stomach from the previous night.

She almost hadn't escaped. Her air element had failed her the moment Katerina had died, and now...the blood red crystal she wore around her neck felt...cold.

For more than ten years, it had protected her, and the connection she'd shared with Katerina had saved her life. The woman had been her sister in every way that counted ever since the fire elemental had plucked Bella off a beach in Mexico, injured and near death. She'd had no memory of who she was or where she'd come from, and her rescuer hadn't cared.

Bella didn't know how she could possibly go on without Katerina. Or why her element, always so strong and reliable, had suddenly failed. She held out her hand, calling upon her unique gifts, but instead of a mini tornado spinning over her palm, she could only manage the barest stirring of the stuffy air in the room.

"I have to get out of here," she said to no one as she pushed to her feet. Mara, the water elemental, had still been alive when Bella had fled, but after absorbing Katerina's fire, would she stay that way? If she didn't, Bowman's entire pack would be coming for her.

Even the *idea* of facing down one of the wolves again left her shaking. The big red one...he'd stared right at her, his luminous green and gold eyes hauntingly familiar and full of rage.

And his scent. A mix of the sea, fresh cut grass, and spice. The water elemental had carried a hint of it. Not as strong as the scent of the alpha, but present, and Bella had been so drawn to it, she'd tried to help Mara just to be closer to it—until Katerina had found out and banished her from the room.

Hours later, Bella could still pick it out among all the other scents surrounding her. She couldn't breathe. Rocking back and forth on the old, cheap bathroom floor, she let her tears fall. A memory nudged at the back of her mind. Arms around her. A man's laugh.

Darkness followed quickly. Fear. Falling. Pain.

Her head hit the edge of the tub, and she collapsed to the floor. "Feckin' hell," she muttered, then drew in a sharp breath. Where had that phrase come from?

Forcing herself up, she swayed slightly and rubbed the rapidly swelling bump north of her temple. It didn't matter. Katerina was dead. She had to pull herself together and run.

If Mara was still alive, she might be able to lead the police to the motel. Every minute Bella stayed here was one she didn't have.

The throbbing pain in her head made it hard to focus as she packed up her few belongings. She couldn't drive like this. Couldn't get on a plane or go to the airport. She was a mess. If her muddled thoughts were any indication, she doubted her ability to form a coherent sentence. TSA would detain her, probably put her on some no-fly list, and then what would she do?

Popping two aspirin from her overnight bag, she crawled onto one of the small, lumpy beds. She could rest for a few minutes. Long enough for the pills to take effect. That was it. After her head no longer felt like it was about to split open, she'd clean herself up and get the hell out of Seattle.

BELLA JERKED UP WITH A GASP. The drapes billowed as her element stirred the air in the room, and beyond the window? Darkness. She'd slept the whole day. And the dream that had woken her? It had felt so real.

Craggy cliffs and loose rocks under her feet. Wind whipping around her, sending her once-reddish brown hair to sting her cheeks. Running. Jumping. Pain. Icy water. Then...nothingness.

The bedside clock confirmed her fears. It was after 2:00 a.m., and she'd slept more than eighteen hours. Though, since the police hadn't shown, Mara either hadn't survived, or didn't know where Katerina had held her.

In the bathroom, Bella squinted in the bright lights, then winced at the black and purple bruise on her forehead. Splashing some water on her face, she rummaged in her overnight bag for concealer—about the only makeup she ever wore—and tried to cover up the worst of it.

But then another whiff of the big red wolf's scent reached her, and she stifled a sob and braced her hands on the sink. Whoever he was, she thought maybe...at one time...they'd known each other, and he'd been nice. But that didn't matter. She'd never see him again, and Seattle wasn't a place she could stay. She had to go back to Phoenix right now.

THE VAN HAD a mind of its own. Why else would she be turning onto Mara's street? Lights blazed in every window of the water elemental's house, and behind the drapes in the woman's bedroom, someone paced. Was it the alpha?

Cutting the headlights, Bella slowed and rolled down the window, inhaling deeply.

He was here. The red wolf.

Her knuckles turned white on the steering wheel, and her whole body started to shake. Until a door shut, startling her. It was him. The tall man with reddish hair strode out of Mara's home. He paused at the house next door, pulled a flyer from a folder tacked to a post, and ran a hand through his locks. They fell past his shoulders, and Bella wondered what it would feel like to touch them.

She extended her hand out the window, palm up. "I call upon the wind," she whispered, "come to me."

A weak breeze ruffled the man's hair, then hers, and she drank in his scent.

"Who are you?" But she kept her voice so quiet, no one could hear her. "Enough," she said as she rolled up the window. It didn't matter how good he smelled. She'd almost killed his alpha's mate, and there was no way she could ever see him again.

Pulling up directions to the airport, she let herself shed a single tear. For everything she'd lost. Including her connection to this handsome and alluring wolf. Once she got back to Phoenix, she'd forget all about him. And that would be a blessing.

April

BELLA HATED herself for being so weak. For running away. But staying in Phoenix without Katerina was too hard. None of the other elementals had ever liked Bella, though for the life of her, she hadn't been able to figure out why.

Maybe because she hated using her air element. Or because she'd never been good at speaking up for herself—relying on Katerina to defend her, to protect her. Now, with the woman she'd considered a sister gone, Bella was drifting. And every time one of the other elementals would come into the occult shop Katerina had run, Flaming Objects, Bella would hide in the back.

Until an earth elemental named Kelly burst through the door and demanded Bella tell her exactly what had happened to Katerina.

The air had whipped around Bella's head, upending books on the shelves, knocking over candles, bundles of sage, and crystals. The power had terrified her. For months, her element had been weak. Almost useless. Just like the red crystal she still wore around her neck. But Kelly's confrontation had stirred something deep inside of Bella, and all of a sudden, it was like she couldn't control herself.

She'd run and left almost everything behind. Half of her clothing, her meager assortment of personal possessions... She'd only taken ten minutes at her apartment to pack, grabbing what little money she'd saved, her cell phone charger, her favorite body lotion, and the white silk drawstring bag she'd kept hidden under her mattress for two years.

Now, sitting on a bus on the way to Seattle of all places, she pulled the bag out of her pocket and loosened the tie.

The smoky quartz pendant tumbled into her hand, and almost instantly, her racing thoughts calmed.

Katerina had taught her all about crystals and their energies, and smoky quartz was used to ease fear, depression, and anxiety, bringing peace to the wearer.

When Bella had purchased the pendant, she'd hid it from Katerina, not wanting to appear ungrateful for the red fire agate crystal the woman had given her the day she'd pulled Bella from the ocean in Mexico and saved her life.

The fiery crystal, which had always been a reassuring warmth against her skin, now weighed her down.

"This fire agate will be your shield," Katerina said as she fastened the necklace around Bella's neck. "It will protect you from anyone who seeks to do you harm and keep you safe under my protection forever."

Staring out the window at the desert landscape she never wanted to see again, Bella swallowed a sob.

I'm sorry, Katerina. It's time for me to be on my own.

As soon as she'd removed the fire agate and replaced it with the smoky quartz, her entire body shuddered.

The heavy weight over her heart lifted, but she couldn't smile. Because a dark sense of foreboding took residence deep in her soul. Was it because of the big red wolf haunting her dreams?

He was the reason she'd decided to go back to Seattle. Despite fearing the alpha's wrath, she had to know why she felt such a draw to the pack's beta. It made no sense. She didn't even know his name.

She knew his body, however. His voice. His scent. They'd shared something long ago.

But what?

CHAPTER TWO

Liam

*H*e balanced on a girder fifty feet in the air, the harness clipped to his belt swinging behind him. A cold, stiff wind ruffled his long reddish hair, barely tamed by the hard hat he wore, and stung his freshly shaven cheeks.

The radio at his hip squawked once, and Peter's voice rang out. "You should be moving a lot faster without that beard weighing you down. It's almost three. I need you in the office to go over the final numbers for the Phinney Ridge bid."

"Will ya' relax? I'm almost done," he said before he drove the last three rivets into the joist.

He never should have grown the beard in the first place. He'd hated it. Itchy, untamed, wild. After four months, he'd finally shaved it off just three days ago.

When he'd come downstairs for breakfast, the entire pack save for Cade and Mara, who'd been at their house next door, had stared at him for a full minute in absolute silence before Livie had burst out in applause.

"Ya' never said ya' hated it," he'd snapped at them. "I'd needed a change. Finally got sick of it."

What he *needed* was a way to forget. To look at Cade and Mara and not see what he could have had with the woman he'd once loved. With his Caitlin.

Unclipping his harness, he headed to the construction elevator with a quick nod to the rest of the crew.

In the past four months, O'Sullivan and Shea, the company he and Peter had formed once the pack resettled in Seattle, had accepted three jobs, including this new condo complex outside of Pioneer Square. They had a dozen men and women working for them, all human, but Liam still liked to get his hands dirty.

Cade, the pack's alpha, had started up his woodworking business again. Shawn had been turning away private accounting clients as tax day was in less than a week, Ollie patrolled for the King County Sheriff's Department, and just ten days ago, Christine had found a naturopathic training program she loved at a local university and would soon be licensed for acupuncture and herbal medicine.

The lot of them were happy here in Seattle. If only Liam could be as well. The weather reminded him of Dublin, and every time he thought of his home, he battled memories of Caitlin.

As he punched the button to take him down to street level, he caught the distinctive scent of fig blossoms.

Shite.

He hadn't smelled fig blossoms in eleven years. Not since his Caitlin had run from him the very day he'd hoped to confess his love for her.

They'd only had two weeks together, but his wolf had known. She was his.

Liam stared out over Puget Sound, the sun making the water sparkle like thousands of diamonds scattered over the landscape. His shoulder ached, and he rubbed the tight muscle. He'd been up late the previous night, plumbing one of the bathrooms in the fixer-upper the pack had purchased next to Cade and Mara's house, and getting under the old sink had been...difficult.

He tugged on his hair until pain prickled along his scalp and a strange sensation skittered over the back of his neck. Gazing down at the street, he narrowed his eyes. A lone woman stood on the sidewalk looking up at him.

Petite. Curvy. Her hair fell in brown waves almost to her shoulders, and Liam's wolfish vision picked out a stud in her nose. Nails painted bright purple.

The wind whipped up, carrying the scent of fig blossoms once again. She took a step closer, and there was something so familiar about the way she moved.

And then he heard a single word float over the air. Soft, light, and the sweetest sound he'd ever heard.

"Liam?"

"Caitlin. Fuck. My Caitlin."

He punched the elevator button harder, but the damn thing took forever to traverse the six floors down to the street.

"Caitlin! Wait!" Liam shouted, desperate, shoving at the gate when he was still three feet off the ground. But by the time he reached the spot where she'd been, he was alone with her tantalizing scent all around him.

"Get the fuck away from her!" Cade growled from the side of the building, sending Liam's heart rate soaring.

As he rounded the corner, he saw Mara with her back against the wall, hands up, and a look of stark terror on her face.

Cade grabbed the woman Liam had seen by the lapels of her green army jacket, and she pulled away, stumbling right into Liam's arms.

Fuck. She felt the same. Smelled the same. And her eyes? They were a rather unnatural shade of purple, but they were definitely Caitlin's.

"What the fuck, Cade? Don't put yer hands on my mate!"

"What?" Mara, Cade, and Caitlin asked in tandem.

His Caitlin backed away, casting glances towards the street, clearly intending to run.

"That isn't your mate, Liam. That's Bella. She helped Katerina kidnap Mara," Cade snapped, advancing on his beta. "She's going to pay for what she did."

"Stop." Liam reached for Cade's arm and took an elbow to the stomach, but he refused to let it deter him. "This—" he turned to his mate, "—is Caitlin Brannigan."

The woman's eyes widened, and she reached for a pale, white crystal hanging at her throat. "No," she whispered. Shaking her head, almost violently, she took off and ran straight into Peter.

"She. Hurt. Mara." His alpha's words held sway, but so did his wolf's *need* to comfort his mate.

Peter took Caitlin by the arms, lifting her until her feet no longer touched the ground. She kicked, connecting with his shin, and a fresh gale, scented with fig blossoms, whipped down the sidewalk.

This couldn't be happening. No one touched Caitlin when he was around. With a half-shout, half-howl, Liam barreled forward, shouldering Peter in the side hard enough he released her and landed on his ass.

Liam wrapped Caitlin in his embrace, though she continued to fight—scratching at his arms and bucking against his hold.

"Caitlin. Luv, no one here is goin' to hurt you. I promise, *mo chuisle, mo chroí.*"

A soft sob escaped her lips, and she calmed, the wind dying down with her fear. "I know those words." Her voice no longer held the heavy brogue that haunted his dreams. Now, there was only a faint lilt to her tone. "How? I shouldn't even know your name, but I do."

Tears brimmed in her eyes, and as she tried to blink them back, Liam realized why their color had changed. Contact lenses.

"I said them to ya' years ago. Ya' don't remember?"

"No."

His heart shattered into pieces. How could his Caitlin ever forget him? Despite the pain, he kept her close, his arm curled protectively around her as he glared at Cade. "She is *not* the air elemental who was with Katerina."

"Yes, she is," Mara said softly. "But she didn't hurt me."

"What?" Cade asked, stiffening. Bright amber and silver flecks glowed in his blue-gray eyes. His alpha's wolf rumbled just under the skin, barely contained. The man was the strongest wolf Liam had ever met. He didn't lose control. Ever.

A few drops of water formed on Mara's pale cheeks. Not tears. Cade's mate was a water elemental, and in times of stress, she could call moisture from the air around her—often without even realizing it. "Bella never hurt me. She was...kind. As kind as Katerina let her be." Combing trembling fingers through her long, red locks, she cleared her throat. "If Liam says she's his mate, we have to hear her out."

"No." Cade hadn't taken his eyes off of Caitlin the whole time, but Mara stepped in front of him, her hands on her hips.

"You remember what happened when Liam threatened me?" she asked.

His only response was a terse nod.

"And what would you have done if he'd tried again?"

"He'd be dead." Cade's reply tore his already broken heart into smaller pieces, even though he understood. Now that he had Caitlin in his arms, he'd protect her with his life—even if that meant leaving his pack.

Mara arched a brow. "I rest my case. Katerina and Jeremy are dead. Bella knows where we live. If she'd wanted to hurt me, showing up *here* seems like a silly idea. Dozens of people around, including Liam and Peter. In the middle of the afternoon. She was running away when she smacked into me, for fuck's sake. Hear her—and Liam—out."

Cade clenched his hands into fists so hard, his knuckles

cracked. "Fine. Pack meeting. Home. Now. She comes with us. Liam, you can follow."

"No fuckin' way." He wasn't letting Caitlin go with his alpha. Not with the mood Cade was in. "She can ride with me."

"Excuse me." Caitlin shoved away from him and drew up to her full height, which was still a good ten inches shorter than Liam's six-foot-four. "*She* is right here and can hear you discussing her like she's invisible." Tugging at her jacket, she glared at Liam. "I'm not going anywhere with any of you. I shouldn't have come at all. I don't know why I did."

She spun on her heel and darted away, and before any of them could stop her, a gust of wind knocked them back, so strong, Cade had to brace Mara so she wouldn't fall over.

By the time they all recovered, Caitlin was gone.

Caitlin

Back in Seattle for only two days, and already, she'd almost died.

No. Almost been killed. She'd felt this tremendous pull all morning. Something she couldn't ignore—and didn't want to—was drawing her closer and closer to the construction site. A sense of home. Of belonging. Of...peace.

Until she'd run right into Mara. The water elemental had screamed, and the alpha had snarled at her so viciously, she knew she was about to die.

But then, Liam had come to her rescue. Liam O'Sullivan. The name felt like second nature to her now. Just like the name he'd used for her. Caitlin Brannigan.

She was Bella. Bella Pond. That was the name Katerina had given her. But it was getting harder and harder to deny that she'd had a life before she'd washed up on that beach in Mexico.

From her hiding place a few blocks away, tucked in a darkened, recessed doorway of an abandoned building, she watched Cade and Mara get into a white Prius. Liam rolled a motorcycle out from behind the construction trailer, and when the engine roared to life, she felt it down to her toes.

Don't go after him. Get out of Seattle. Go back to Mexico. Or South America. Anywhere but here.

Too bad every fiber of her being, every cell from head to toe was drawn to Liam. If for no other reason than to find answers. He could tell her who she'd once been. And maybe, what had happened to her.

CHAPTER THREE

Liam

*P*ack meetings were usually raucous, jovial affairs, often featuring an abundance of pizza and brews. But tonight, the house was almost silent.

Only Serena, Livie and Shawn's three-month-old daughter made any noise. The baby was fussy, likely picking up on the tension filling the room.

At the large dining table, Livie bounced the baby on her knee while Shawn stood behind them, ready to whisk his mate and pup away the minute a fight broke out.

And it would. Liam was ready to snap, and he doubted Cade was much calmer. If at all.

"Hush, sweetie. Mama's not going to let anything bad happen," Livie cooed to the baby. Serena squeezed her bright blue eyes shut and let out an ear-piercing wail.

Shawn grinned. "That's my girl."

"Don't encourage her," Livie said, elbowing her mate in the stomach. "She can't be an alpha until she finds her own pack."

Mara held out her arms. "I can take her for a bit." Within seconds of settling against Mara's hip, Serena quieted. "I realize this has nothing to do with me. It's just Cade's scent on me. But... being able to calm her like this? It's kind of a rush," Mara said.

Even as young as she was, the baby recognized her alpha, and she never cried when Cade or Mara held her.

Dipping her head, Mara inhaled Serena's scent, and the lines of strain that had deepened around her eyes since the incident with Caitlin faded away.

"You're a natural with her." Livie sighed as Shawn started massaging her shoulders. "When are you and Cade going to...?"

"Oh! Not for a while, I hope." Mara's cheeks flushed bright red. "It's only been a few months—"

The front door slammed as Cade entered, his eyes still shifting between steel blue and amber as he focused on Liam. "Want to explain how a dead woman ended up working with the bitch who almost killed all of us?"

Liam pushed off the wall and approached his alpha, keeping his gaze on the man's shoes. "I don't know." With a quick shake of his head, he continued, "Eleven years ago, we were in Dublin together. The full moon was only a week away, and I'd planned on askin' her to be mine. But somethin' happened. I don't know what. One moment we were walkin' hand in hand down the street and the next, she was terrified."

He'd never forget the look on her face. The tremor in her voice. "That's when I found out my Caitlin had secrets. Dangerous ones. Somethin' about another elemental—earth, I think—who'd bound her."

"That's not possible, is it?" Mara asked.

"Caitlin claimed it was. She ran from me. Used her charms to distract me until she was too far away for me to track. I searched everywhere from Dublin to Cork for 'er. A few weeks after I got back to the States, a letter came."

Pulling a small leather pouch from his pocket, he swallowed the lump in his throat. It was virtually waterproof, meant to hold precious family photos, but Liam carried only one thing inside. Caitlin's letter.

For five years, it had always been in his pocket, until he couldn't stand to look at it any longer. A few months before the fire in Bellingham, he'd put it in a safe deposit box. Thank God he had, or it would have been lost.

He'd never shown anyone. Not even Cade. But now, he passed it over, his nerves a tight, icy ball in his gut.

Liam,

I'm sorry, my love. For running. For hiding this secret until it was too late. I only made it to the edge of town before he found me, and when he did... I can't tell you what happened. It shames me too much.

Fergus will see me dead before he lets me go, and he'll kill anyone who gets in his way. He knows I was with someone. That I found love. I barely stopped him from going after you, and the price I paid was too dear.

You were the best part of my life. With you, I was who I was meant to be.

By the time you read this, I will have given myself to the sea. Don't be sad. I'll finally be free of him.

Yours,

Caitlin

After a quick glance to ask his permission, Mara read the note aloud, and Liam squeezed his eyes shut against the pain of Caitlin's final words.

"I don't know how she got caught up with Katerina," Liam said. "But that woman—Bella—she's Caitlin Brannigan. I'd bet my life on it."

"I don't care what her name is," Cade growled. "She hurt Mara."

"No. She didn't—"

The punch snapped Liam's head back, pain shooting from his jaw to his temple. Without thinking, he tackled Cade, and the two of them crashed into the dining room wall.

Yelping, Livie snatched Serena from Mara's arms, fleeing with her up the back stairs to the suite she and Shawn claimed on the top floor. Peter and Ollie tried to separate alpha and beta, but though Cade was in charge, Liam's size gave him the advantage.

Until Cade roared with the strength only the start of a shift could provide and threw Liam into the table. One of its legs cracked in two, and the large polished wood bowl in the center clocked Liam in the back of the head, stunning him just enough for Peter and Ollie to haul him up by his arms.

"Will you both stop this bullshit?" Mara said from the threshold. When everyone turned to her, she huffed. "You're all adults. Or I thought you were. Is there some reason you can't use your words? Bella—or Caitlin, whatever her name is—didn't hurt me. I don't remember everything from that time—I was too sick, but I remember that."

Cade leapt up and headed for her, but Mara waved him off. The air thickened, humidity filling the room, along with Mara's unique scent. But there was something else as well. Mara's fear.

"I was gagged and tied up," she said quietly. "In a bathtub. They had a hotel room somewhere on Highway 99. I couldn't move, and I was burning. Katerina's charms..." She shuddered, and a single tear tumbled down her cheek. The room was so quiet, Liam heard the drop hit the hardwood floor. "It was like all those months I was sick, played out on fast forward, and I knew I was going to die. Until Bella came in with a damp cloth. More than once. She tried to keep me alive. Comfortable. Or...at least not in quite as much agony."

Shawn cleared his throat. "Did she hurt anyone when we fought Katerina at Gasworks Park?" One by one, the wolves shook their heads, and he met Cade's eyes. "All the charms I saw her use? They were only defensive."

"So, can we put aside how she came to be with Katerina and what you all assumed she did, and talk about the real problem?" Mara arched her red brows.

Everyone in the pack, except Cade, stared down at the floor.

"What's that?" he asked.

"How do we find her again? We have to know if she really is Liam's mate. Because if she is, you—" she pointed at Cade, "—can't keep them apart."

"The hell I—"

"You were ready to beat the crap out of any of them—all of them—for even looking at me sideways," Mara said, lacing her fingers with Cade's and guiding his hands to her waist. "Can't you see Liam feels the same way? He thought she was dead. We have to help him. That's what family does."

Water ran in the kitchen, and a moment later, Christine approached Liam with a wet cloth. "Mara's a damn good peacemaker. Sit down and let me take care of that."

He hadn't even realized he was bleeding, but with the momentary dip in the tension filling the room, his split lip started to throb. Blood dripped down his chin onto his blue flannel shirt.

Hissing out a breath when the pack's healer pressed the towel to the wound, he stared down at the floor. Whatever happened now—whatever Cade decided—would determine whether Liam still had a family at the end of this mess.

He loved them. All of them. But he'd walk away if it meant he could be with Caitlin again.

"I'd stay with ya' forever if I could."

Caitlin's last words back in Dublin floated through his memories. He wanted forever. Needed it.

Heavy footsteps thudded across the floor, and Liam forced his gaze up to see Cade headed from the room. "I need a few minutes to think. Liam, you stay put." Holding out his hand, he waited for Mara to join him, and the two retreated to their own house next door.

"Thanks, Chrissy," Liam said. "Ya' don't need to mind me. I won't go anywhere."

The rest of the pack filed out one by one, leaving him alone at the broken dining room table.

What the hell was he going to do now?

AN HOUR LATER, Liam had just finished reinforcing the table leg with a bracket when he looked up and found Cade watching him.

His alpha was calm. In total control of his wolf. Mara had done that. Chrissy was right. She was good for Cade—and for the pack.

"Cade."

"You want a drink?" Cade asked as he headed for the kitchen and pulled a bottle of whiskey from the cabinet, along with two glasses.

"We drinkin' to say goodbye or make peace?"

"Sit." It wasn't a request, and the order carried a physical weight Liam couldn't ignore.

"*Sláinte*," Liam said as he raised his glass to his alpha.

"*Sláinte agatsa.*" At his shocked expression, Cade arched a brow. "What? Is it so hard to believe I learned the response to a proper Irish toast? You're my best friend, Liam. My brother in every way that counts."

With a nod, Liam drained his glass and Cade poured them both another shot. Werewolves burned off the alcohol in minutes, a fact Liam had often lamented—usually around the anniversary of Caitlin's death when all he wanted to do was drink himself into a stupor. Something he'd never managed to do.

"Mara's right." Cade's expression carried equal parts pride and frustration, and he stared at the whiskey in his glass, swirling it around and releasing the sweet, spicy scent into the room. "You have to find out if that woman is your Caitlin."

"But do I have yer blessin'?" Liam couldn't meet his alpha's gaze. The pack was his family. He'd been born to lead. His parents had expected him to become an alpha, just as his father had been. But after losing his Caitlin, he'd known. That life wasn't for him. But this one...beta to one of the best men he'd ever met? He didn't want to give it up.

"Yes." The word escaped on a rough whisper, and Cade drained the rest of the drink. "But there are rules, Liam."

"Name them." Straightening in his chair, he felt a small ember of hope starting to burn under the shattered remains of his heart.

"When you find her, you bring her back here. I want to know how she came to be with Katerina. All of it."

"Do I have yer promise she'll be safe—?"

Cade slammed the glass down on the table hard enough it cracked into three pieces. "Fuck. Mara bought us those glasses." Sweeping the remnants into his palm, he strode into the kitchen and tossed them in the trash, then braced his hands on the sink to stare out the window. "You should know me better than that."

"And ya' shoulda' known me better too," Liam said quietly. "But I threatened Mara, and it almost killed her. I need yer promise, Cade. That ya' won't be as stupid as I was. I understand now. How ya' felt when ya' saw my wolf standin' in front of her. Why ya' almost kicked me out of the pack. So I'll ask ya' again. Will Caitlin be safe if I bring her here?"

"Yes." Cade turned, pain etched around his eyes. "No harm will come to her in this house or mine. But I make no promise to accept her as your mate. If I'm not satisfied with her answers, she's gone, and I don't want her anywhere around the pack again. What happens after that? It's on you. Understood?"

"Understood."

Cade headed for the front door, but stopped to rest a hand on Liam's shoulder. "You're my brother. My best friend. My beta. I don't want to lose you. But Mara comes first. If Caitlin's your mate, and you have to make the same choice...I won't like it. But I'll understand."

CHAPTER FOUR

Caitlin

$\mathcal{F}$rom her position behind a large oak tree at the end of the street, Caitlin heard the rumble of the motorcycle. Why had she come here? Any of the wolves could probably scent her.

At the construction site, the alpha had looked like he'd wanted to tear her apart. Not that she could blame him. She'd almost killed his mate. Even though it had been Katerina's idea—the fire elemental's desperate need for vengeance driving her well past the point of sanity—even though Caitlin had done everything she could to keep Mara alive, Bowman could—and probably should—end her.

And now she was outside his house hoping for a single glimpse of the red wolf? Katerina had always told her that her heart would get her in trouble.

Bella—or *was* she Caitlin?—wished she had just a fraction of Katerina's power. Of her protection. From the moment she'd taken off the blood red crystal, she'd been having memories of another time. What felt like a whole other *life* she'd lived.

A life that included the Irishman.

Liam O'Sullivan.

The motorcycle's engine revved louder, and a moment later, a dark-clad figure sped past. Liam's unique scent floated to her when she called upon her air, and even though he'd been mostly hidden by the black leather jacket, black pants, and the large helmet, she knew it was him. No one smelled like that. Like the sea after a storm mixed with a fresh cut pine tree.

In the beat-up Honda Civic she'd found on Craigslist for two hundred dollars, she followed him, keeping her window rolled down so she could track his scent. He turned, heading for the hill that led to the lake.

Caitlin had gone there the day she'd arrived in Seattle, and had gotten the shock of her life when Mara had run right past her. Then, horror had set in.

The water elemental was sick.

She'd bet her life on it. Katerina's fire was still alive somehow *inside* Mara.

Deep down, a warning echoed in Caitlin's mind.

Two elements cannot coexist in harmony. One will always overwhelm the other, and only the strongest elementals can survive.

"Shit," Caitlin whispered to no one. "The strongest...they can survive, but they won't stay sane."

Yet one more piece of wisdom she had no reason to know and couldn't remember how or why she'd ever learned.

The sound of the bike faded away, replaced by footsteps crunching across the rocky path.

Emboldened by a force she couldn't control, she followed him, all the way down to the dock stretching out over the water. To a wooden bench at the end that was now empty, but carried his scent so strongly, he'd been here moments earlier.

"Followin' me now, are ya'?"

Her heart leapt into her throat. Whirling, she caught her foot on an uneven board and went down, toppling over the side of the dock and into the icy water.

"Caitlin!"

She came up spitting, her teeth chattering, fighting against slimy, slippery vines of algae beneath the surface to hear the splash as Liam jumped in next to her and wrapped his arm around her waist.

"Let go of me, ya' big oaf!" Her voice didn't sound like her own any more. Or maybe it did, because the accent mirrored his and she felt like she'd carried it all her life.

"Fine. Suit yerself."

The loss of his strong arm, of his warmth, shocked her as he strode for the shore, and Caitlin—for she was damn certain her name wasn't Bella now—followed him. Though she had to swim at least half the distance being so much shorter than he was.

Liam shook himself from head to toe once he was back on the sandy beach, and when Caitlin stood in front of him, dripping wet, she called on her element to wick away the water. But she was weak. Had been ever since Katerina's death, and all she managed to do was dry her green army jacket and the ends of her hair.

"Yer goin' to talk to me." Liam shoved his hands into the pockets of his leather jacket and strode over to a stone wall at the edge of the beach where he sunk down and waited, watching, until she approached.

The whole wall was only four feet long, the rest of it covered by blackberry brambles, and he hadn't left much space next to him. Probably on purpose. "Scoot over."

"I like it here."

The bastard. "Stuff it, Liam. Move the fuck over. I'm here. That's what you wanted, yeah? That's all ya' get until ya' give me some answers."

His head snapped up. "I swear, luv. It's like ye're two different women. Even yer voice changes. And my Caitlin never would have said that to me. I only heard her swear once in the weeks we had together."

"Well, I'm not your Caitlin. I don't know who the hell I am, but I'm *not* yours." She shoved at his shoulder, and he moved a few inches, giving her just enough space to sit next to him, even though the outsides of their thighs were so close, his heat warmed her.

"I didn't say I didn't like it," he said quietly. "Ya' have some spirit to ya' now. Some fight. Maybe if you'd had that before..." His voice dropped, so low she had to strain to hear it. "Fuck me. I'm sorry. That was a shite thing to say."

"Doesn't make it less true." She sighed, leaning forward with her elbows on her knees, letting the subtle lap of the water against the shore calm her. At least the night was warm, because sitting in wet jeans, her blouse plastered to her breasts under her jacket, left her feeling exposed in a way she feared was dangerous around the sexy beta wolf.

"Talk to me, Caitlin." His deep voice did things to her. Stirred memories she wasn't prepared to face, but could no longer ignore.

"You're sure I'm her?" Peering up at him briefly, she met pale green eyes that were so familiar, she wanted to lose herself in them.

"I am. But if ya' want proof..." Liam turned towards her and held out his hand. "Caitlin had a scar on her right arm, a few inches above her wrist. The length of my thumb. I used to tell her it proved—"

"—that I was real." A sob broke from her lips as she shed her jacket and yanked up the sleeve of her black shirt. The thick scar almost glowed in the moonlight. When Liam traced it with a calloused finger, his touch sent sparks racing all the way to her core. "I don't even know how I got it."

"Ya' never did say. I got the sense it wasn't a good story."

His hand was warm. Wolves ran hot. She remembered now. A little. How he used to hold her. Like he was a big, burly blanket. One who would keep all the bad things far away from her.

"I've missed ya', luv. Every single day for eleven years. When I got yer letter...it broke me."

"What letter?"

She still wasn't certain she trusted this werewolf, but she couldn't deny they'd shared something. A relationship. A life, even?

Liam reached into the pocket of his jacket and swore under his breath. The leather billfold was damp, and as he opened it, he breathed a sigh of relief. "Thank fuck. It didn't get wet."

Carefully unfolding the heavy piece of stationery, he passed it to her.

"This is my handwriting." As she read, a cold chill spread from the top of her head to her toes, and she shivered. "Who's...Fergus?" Even saying the name felt wrong. "Why can't I remember?" Tears burned her eyes, but she wouldn't let them fall. Not in front of this man she was pretty sure she'd loved.

She felt it. Their connection. Their history.

It buzzed under her skin, energizing her, terrifying her, and making her want to run as far and as fast as she could to get away from him.

"Come back to the house with me, Caitlin. Please. Ye're freezing. I'll tell ya' everythin' I remember about...us. And what little I know about this Fergus bloke." Liam grabbed her hands and held on tight, his green eyes shimmering with gold and amber from the lights around the lake's walking path.

His wolf.

Panic flooded her, and her breath caught in her throat. "Let...go."

He did, but didn't move away, and the look on his face...was pure agony.

"What—" her voice cracked. "What am I supposed to do with

all of this? It's been eleven years. I never had a single memory from my life before…from this life you say we had together until…" Springing up, she started to pace the small stretch of beach.

"Until what?" he asked.

"Until Katerina died. Ever since that day, I have these dreams, these nightmares, these *feelings* I don't understand." Her fingers brushed the hollow of her throat, but the quartz brought her little comfort. She wanted her anonymity back. Her blissful ignorance.

"Ya' know I loved ya'."

"That doesn't tell me anything, wolf," she snapped.

Her wolf—because he *was* hers, even though she had no idea how—sprang for her, hauling her against his body, threading his fingers through her hair, and angling her head so she had to look him in the eyes. "I have a name. Use it."

His warmth spread through her, and she wanted to stay with him. So familiar. So comforting. He'd shocked her with his speed and the gritty desire in his voice, but his hold was gentle, protective, and not entirely unwelcome. "Liam."

"Shite, luv. Every night I hear ya' in my dreams. I never once thought I'd be able to hold ya' again. Touch ya'." From his tone, he was barely keeping it together, and Caitlin rested her cheek against his chest, listening to the steady beat of his heart.

After several long moments, he eased her back slightly and ran his nose along the curve of her neck. "I'll help ya' find the answers ya' need, Caitlin. Even if ya' can't stay with me once ya' know. But will ya' do one thing for me?"

"What?" she whispered, afraid if she spoke any louder, this moment would shatter and she'd be alone again.

"Apologize to Cade and Mara. Tell them how ya' came to be with Katerina. Explain yer part in what happened."

"Cade wants to kill me," she said, shaking her head and trying to extricate herself from his embrace.

"He won't. He gave me his blessin' to try to find ya'." One corner of Liam's mouth turned up. "I woulda' done it anyway."

"You never did like to follow the rules." How did she know that? Did it even matter? "You're sure he won't...it won't be like this afternoon?"

"I promise, luv. Ye're mine. No one would dare." Liam offered her his hand. "Will ya' trust me?"

She was going to regret this. She knew it. But despite her fears, she *did* trust this man. With her life. "Let's go."

LIAM TRIED to convince her to leave the beat-up old hatchback and ride with him on his bike, but as much as Caitlin wanted to spend a few minutes with her arms wrapped around this big, strong wolf, she wouldn't abandon her only means of escape two miles from Bowman's house.

So she followed him, her heart pounding in her chest the whole time. After parking in the pack house driveway, he waited for her to join him before wrapping gentle fingers around her elbow and guiding her next door.

"This was a mistake," Caitlin said as a stiff breeze surrounded them, raising gooseflesh on the back of her neck.

"I won't let them harm ya'," Liam said, and she tried to take comfort from his strong, deep voice, his scent. But after what she'd done...

She had to fight the urge to bolt as the door swung open. Cade wore only a pair of flannel pajama pants, his steel and flax hair sticking up in odd directions. "Well, that didn't take long." He ran a hand through the shaggy strands. "She's not welcome in this house. Take her next door."

"Cade?" Mara belted a robe tightly while peering around her mate's chiseled torso. "It's late. Let them come in."

"You can't be serious," Cade growled.

43

"I am. We're all tired, and Caitlin would be a fool to try anything with you right next to me. Whoever she is, whatever reasons she had for helping my sister, I don't think she's a fool. I'll start a pot of coffee."

"Fine. But if I feel even a hint of an air charm..."

Caitlin shivered, her clothes still damp, but it was Cade's tone that had sent the cold chill down her spine. "I mean you no harm," she said. "I just want to figure out who I am."

When Cade moved aside, Liam crossed the threshold, Caitlin's hand held tightly in his.

"Sit down," the alpha ordered, but Caitlin shook her head and ducked behind Liam.

"Um, I sort of fell into the lake. My clothes are still wet. I don't want to ruin your furniture."

"Come with me. I have something that should fit you." Mara headed down the hall, tossing a glance over her shoulder as she went. "Liam, can you start the coffee, please?"

Caitlin didn't want to go anywhere without him, and it was pretty damn obvious the alpha wasn't happy Mara was heading for their bedroom. But she followed a few steps behind the water elemental, hovering in the doorway in full view of the men as Mara dug around in her closet.

"They're not particularly stylish, but they'll do well enough," she said as she handed Caitlin a pair of gray fleece pants and a sweatshirt. "Bathroom's down the hall."

"Why are you being so...nice to me?" Hugging the soft material to her chest, she swallowed hard as Mara stared her up and down, those green eyes sharp, even with the bags under them larger than they'd been just this afternoon.

"Because I didn't know my sister well, but I know she had...problems. Our mother's death broke her in ways I'll never understand. I was just a baby, and unlike Katerina, I was adopted by a loving family. I guess...I'm hoping you can help me understand her a little better. Maybe then, I can understand...other things." Mara absently rubbed a spot between her breasts, a pained expression tightening her features.

"And I know one more thing. You *are* the woman who called herself Bella. Physically. But where it counts? Here?" Mara moved her hand to her heart. "You've changed. It's in your eyes. And I don't mean the lack of contact lenses. You're Caitlin again, aren't you?"

"I...I want to be," Caitlin whispered. "But who is she?"

"You don't know?" Mara's reddish brows lifted, surprise coloring her tone. "Get changed. Then Liam can tell you."

CHAPTER FIVE

Liam

*C*aitlin emerged from the bathroom looking like she was about to be led to the slaughterhouse. The gray sweatshirt dwarfed her, and she fiddled with the pale white crystal at her throat.

"I can put your clothes in the dryer," Mara said, holding out her hands for the damp bundle, but before she reached Caitlin's side, she stumbled and, with a little moan, sank to her knees.

"Mara!" Cade raced to her side and swept her up against his chest, carrying her to one of the love seats where he smoothed a hand over her hair. "You're shaking, honey. What's wrong?"

"I'm okay," Mara said. Her voice was weak, and worry sat like a stone in Liam's gut. His alpha's mate was sick again. He'd bet his life on it. Her scent, usually so strong in this house, had faded, and was now tinged with a hint of smoke. "Just a little spark of my sister's fire. Made me dizzy."

"Dammit. That hasn't happened in months," Cade muttered, and Mara looked away. "It hasn't, has it?"

"Maybe once or twice," she admitted. "I'm using my element. There's nothing to worry about. I won't let her fire overwhelm me again."

Cade didn't look convinced, but Mara cupped his cheek. "Get the coffee. I'll be fine, shaggy man." With a gentle brush of her lips to Cade's, she settled the man in a way Liam hadn't thought possible. "I need the caffeine."

With a pointed stare at Caitlin, then Liam, Cade nodded. "She doesn't move."

"Don't give her orders. She's not pack," he snapped.

Not yet, at least.

"Liam, don't test me on this." The warning growl set the hair on the back of Liam's neck on edge, and he ached to fight. To protect his mate. But Cade was his alpha, and he respected Mara too damn much to destroy her living room.

Mara offered Caitlin a weak smile. "Wolves. Not always good with their words, are they?"

"I...wouldn't know."

Fuck. Her voice was so tentative. So uncertain. And she appeared unwilling to move from her spot in the hall.

With a wave of her hand, Mara continued. "Sit, please. Cade didn't mean for you to stand all the way over there all night. He's just being...overprotective."

Caitlin spared Cade a brief, fearful glance before setting her wet clothes on the hearth and perching on the edge of the love seat.

Liam sank down next to her and linked their fingers. Hers were cold, but she didn't pull away, and when she met his gaze, her blue eyes searched his, looking for something...anything to hold on to.

Cade joined them a minute later with four cups of coffee held awkwardly in his scarred hands.

The sight of the burned skin, still shiny and without much sensation even after all this time, shook Liam to his core. How could he ask his alpha to accept Caitlin into the pack after what Katerina had done to him?

Liam forgot so often. How the fire elemental had tortured Cade for close to a year, starving him, feeding him nothing but rotten meat—and not much of it. In the months since Cade had escaped, found Mara, and broken free from the charm trapping him as his wolf, he'd put on twenty pounds of solid muscle, but he was still thinner than he'd been before.

And there were times his alpha's eyes were still so very haunted, and those days, only Mara could reach him.

"All right. Talk," Cade ordered.

"Oh, for fuck's sake—" Mara slapped her hand to Cade's chest, "—calm down. Yes, Caitlin needs to explain a lot of things, but all this grunting and growling at her isn't going to help."

"She. Hurt. You."

"Katerina hurt me. Bella helped, yes. But look at her, Cade. *That* isn't Bella. Not anymore." Mara huffed as she cupped the coffee in her hands and inhaled deeply.

"Will someone please tell me what the fuck is goin' on?" Liam asked. "How can she be two different people?"

"Until Katerina died," Caitlin said quietly, "I *was* Bella. I didn't have any memories of Liam. Or of any part of my life before Katerina."

"But how, luv? How could you forget...*us*?" Desperate to understand, Liam scooted even closer to his mate, and she stiffened and shook her head.

"I don't know. But Katerina wasn't *just* an elemental. She studied runes, spells, hexes...anything she thought might augment her power and...oh, shite." Her hand flew up to cover her mouth, and she looked from Mara to Liam and back again, tears shining in her eyes. "She did it all to protect us. From... something. Her necklace. The fire agate crystal. It was like her own personal talisman, and we all had one."

"Who's 'we all'?" Cade asked, his eyes keenly focused on Caitlin.

"Me, Jeremy. The other elementals in Phoenix. We had a handful of fire and earth in the area. Water and air elementals tend to prefer cooler weather."

"I remember it," Mara said bitterly. "When you were trying to help me. You're so pale, it looked almost black against your skin." Leaning forward, she pulled at the neck of her robe to reveal the top of an angry scar between her breasts. When she'd fought Katerina, she'd absorbed the woman's fire element, and the scar had taken months to heal. Even now, it was still redder than Liam thought it should be. As Mara moved, the light caught a shard of something embedded in her skin.

"Mara?" Liam asked. "Is that...?"

"The crystal? Yes." Mara shuddered, and Cade wrapped his arm around her shoulders. "Sorry. I don't like remembering." After a sip of coffee, she blew out a breath. "It was like all of my sister's fire concentrated in the—what did you say it was? Fire agate?—in the fire agate, and that's how it...entered me. It felt like someone was shooting a laser straight into my chest."

Cade reached over and gently closed her robe, and the look in her eyes...pure, perfect love. The two of them were made for one another, and fuck. Liam wanted the same feeling. He'd had It. For all of two weeks before Caitlin had fled Dublin.

Now, his mate pulled her hand from Liam's and hugged herself tightly. "I'm so sorry. I never wanted anyone to die. But Katerina saved my life. At least, I think she did."

"You think?" Cade asked.

Straightening, Caitlin drew in a deep breath. "Until Katerina died, my first memories—my only memories—were of waking up in a hospital in Mexico. Eleven years ago. She was sitting next to my bed, and I was so confused. I didn't know my name, or what had happened to me. Why every part of me hurt. But Katerina told me I didn't have to worry anymore. That she'd protect me. I trusted her. I was already wearin' the fire agate crystal, and fuck. I didn't even question where it had come from. Who *does* that? Who lets a complete stranger take over her life? I couldn't remember my name, and she told me she'd give me a new one. Bella."

"My sister had *talents*. You said it yourself. She wasn't just an elemental. She came to see me once when I was sixteen, and the whole time she was in the room, I could feel this *presence*. This overwhelming urge to believe her. It made me sick. So I threw her out."

"I wish I'd done the same." Shame tinged Caitlin's tone, and she shook her head. "I'm so sorry. When she told me she'd found 'the wolf' and she needed my help to trap you, I didn't even question her."

A low, angry sound rumbled in Cade's throat, and Mara started rubbing his thigh. "And now?" the alpha wolf asked.

"Now? I don't know a feckin' thing. Shite. Shit. I can't even be sure what's going to come out of my mouth. What the fuck does 'feckin' mean?" Caitlin turned to Liam. "And this Fergus? You know more about him than I do!" A gentle breeze stirred a few strands of her hair, and she dug her fingers into her thighs.

Liam ached to comfort her. To wrap her in his arms and tell her that no one would ever hurt her again. Taking a risk, he laid his hand over hers, and she stiffened but didn't pull away. "He was an earth elemental. And, luv, ya' said he'd bound ya' somehow. That he could find ya' anywhere. That ya'd never be free of him."

"Then why hasn't he come for me in eleven years?" she asked. "Because Katerina never once mentioned his name. No one's ever come looking for me."

Mara leaned forward, her brows drawn together. "What happened to the crystal my sister gave you?"

"It stopped working. Changed, somehow. It was always warm, but when she died, it turned cold." Caitlin's fingers trembled as she stroked the pale white pendant at the hollow of her throat. "I took it off when I left Phoenix and swapped it for this smoky quartz. I bought this on my own and hid it from her. Maybe... deep down...a part of me knew something wasn't right."

"When did you start to remember?" Mara asked.

"After she died. I think. Maybe before? I could smell Liam on you." Caitlin's cheeks flushed bright red, and she fixed her gaze on Mara's coffee table. "When we all fought...shit. Katerina told me and Jeremy to kill all of you, but I...I couldn't. The next night, I started to see Liam in my dreams."

"That was four months ago." Fuck. Why had she waited so long? Liam had so many questions, but if he demanded answers, he was afraid Caitlin would run so far and so fast, he'd never find her again.

"I tried to forget. Or...not remember." A single tear balanced on her lashes, and he wanted to dash it away, but suspected the touch wouldn't be welcome. Not now. "I shouldn't have come. I don't belong here. I'll go back to Phoenix." Shooting Cade and Mara a glance, she swallowed hard. "You'll never see me again. I swear it."

His mate pushed to her feet, but Liam leapt up and blocked her way, his hands on her shoulders. "Ya' don't belong in Phoenix, Caitlin. I can tell ya' that for damn sure. Don't leave me again. Please."

"I don't remember leaving ya' the last time!" She balled her hands into fists, and the drapes billowed.

"Goddammit, Liam. I won't have her using her element in this house! Get her the fuck out of here before I do it for you," Cade shouted, angling his body in front of Mara's while the water elemental clutched at his shoulder.

His alpha's tone made him flinch, and Caitlin used that single moment of distraction to slip past him and race for the door. Before he could take more than two steps, he heard her car start, the belts making a high-pitched whining noise. A death trap it was. He should have insisted she ride with him.

"Ya' said ya' would listen!" Liam roared. The two men stood, barely a foot apart, both ready for a fight, until Mara, who'd risen alongside Cade, took a single step towards them, then collapsed into a heap on the floor.

CHAPTER SIX

Caitlin

She needed air. Needed to know she could call on her element to protect her, and inside that house with the alpha looking like he wanted to tear her limb from limb...she couldn't think.

Mara hadn't been well, and the same words Caitlin had recalled earlier echoed in her mind. In her own voice, no less.

Two elements cannot coexist. One will always overwhelm the other, and only the strongest elementals can survive.

She'd said those words to someone. A dark, shadowy figure. Tall. Bulky. Not Liam. Fergus?

Pressing her fists to her eyes, she tried to see his face, but it was shrouded. Haunted. Like one of those twisted Halloween masks the kids always wore when they'd come to Katerina's occult shop.

With all the windows in her little car rolled down, she let the cool, night air waft over her and felt marginally better. Until she realized her mistake.

Her clothes were still at the alpha's house. "Blast it! I liked that jacket." She'd had the presence of mind to tuck her keys and her wallet in the pocket of the fleece pants Mara had lent her. But the one thing she'd left behind? Katerina's fire agate crystal. Her last connection to the woman who'd saved her life.

It was dead now. Ineffective. Useless. But despite that, tears sprang to her eyes. She'd never see it again, and it was like losing Katerina a second time.

By the time Caitlin reached the run-down extended-stay hotel room she'd rented when she'd arrived in Seattle, exhaustion weighed her down. Locking the door, she made a beeline for the only item in the kitchenette. A bottle of whiskey.

Three shots in, she knew she was headed for a world of hurt, but what else was she supposed to do? Let her memories of Liam —and there were more of them every hour now—drive her back into his arms?

No. Because she could *feel* darkness coming for her. It had a name. One that made her shiver. Fergus. Fergus Tharp.

Sitting cross-legged on the bed, she opened her used laptop and searched for him. Or tried to. The drink made her fingers clumsy, and she kept misspelling his name. When she finally got it right and found a grainy photo of a lone man standing close to the edge of the Cliffs of Moher, something broke inside her.

Fergus Tharp mourns the loss of his love, Caitlin Brannigan. The young woman threw herself off the cliffs three days ago, and her body has yet to be recovered.

"My Caitie was troubled," Tharp said when asked if he suspected Miss Brannigan was suicidal. "But no. I never thought she'd do this. We were happy together. She was my air."

"His air?" Caitlin said, her tongue thick and unwieldy. Shit. She had to sober up. Stumbling into the kitchen area, she started a pot of crappy hotel coffee, hoping it would help clear her head. Because she wasn't Fergus's air. Not the way he'd implied.

She understood now. Why she'd told Liam she was bound to

Fergus. How he always managed to find her. Why she'd never be free.

Fergus Tharp had used a spell to *steal* her element. He'd *taken* her air, left her weak and at his mercy. That's why she'd tried to end her life. Because he wouldn't—couldn't even—let her go. The spell wasn't his. And while he had the power to wield it, once he had, it had taken on a life of its own.

A memory fought its way to the surface of her muddled thoughts.

"You're mine, Caitie. No one can protect you like I can. Can't ya see that?"

She sobbed, cowering against the wall, the stale, unmoving air sapping her strength. "I'm sorry. I won't run again. Ye're so good to me, why would I ever leave?" The lie rolled easily off her tongue, though she struggled to force the words out of swollen and bloodied lips.

"I can smell him all over ya'. What did he do for ya' that I can't? Did he fuck ya'? Tell me how to find him, and I'll ease yer pain. What's his name, Caitie?"

The compulsion charm settled over her, urging her to confess everything. But enough of her own power remained to keep Liam safe, and she stared up at the wild eyes, the tufted black hair, and the snarling, twisted face. He'd been handsome once. Sweet. That boy still existed within the madman—but she couldn't find him now. "There's no one. No one but you."

With a yelp, she dropped the coffee cup, and the damn thing shattered into a dozen pieces. It didn't matter. Her stomach pitched and roiled, and she ran for the bathroom, falling to her knees in front of the toilet seconds before the whiskey came back up, violently.

Without Katerina's protection, Fergus could—and would— find her again. Hell, he might already know where she was. Shite. How much longer did she have? Days? Weeks?

As she collapsed against the wall, she only had one thought.

If Fergus found her with Liam, he'd kill the werewolf. Slowly. Painfully.

She had to run. Fergus's element was earth, so he'd have a hard time flying. But her air—her stolen element—would allow him to live through a flight, maybe even long enough to get from Ireland to the States.

And if he'd managed to get his hands on any other elements in the past eleven years...well...he could be unstoppable.

New Zealand. She couldn't go any farther. Not unless she somehow expected to live on the South Pole. Even there, she might not be safe. But it was her only hope.

Liam

The minutes ticked by, so slowly, he thought the clock was moving backwards. He'd been pacing for over an hour now, and Cade still hadn't come out of the bedroom.

His alpha's voice carried through the door every now and again, but though Liam wanted to eavesdrop, he wouldn't.

Mara had come to after a few moments, but she'd been unable to do more than say Cade's name and ask for water. If Caitlin had done this to her, triggered her illness again, Liam could kiss any hope of staying in the pack goodbye.

And could he truly mate himself to Caitlin knowing she was the type of person who'd purposely hurt Mara? His instincts said yes, he could. And no, she wasn't. But his heart? That was an entirely different matter.

The bedroom door opened, and a burst of humidity filled the house. Mara shook off Cade's arm around her waist and shuffled over to the hearth where Caitlin's folded clothes lay.

"Honey, don't. Let me," Cade said as he sidestepped her and grabbed the bundle.

She rolled her eyes. "I'm not going to shatter, you know."

"What's going on?" Liam asked as Cade spread the green army jacket out on the table and searched through the pockets.

"This." Holding up a white silk pouch, Cade glared at Liam as he fished out a dark red crystal. "This belonged to Katerina."

"Fuck me. Caitlin said it stopped workin'."

"It did." From the love seat, Mara held out her hand, and when her mate didn't move, she sighed. "Give it to me, Cade. I can handle it now."

"No. I'm taking it to Livie. She can shift and run for an hour, then drop it somewhere it won't hurt you again."

"You'll do no such thing." Pushing to her feet, Mara shuffled over to him and eased the blood red stone from his hand. "See? I'm fine."

Liam would bet his life she was lying. Her skin had paled, her lips turning almost bluish in the light from the kitchen. But as he watched, Mara called on her element and droplets of water gathered all over the crystal.

"There's a small amount of my sister's power left in the stone," Mara said. "Enough that I could feel it earlier."

"Feel it? You passed out!" Cade plucked the crystal from her palm and shoved it into his pocket. "I'm not losing you to this fucking fire element."

"Do you think I want to die? I don't. But I do want to figure out what the hell is going on. And there's only one way to do that. We have to find Caitlin." Mara turned to Liam. "You don't have any idea where she might be, do you?"

His shoulders slumped, and he shook his head. "No. She found me at the lake earlier. But she has a car, and even as my wolf...unless she's close, I won't be able to scent her."

"Try it," Cade growled. "I'm going to get Christine to stay with Mara and I'll join you."

Shock left Liam speechless as Cade strode from the house. His alpha rarely shifted anymore.

"He's worried," Mara said softly as she retreated back to the love seat and tucked her legs under her. "He still doesn't trust his wolf. Not completely. Not after…"

"After bein' trapped for so long."

Patting the cushion next to her, Mara waited for Liam to join her. He kept as much distance between them as he could, not wanting to face Cade's wrath. Wolves were territorial and possessive with their mates, especially for the first year, and if Liam so much as put a hand on Mara, Cade would be within his rights to beat the crap out of him.

"I had a good couple of months," Mara said as she played with the belt of her robe. "For all of January and February, I felt great. But a few weeks ago, something changed."

Liam glanced over at Mara. Her eyes were unfocused, her lips parted slightly. "Are ya' okay?"

She shook her head like she'd just realized he was in the room. "Sorry. This keeps happening."

"What?"

"I lose time," Mara whispered. "Sometimes seconds, like now. But…once, it was over an hour."

"Fuck me. And ya' never told Cade?" Liam clenched his fists hard enough his knuckles cracked, and the urge to find his alpha and tell the man he could never leave Mara's side almost overwhelmed him.

"Not until tonight, no." Shame tinged her voice, and she ran a hand through her red locks. The faint scent of smoke, of the remnants of a fire, wafted over Liam. "Eleanor—the air elemental who lives in Oregon?—she suggested I come down to visit her for a few weeks. There's a whole community of elementals in Cannon Beach, including a group of elders. Like…elemental royalty, I guess."

"Have Cade take ya'. I can handle pack business." He didn't know what the fuck he'd do about Caitlin, but his alpha's mate was sick—and scared—and he had to help. It was his place. His duty.

"They said Cade wasn't welcome. I'd have to come alone. So they could protect me. Something about it feels...*wrong*, Liam. And now that we know this is tied to my sister's element? We need to find Caitlin. If anyone has answers, she does."

Mara sank back against the cushions, her eyes fluttering closed. "Go with Cade. Make sure he's safe." A tear glistened on her cheek, and she swiped it away with a trembling hand. "Make sure he comes back to me. Comes back from being his wolf. Please."

"I will, Mara. I promise. Ye'll rest? Listen to Christine and let her give ya' somethin' to help cool ya'?"

His alpha's mate nodded and pulled a blanket from the back of the love seat. "I will. Go. Go now before you lose her scent completely."

Caitlin

She tried, desperately, to distract herself. But the television was conspiring against her. She flipped channels for half an hour and all she found were romantic comedies and horror movies.

Still too drunk to drive, she burrowed under the covers and tried to ignore the ever-growing sense of foreboding filling the room. Until a tentative knock sounded at her door.

No one knows you're here. It's probably just housekeeping.

At midnight? Maybe if she stayed quiet, they'd go away. Bracing herself against the side of the couch, she called upon her element, creating a mini-tornado between her hands.

"Caitlin? It's Mara. Please...let me in?"

Mara? What was the water elemental doing *here*? And how had she tracked Caitlin in the first place?

Tiptoeing to the door, she checked the peephole. Mara stood a few steps back, alone, looking like she was about to fall over.

"Shite. What's wrong?" Caitlin asked as Mara trudged inside and made a beeline for the chair next to the window.

"I don't know." Mara's green eyes were bloodshot, and the dark, puffy bags underneath were so much worse than they'd been just two hours ago. Her face was flushed, like she'd been out in the sun for hours.

Quickly, Caitlin removed the smoky quartz pendant from around her neck and pressed it into Mara's palm. "Take this. It should be cooling and detoxifying."

Within seconds, Mara's cheeks paled back to their normal color, and the stress lines bracketing her lips eased slightly. "That's...amazing."

"I can't do what Katerina could. With runes and spells and enchantments. But I know a little. Put the necklace on and give me your hand." Kneeling, Caitlin waited for Mara to fasten the clasp, then linked their fingers. Dammit. Mara was burning up.

"Call on your water element as I pull some of my air. The two together should help cool the fire within you."

Mara closed her eyes, and a few drops of water gathered on her cheeks.

"I call upon the air. With water at its side, it will quench the flames burning where they do not belong," Caitlin murmured, and the drapes billowed gently, the temperature in the room dropping ten degrees in a matter of seconds. "Better?" she asked.

"It won't last," Mara said. "But I'll take it."

"How did you find me? Is Liam—?"

The water elemental shook her head. "Cade and Liam are trying to track you by scent, but neither of them *really* believe they'll be successful. I think...I'm pretty sure I came alone."

Caitlin's fear spiked, and she clutched Mara's hand tightly. "You think...?"

"I don't remember how I got here. Not really. I drove. I have my car keys." She dug into her pocket and withdrew the key fob for the Prius. "I was at home with Christine, and I went into the bedroom. After that...the next memory I have is of getting out of my car in the motel parking lot. And *feeling* you." She shook her head. "No, not you. Not exactly. More like...whatever hold my sister had over you. It's still there. Faint. Fading fast, now. But I just sort of...followed it. Like this string connecting us." She loosened the top two buttons of her flannel shirt to show Caitlin her scar. The red crystal shard glowed, and when Caitlin approached, Mara hissed out a breath.

"We need to get that thing out of you. Now." Caitlin rummaged in her backpack for her pocket knife, but Mara held up her hand.

"You can't. We've tried." She huffed out what might have been a laugh. "I asked Christine—the pack's healer—a dozen times, and she refused. Cade was too scared of hurting me. Until the day they found me holding an ice pack to my chest with a sterilized scalpel on a tray in front of me."

Caitlin gasped. "Shite. That's..."

"I'm a nurse. I thought I could excise it easily. But it's embedded in my sternum." She sat back with a sigh. "When I couldn't cut it out of me, I snuck into the hospital where I used to work and used the ultrasound machine."

"I need another drink." In truth, it was the last thing she needed, but all of this was simply too much. If Mara could track her by her element—or by Katerina's—Fergus could certainly find her. "Ya' want one?"

"No. I have to drive myself back home soon. Cade and Liam won't stay out forever, and if he finds out I'm gone, he'll...well... he'll be very *put out*."

"I remember a little. Wolves and their protectiveness. How angry Liam was when I told him about Fergus. I only have these bits and pieces," Caitlin said before she poured herself another shot of whiskey and drained it in a single swallow. The alcohol burned, giving her something to focus on besides her fears. "Moments. With these big blank spots in between."

"Come back to the house with me." Mara pushed to her feet and swayed slightly before steadying.

"No. I can't put Liam in danger. Fergus will find me. He'll call to me, and if he's powerful enough, he might be able to tell that Liam's with me." Her brain felt like Swiss cheese—more holes than actual memories at the moment, but she *knew* Fergus would come for her. "He wanted to kill Liam once before." Shuddering, she gripped the glass hard enough her knuckles paled. "I remember him beating me. Tryin' to get me to tell him where Liam was. *Who* he was. And shite. I wanted to tell him. That's how strong his hold over me is."

"Oh, my God. That's why you tried to kill yourself?" Mara's horror pulled water from the air, and several droplets landed on the old, scarred counter. "Because you didn't think you could resist him any longer?"

Caitlin nodded. "He can compel me. Force me to bend to his will." Tears burned her eyes, and she sank down to the floor and covered her face with her hands. "I helped him *hurt* other elementals. He wants...he wants..." She couldn't tease that last bit of knowledge from her memories. Other elementals had died. Right in front of her. But why? Had Fergus been trying to take their elements too?

"Caitlin, please. I know you're scared. So am I. You're the only link I have to my sister." Mara's voice wasn't steady, and she knelt next to Caitlin. "She did something to me. Or...I did something to her when I took in her element. And whatever that was—is—it's killing me."

"Killing you?" Even though she'd only known Mara for a few hours, she felt a connection to the water elemental she couldn't explain. Whether it was guilt over helping Katerina or something deeper, Caitlin didn't know, but she didn't want Mara to die.

Memories tickled the back of Caitlin's mind. A thick accent. Not Irish. Scottish if she had to guess. Screaming.

"You've failed. Four times now. The next one you find, you will bring to us and we will do what you cannot."

What did it mean?

"Caitlin?" Mara's warm fingers touched her wrist, and Caitlin jerked back with a tiny yelp. "Where did you go?"

"Fergus isn't the only one we have to be afraid of." Meeting the water elemental's gaze, Caitlin set her shoulders and rose. "We have to go back to your house. Right now."

CHAPTER SEVEN

Liam

*T*hey'd run for over an hour, and though he'd wanted to split up to cover more ground, Mara's words echoed in his head. *"Go with Cade. Make sure he's safe."*

So he had. Stayed by his alpha's side as they'd searched every street around Green Lake, hoping to catch something of Caitlin's scent.

Despite the miles they'd covered, he wasn't tired. Not physically. It had been more than a week since the full moon. When they'd lived in Bellingham, there had been times Liam had run for hours every night just to try to escape his memories.

Now, they only ran as a pack on the full moon, and while Seattle was rife with greenbelts and wooded areas their wolves could hide, it was nothing like the forests up north.

Padding through the back gate of the pack house, Liam froze and scented the air. At his side, Cade did the same with an inquisitive—yet somehow still angry—sound.

Fig blossoms. And...Mara.

The two wolves dropped down to their haunches and closed their eyes. Shifting was instinctual. All Liam had to do was reach for the man inside, and his bones started to pop and crack, his fur receded, and his tail shrank away to nothing.

He howled, muffling the sound with his front legs crossed over his muzzle. The pain was almost overwhelming, every time, but along with it came the most exhilarating sensation. He welcomed the agony of his lupine teeth being absorbed back into his jaw and his human incisors fighting their way to the surface.

In under a minute, the two men lay naked on the grass, both panting, their bodies trembling.

Cade recovered first and pushed to his hands and knees. "If she's hurt Mara—"

With a grunt, Liam got to his feet and snagged his pants from the chair on the back patio. "She wouldn't. Not my Caitlin. And yer not goin' in there buck-arse naked."

Cade was already halfway to the sliding glass door and showed no signs of stopping, so Liam balled up the man's shirt and lobbed it at his back.

"Don't," Cade growled.

"And if I'd strode into yer house naked the first day?" The realization hit both of them at the same time. Liam had done just that, and Cade had almost kicked him out of the pack for it.

"Fuck," the alpha muttered as he yanked on his pants and shrugged into his shirt. "But you had better be right about her."

Shite. The scent of fig blossoms filled the pack house kitchen, and at the wobbly dining room table, Caitlin sat huddled in the sweatshirt Mara had loaned her, a cup of tea in her hands, with the entire pack gathered along the perimeter of the room.

Across from her, Mara held her own mug, and Liam's gaze went to the crystal at Mara's throat. Caitlin's crystal.

"What the fuck is going on here?" Cade's voice had taken on a rough, guttural tone, and he raced to Mara's side and dropped to a knee next to her. "Why are you out of bed?"

"Because someone had to find Caitlin, and clearly the two of you weren't the ones to do it." She gave her mate a half-smile, but he just growled in return.

"You swore to me you'd stay put. That you'd rest." Cade glared at Christine. "And you were supposed to watch over her."

"Don't blame her." Mara ran a hand through her hair and nodded to the chair next to her. "You're going to want to sit down for this."

"Fuck, no."

Liam couldn't blame his alpha. Mara looked decidedly guilty. And worried.

"I, um...lost time again," she said quietly. "And I found myself outside Caitlin's hotel room."

Cade pushed to his feet and started to pace. His knuckles turned white as he practically vibrated with a mix of anger, fear, and frustration.

"It's not like I *planned* it," she said. "Caitlin helped me, and I'm fine now."

He grabbed her hand and brought the inside of her wrist to his nose, inhaling deeply. "The hell you are. I can smell the fire, honey. It's stronger now than when you passed out!"

"That doesn't matter." At Cade's incredulous stare, Mara nodded at Caitlin. "We have a bigger problem."

"There is no bigger problem than this," Cade growled. "What am I supposed to do? Tie you to the bed every time I leave so you don't accidentally walk in front of a bus?"

Mara's eyes darkened, and a wave of humidity infused the room. "You're the alpha of this pack. That doesn't give you the right to take that tone with me. I'm not a wolf. I'm your wife. Remember?"

"Yes. I remember. And you're my *mate*, Mara. I won't survive losing you, and you can be damn sure I'm going to do whatever I can to keep you safe."

The other members of the pack stilled, the silence so total, Liam could hear the rapid, fearful beat of Caitlin's heart.

After what seemed like forever but was probably only a minute, Mara rose and crossed to Cade, framing his face with her hands. "You're not going to lose me. I promise. Now will you sit down and listen to what Caitlin has to say? It's important." Reluctantly, Cade led her back to the table and pulled out a chair next to her. With a glance at the air elemental, Mara said, "Go ahead. Tell them. Tell all of them what you remember."

Caitlin took a sip of tea—mint, from the scent that wafted over Liam—and then reached for his hand. Her touch was like a balm to his battered heart. As well as a shot of pure need to his dick.

Fuck. This was not the time for his mating drive to take over, but controlling himself after eleven years was the hardest thing he'd ever done—save accepting Caitlin's death in the first place.

"I remember you, Liam." Her voice held a hint of Ireland, the lilting melody so like his dreams. But it was her words that brought him the most peace. "I cared for you once. I know that much."

"And now?" He had to force the question out over the lump in his throat.

"Now? I don't know ya'. I barely know myself." Tightening her grip on his fingers, she sighed and held his gaze. "I can't tell ya' what happened when Fergus found me. Not yet. But I can tell ya' how he found me. And why Mara's in terrible danger if this fire inside her continues to grow."

She paused, chewing on her lip for a moment, and Liam squeezed her fingers.

"Go on, luv. We'll listen." With a sweeping gaze, he took in the rest of the wolves in the room. His pack. His brothers and sisters. When he met Cade's eyes, the alpha gave him a terse nod. It wasn't the warm welcome Liam would have liked for his mate, but a gesture that told every member of the pack they weren't to interrupt or threaten Caitlin unless he gave the word. Grateful, Liam nodded back. "All of us."

Caitlin

She couldn't believe she was sitting here surrounded by seven werewolves—all but one of whom definitely wanted her dead—and about to tell them her greatest shame. How stupid she'd been as a young girl, and how one decision had set the course of her entire life.

"I grew up in a little town in Ireland. Doolin," she said, staring into the mug of tea. Looking at any of the wolves—especially Liam—was too painful. "There were a handful of elementals in Doolin. Air, water, and earth. No fire that I can remember. Fergus was the most handsome boy in town. Or so I thought. He was two years older than me. My first crush, I suppose."

Next to her, Liam let out a low growl, and she flinched.

"I can't help it, luv. Ye're mine."

"I'm not. Yet, anyway," she shot back. "And you don't get to decide that for me."

He stared down at their joined hands, then muttered, "My wolf claimed ya' eleven years ago. Even if ya' reject me, Caitlin, he'll still be yers. I'll still be yers. Always."

Mara cleared her throat. "Liam, please don't take this the wrong way, but your wolf needs to shut up and let Caitlin speak."

Gaping at Mara, Caitlin didn't know what to say. The water elemental's words held power over the entire pack, especially Liam. The man who wanted to be her mate hung his head, but didn't let go of her hand.

"Fergus was earth. Is earth." Caitlin could feel him now. His presence. The way he tugged on her element, like she was a fish caught on his hook and he was desperately trying to reel her in.

"When he was seventeen, his father moved him to Scotland. I was a teenager who thought she was in love. I rebelled against my mum, told her she didn't understand me, all the while writin' Fergus letters and begging him to come back for me. I was so stupid."

"Stupid?" a female wolf with blond hair and a baby balanced on her hip asked.

"When Fergus came back, he said he wanted to see the world with me. He'd take me away from Doolin, take care of me. We could be together if I'd just give him my element."

"Give him your air?" Mara asked. "How would that even work?"

"He had a spell. He said he'd learned it while he'd been away. That he'd learned so much and he wanted to share it with me. I didn't question him. He made it sound so exciting. So romantic. It wasn't any of those things."

The tea was gone now, and she had nothing to distract her as she let herself sink deep into her memories.

"Give me yer hands, Caitie. When we're done, we'll be closer than any two people have ever been. Are ya' ready?"

Breathless, excited, Caitlin held on tight. She wanted this, wanted him. "Ya' won't leave me?"

"Never, lass. Ye'll be my first." His dark gaze searched hers, as if he might be having second thoughts, but then he shook his head and his eyes turned cold.

First what? she wondered. He started to chant and nodded towards the paper he'd set in her lap. She brushed her worry aside. Fergus loved her, and she loved him. They'd be together forever.

A lock of black hair fell over his forehead as he continued to chant, "Air to Earth, Fire to Water. Four become one. Do ya' give me this gift freely?"

"I do." She read aloud from the words he'd written for her. "My heart to your heart. My air to your earth. My strength to your strength. What was two will be one."

Fergus threw his head back as power thrummed through their joined hands. "Yes! More!"

White hot pain cleaved her heart in two. A vise tightened around her lungs, and she pulled her hands away, but it was too late. She couldn't breathe, couldn't call on her element, could barely move. Clutching at her throat, she stared up at Fergus's face. So handsome. She wanted to kiss him. To feel his arms around her. But something was so wrong. So very wrong.

"Let go, Caitie. Give me yer air, and I will live forever!"

Her entire being railed. Choking, she clawed at the floor, inching away from the man whose face now lit up with glee. Fire burned deep inside her soul, the void spreading through her chest, her arms, her legs, all the way to her fingers and toes. She felt nothing but agony, heard nothing but the dull roar of her heartbeat in her ears, saw nothing but his eyes, glowing bright white. Darkness closed in on her, and he roared with laughter, his fists raised triumphantly.

As her consciousness left her, his words floated in the air. "Two down. Two to go."

Caitlin didn't know when Liam had pulled her into his arms or how long she'd clung to him, but his shirt was soaked from her tears, and the entire pack was completely silent. She inhaled his scent. Pine and the sea and strength. Home.

"Are ya' back with me, luv?" he asked, his deep voice rumbling in his chest.

"Y-yes. What happened?" Unwilling to risk meeting his gaze, too ashamed of what she'd done, of what she'd let Fergus do to her, she kept her face buried against his neck. Even though she'd never be his, never be free, she needed this small bit of comfort. This stolen moment to keep tucked away in her mind for however long she had left to live.

"Ya' were tellin' us about the charm. And all of a sudden, it was like ya' couldn't breathe." He pressed a kiss to the top of her head, and the strain in his voice made her heart ache. "I thought I'd lost ya'."

"You will," she whispered, finally gathering the strength to raise her head and face the rest of his pack. "I can't stop him from finding me, Liam. Katerina's magic is gone now. He'll know I'm alive. And he'll come for me."

"He'll have to go through me."

Her wolf was so confident, she wanted to believe him. But she knew better. "If you fight him, you'll lose, Liam." Extricating herself from his arms, she returned to her chair, though the idea of being parted from him for even a minute set her on edge.

"I've only been strong enough to fight him once, and even then...it was because I knew if I were quick about it, I could end my life before he could stop me."

Liam cupped the back of her neck, urging her to look at him again. His fingers were so warm, so strong, and she wanted to stay with him more than anything.

"Ye're not alone any more, Caitlin. Ya' have me." He paused for a moment, flicking his gaze to his alpha, then back to hers. "And the pack."

"It won't be enough. Because it's not just Fergus." The wolves exchanged glances, and Liam's eyes hardened. She rushed to continue, afraid if she didn't get it all out right now, she never would. "The spell Fergus used? It came from a very powerful group of practitioners." At Liam's confusion, she added, "Witches. Mages."

"So?" Liam asked. "I don't care who he had helpin' him. I'll kill anyone who tries to harm ya'."

"You don't understand." Shit. She was making a mess of this, all because she was terrified of her own memories. "The practitioners think they can use Fergus to get all four elements together in one person."

"If I'm unstable with two," Mara said quietly, "what would four do to someone?"

Caitlin shook her head. "That's just it. Four elements...might actually be stable. But it would be much *more* than stable. There's a fifth element. Spirit. It's...like the total harmony of body and soul, of this life and the next. The practitioners—the Thirteen, they call themselves—believe if they can achieve this state, their magic will be unstoppable. No elemental on earth would be safe from them."

Staring at each wolf in turn, Caitlin's frustration rose. They didn't appear to grasp how serious this was. "Ya' have two elements already, Mara. The two Fergus *doesn't* have. If he finds out about that, he'll want ya'. He'll try to take your water and your fire."

"A part of me thinks that wouldn't be so terrible," Mara said, almost to herself. "I want to be...normal."

Caitlin pushed up from the table, clenching her hands into fists and battling the overwhelming urge to let her element free. To use a compulsion charm like she had so many times while under Katerina's thrall, or Fergus's harsh control. "The spell worked with me. But the pain was like nothin' I've ever felt before or since. I almost didn't survive. After Fergus could compel me with my own feckin' element, he found others—or made me find them—and then he'd use my air to convince them to give up their elements as well."

"But you said you didn't think the practitioners had been successful." Cade leaned forward, his steely blue eyes narrowed. "If this Fergus asshole took other elements—"

"Because every single one of those elementals died!" Tears sprang to Caitlin's eyes and she didn't think she could hold her emotions in check a moment longer. "There's a problem with the spell. Or was. It only worked with me. But Fergus kept tryin'. Over and over again. Until the practitioners demanded that the next elemental he found, he bring straight to them."

"I still don't understand why this is something we need to be so worried about," Liam said.

Her frustration spilled over, and power gathered between her fingers, itching to be released. "Fergus was no good to them with my element hidden from him. But now? They can finally get what they want. The four elements. All by getting to Mara."

The room exploded into chaos. The alpha wolf leapt to his feet, pulling Mara up with him as he wrapped his arms around her, two of the other males formed a wall in front of the pair, presumably to stop Caitlin from taking Mara away—and apparently ignoring the fact that she'd been the one to help Mara not more than an hour ago, and Liam simply stared up at her, his green eyes filled with horror—and a hint of understanding.

This was the only chance she'd have. She knew it as well as she knew her own name...now. Weaving the compulsion charm with her hands at her sides, she took one step back. Then another. And another.

"You will all hide Mara. Keep her safe. You won't let her use her element. Run, if you must, but never allow anyone to know what she can do. And don't try to follow me. None of you will move until you can no longer scent me. Let me die before Fergus uses me to kill all of you." Sending the charm swirling around the room, she watched as their eyes went glassy and their voices died down.

"I'm so sorry, Liam," Caitlin whispered, then ran.

CHAPTER EIGHT

Liam

*N*o one moved for a full five minutes. He could see Cade's eyes, the pained expression on Mara's face. Peter growled quietly behind him, straining to escape from Caitlin's charm, but Liam didn't have any fight left in him.

His mate had rejected him. Again.

Serena let out a wail, and the baby's cry shattered the preternatural stillness infusing the room. Cade was across the table in two seconds, knocking Caitlin's mug to the floor and tackling Liam hard enough to drive the air from his lungs.

"You swore to me," he spat, holding Liam down while his eyes glowed.

"She's terrified." Mara's quiet voice stopped Cade with his arm cocked, ready to punch Liam in the jaw before he beat the crap out of him.

"I. Don't. Care." Yet, Cade got to his feet and went to his mate's side. "I told her earlier. No charms. And yet she did it again. What's worse, she *compelled* us."

"You didn't see her at the hotel." Mara gave Liam a pointed gaze. "When I looked up and found myself at the University Extended Stay, I was ready to give up fighting. I can't *stand* not being...me. I thought dying was terrible. This...this is worse. Because when I'm not in control? There's this little sliver of me that *knows* what's going on. *Knows* I'm not me. Like a shadow. Fighting to get out of this terrible, horrible box my sister—or her element at least—is using to trap me." Tears tumbled down her cheeks—cheeks that were too flushed, yet almost hollow.

She took a deep, shuddering breath and reached for Cade. Winding her arms around his waist, she leaned into him, and the pain in her eyes eased slightly, but her shoulders were still stiff, hiked up around her ears.

"Caitlin helped me. She used her element. Joined it with mine to strengthen my water and dampen the fire. And she gave me this." Her fingers curled around the quartz pendant. "It's grounding. I don't feel like I'm standing on the edge of a cliff anymore. It's precious to her, but she handed it over without a second thought because I needed it."

"And that's supposed to make up for what she just did?" Peter asked, his voice hoarse. He took two uneven steps, then braced himself against the counter. Ever since the fire, since Katerina's charms had stopped him and Livie from shifting back into their human forms—an act that would heal almost any injury a wolf sustained—he'd suffered. Physically and emotionally. Liam knew it, and yet he'd kept his distance. They worked together every damn day, but rarely spoke about anything besides the job. Now, the man looked at Liam like they were strangers.

"Yes." Mara peered up at Cade, and the moment that passed between them seemed to fill the room with its intensity. Pure, perfect love, but also desperation. Fear. Pain. "What she did to us just now? Does anyone remember her words?"

One by one, the wolves shook their heads.

"Let me die before Fergus uses me to kill all of you."

Agony caught fire in Liam's chest, consuming his battered heart before it turned to anger. Rage. Despair. His mate was going to sacrifice herself again. And this time, he'd bet his life she wouldn't fail.

"Eleanor told me a little bit about what air elementals can do," Mara continued. "When she was training me before you all arrived. They can compel, yes. But they can also track. Anyone. All they need is the barest hint of a person. Of their scent. Their... unique essence. If Fergus gets his hands on Caitlin again, he'll be able to find me."

A growl rumbled in Cade's chest, and he stood a little taller. Mara slid her hand around his waist and settled even closer to him, eyelids heavy, exhaustion and defeat playing over her features.

"That's why she's doing this. Well, one of the reasons. To protect me. A woman she doesn't know, who's mated to a man who wants her dead. And to protect all the other elementals the practitioners might go after. Might kill."

"And you're sure about all of this?" Cade asked, crouching down next to her chair and taking her hands.

"Almost as sure as I am that you love me."

The two didn't move for several seconds, holding one another's gaze, sharing something Liam could only dream of having one day. A bond so strong, so instinctual, words could never do it justice.

Cade rose again, the alpha wolf rearing up in his eyes. "When Liam...*questioned* Mara's intentions months ago, I kicked him out of the pack."

No one dared breathe. They never spoke about that fight. About Cade's words moments before Livie had come back to tell them Katerina had taken Mara.

"But then he risked his life for her. For all of us. Fought alongside us when he had no obligation to stay." Cade held up his hand before Liam could interrupt him. "That's what family does.

Family sticks. We fight, but then we forgive."

Peter pushed off the wall, rage filling his brown eyes, but one growl from Cade had him hunching his shoulders and stepping back again.

"Caitlin and Liam never formally mated," Cade said. "That chance was stolen from them by some Irish bastard with magic on his side. But Livie, Shawn? You know as well as I do. Completing the mating bond? It's a formality. Ceremony. Tradition."

Finding Mara's hand, Cade brought it to his heart. "Liam's mate needs our help. She's a part of this family. I may want to kick her ass right now, but I won't. Because family sticks. And family forgives."

"Cade, does that mean…" Liam swallowed hard in a vain attempt to force the rest of his plea from of a throat that was suddenly too tight for him to breathe.

"Go after her. Keep her alive. Bring her back here where she won't have to fight alone."

As he strode for the door—headed for his bike and his mate—Liam paused to clap his hand on Cade's shoulder. "I'll never be able to repay ya' for this."

"Family doesn't ask you to." His alpha pulled Liam into a quick, one-armed hug, and as Liam shut the front door behind him, he heard Cade's voice once more.

"The rest of you, listen up. I know everyone's exhausted, but we need a plan to protect Mara, and we need it right fucking now."

Caitlin

She still had a mile to go when the rain started, and she began to run. Calling a Lyft would have taken too much time, so once she'd left the pack house, she'd taken off at a jog.

Her charm would hold. It had to. Mara knew where she was staying, and she figured she had at most twenty minutes before someone showed up looking for her.

She didn't care who it was—Liam, Mara, or Cade. She didn't want to see any of them. She couldn't. They'd try to change her mind. Or in the case of the alpha, probably kill her.

Though at least then, she wouldn't have to worry about doing it herself.

Keeping her head down, she turned onto 15th and made a beeline for the hotel, only to smack into a steaming brick wall right outside her room.

With a yelp, she tried to pull away, but a strong arm steadied her.

"Easy, luv. I have ya' now."

Oh God. She'd been too slow. Liam's gentle words warred with the harshness of his tone, and when he tipped her chin up to force her to meet his gaze, she found his moss and amber eyes hard and unforgiving.

"Let me go."

Liam stepped back so she could pass, but he didn't leave, waiting until she'd unlocked the hotel room door before he spoke again. "Do ya' think I'm a proper idiot?"

Of all the questions he could have asked, she hadn't expected that one. "No."

"Then why," he said, following her in and locking the door behind him, "did ya' expect me to let ya' face that bastard alone?"

"Because if ya' don't run—if you don't take Mara and keep her hidden until someone, somewhere finds a way to separate elements safely, you're going to die. I won't be able to stop it."

"And what about you?" He reached for her, but she darted

around the countertop in the small kitchenette to keep some space between them. He smelled so good, and he'd been so warm, and all she wanted to do was let herself have a few minutes where she could be free—be herself—with Liam.

"Me? I'm already dead." Caitlin grabbed the bottle of whiskey and shoved it into her small duffel bag before ducking under his arm and heading for the pile of clothes she'd left on top of the dresser.

"Ya' look full of life to me." His voice softened, and he skimmed a knuckle along her jaw. "Don't run, Caitlin. Please."

For a single moment, their gazes locked, and Caitlin's heart ached. Once, Liam had been all she'd ever wanted. Was he still? He'd changed. Eleven years would change anyone. But under the strong, cocky, beta wolf, she could still see the sweet, protective man she'd fallen for.

And now, she had to break his heart.

"I don't love ya', Liam. I didn't eleven years ago, and I certainly don't now. We had some fun together, I'll give ya' that, but there's nothin' between us."

Don't back down. Don't let him see the truth.

"Ye're lyin' to me." Liam wrapped strong fingers around her upper arm, his hold firm, but not so tight he was hurting her.

"What? No." Caitlin tried to shake him off, but he didn't budge.

"Prove it." The dare flashed in his eyes, amber streaks amid the green, and the corner of his mouth turned up slightly.

"There is nothing I could possibly say that would prove how I *don't* feel about ya'." Shit. She needed to get her emotions under control. A hint of her Irish accent kept slipping through, and that would only spur him on.

"Say? No, luv. Ye're right about that. But if ya' feel nothin' for me, then kiss me goodbye. One last kindness, yeah?"

The dare turned to an amused glint, and Caitlin clenched her fists at her sides. He was maddening. "Fine. One kiss."

Despite the overwhelming desire to burst into tears, to mourn the loss of the man she'd once cared so deeply for—the man she thought she might have *loved*—for a second time, she could hold it together for another five minutes before she'd make him leave.

"Come here, then." He traced the curve of her cheek, then threaded his fingers into her hair. "Ye're the only woman I've ever loved, Caitlin."

As he leaned closer, she inhaled his scent, and shit. She never wanted to leave him. His other hand pressed lightly to the small of her back, and she fought to trap a whimper behind her lips.

Arousal flooded her, and Liam grinned. Damn werewolves and their keen sense of smell.

"Breathe," he whispered.

When had she stopped? Right about the time he nuzzled the spot behind her ear she'd forgotten he loved so very much.

"Liam..." Unable to keep her hands to herself, she gripped the sleeves of his leather jacket.

"I love hearin' ya' say my name." His hard length pressed against her hip, and she shuddered. She *had* loved him once. Denying it was only causing her more pain. If only she were free...

"Do ya' want this?" he asked, his lips skimming the corner of her mouth.

With all my heart. She couldn't tell him the truth. Not with Fergus out there. Every minute, the earth elemental's call grew stronger. He hadn't sent out a locator charm for her yet, but he would. Soon. And when he did...she'd have no choice but to go to him.

"I can't..." she whispered.

"That's not an answer." Liam pulled back to meet her gaze, the sudden chill against her skin almost a physical blow. "Why did ya' run, Caitlin? Answer me."

"To save you."

"I don't need savin'." Shoulders stiff and straight, he shoved his hands into his pockets. "And I'm fuckin' tired of ya' keepin' secrets from me."

Frustration thrummed through her, and Caitlin stalked over to the dresser and shoved the last of her belongings into her bag. "You don't know him. Fergus Tharp is a crazy bastard who thinks he owns me. And...fuck. He does."

Liam growled, yanking her into his arms and holding her against him as she desperately tried to maintain control of her emotions.

"He took my element. Convinced me he loved me so he could use the practitioners' spell, and now...he can wield my air against me whenever he wants. I'm powerless against it. Against him. With the practitioners supporting him...he's unstoppable. I have to end this. Now. And the only way I can do that..."

"Is to die." Liam's voice took on a rough, guttural tone, and he held her tighter, burying his nose in her hair.

"*Mo chuisle, mo chroí,*" Caitlin whispered, and Liam drew back enough to meet her eyes. "I know what it means now. I remember. I remember *you*. I died to protect you once. I'll do it again."

CHAPTER NINE

Liam

"The hell ya' will." He would *not* let his Caitlin sacrifice herself to save him. Not again. If he were home, at the pack's house, his fist would already be through the wall, but here...with his Caitlin trembling in front of him like she *expected* him to lose his shit, *expected* him to be angry with her, he blew out a breath and his shoulders slumped.

"I failed ya' all those years ago, luv. If I'd been stronger—" he held out his hand, hoping she'd grant him this one indulgence, and when she did, electricity raced up his arm. "I won't lose ya' again. If ya' don't love me now, if ya' don't see a future with me, then I'll walk away as soon as ye're safe. But that fuckin' arsehole will not take one more minute of yer life if I can help it."

Caitlin chewed on her lip, her blue eyes shining. "I could make you forget..."

"No. Ya' couldn't. I'm here, yeah? Despite the charm ya' tried earlier?" He tucked a lock of wet hair behind her ear, letting his gaze rove down her body. Under the sweatshirt, her nipples pebbled, and an appreciative purr rumbled in his chest. "Nothin' could make me forget ya', Caitlin."

Slipping his hands under the fleece, he found cool, soft skin, and Caitlin shuddered under his touch. Taking a risk, he let his fingers trail up her sides until he cupped her breasts. Fuck. Lace covered perfect handfuls, and his thumbs brushed those tight nubs.

She tipped her head back with a moan. Did she know? That this was as far as they'd ever taken things before? Despite his throbbing cock, the raw, desperate need eleven years of blue balls could give a man, he lowered his hands and cupped her arse, pulling her against him and claiming her lips.

She melted in his arms, and her taste was everything he remembered and more. He traced the seam of her lips, no longer gentle, but possessive, and she yielded to him, clutching at his arms, his back, like she was terrified he'd just disappear.

Scooping her up, he carried her to the old, worn couch and sat with her on his lap. He knew the moment she felt his length pressing against her arse, and her eyes flew open, her cheeks flushed. "Liam...I..."

"Shhh, luv." He shifted her just enough to grant them both a measure of relief. "Nothin' happens ya' aren't ready for."

Tears gathered at the corners of her eyes. "When you're here... when you're right next to me, I can almost believe everything will be okay."

"Make me a promise, Caitlin. Just one." He took that moment to memorize her features. How much she'd changed, but how much had stayed the same. Her hair, shorter now, but still just as soft. Her eyes. Sadder. Weary. Her lips. Full, slightly swollen from their kiss, and trembling.

"What?"

"Don't run. Don't run, and we'll find a way to be together." Forcing the words out almost broke him. If she left him again, he wasn't sure he'd survive. "Ye're my mate. Even if we never seal our bond under the moon, even if ya' decide once ye're free that ya' don't want me, I will never love another."

She answered him with a searing kiss, and it wasn't until she had him on his back, straddling him with her hands carding through his hair that he realized she hadn't given him her promise.

"Caitlin." Her name escaped on a groan, and shite. He needed her like he needed his next breath. Like he needed his heart to beat. But he couldn't use her for a casual fuck. Wouldn't. "Stop."

"Give me this," she demanded even as he pushed himself up on an elbow. "Give me this one night before I have to go."

"Not unless ya' promise me." Getting to his feet was the hardest thing he'd ever done. Harder even than leaving Ireland and abandoning all hope of finding her. "Wolves mate for life, luv. The moon's but a week away. If I get a taste of ya', I won't ever want to let ya' go, and my wolf...it'll be the death of him."

A single tear tumbled down her cheek, and she reached for him, but he took another step back.

"Do ya' want this? Us?"

His entire body hummed with raw need, his muscles so tight, he feared they'd snap. Until she met his gaze and nodded.

"I need to hear ya' say it. And I need yer promise." His wolf railed, demanding he claim his Caitlin. That he take her to bed and ravish her body until she was nothing but a quivering mess —not that he'd be any different. But the man in control knew he couldn't. Not unless she agreed to give them a chance at happiness.

"I want...you." The single word escaped dripping with desire, and the scent of her—of her need—filled the hotel room.

"That's not a promise."

Her lower lip quivered, and quicker than he thought possible, she launched herself at him, winding her arms around his neck and grinding her hips against his. "I promise." Her tears flowed freely, and he dashed them away with his thumbs, cupping her cheeks and holding her still.

"Promise what?"

"I won't run. Shite, Liam. I should. Everything in me is screaming to charm ya' and run as far and as fast as I can. But...I lied earlier. I *did* love ya' eleven years ago, and I want to see if I can love ya' again."

That was all he needed. Everything he needed. Stripping off her sweatshirt, he growled at the sight of the black lace bra. Her perfect breasts begging for his touch. The catch released with a flick of his fingers, and the delicate material fluttered to the floor.

Swirling his tongue around a nipple, he pulled back, seeking out her gaze as he blew on the hard nub. Caitlin whimpered softly, and he turned his attention to the other breast, savoring each taste, each new thing he learned about his love.

The fleece pants fell next, and he slid a finger under the seam of her panties. "Shite. Ye're so wet," he whispered as her knees buckled. Catching her in his arms, he carried her over to the bed where he laid her out like a banquet before tearing through the lace covering the one place he was most desperate to be.

She strained to reach the button on his jeans, but he captured her hands and pinned them to the mattress.

"Easy now. Once ya' touch me, luv, the only way I'll be able to stop is if ya' tell me to. And I won't last. Not after eleven years of fantasizin' about this moment. So no touchin' until I'm well and truly done with ya'."

"Liam—"

God, he loved how she said his name. Always had. Even now, with her accent such a tenuous thing, he couldn't get enough of it. Positioning himself between her thighs, he inhaled her scent, trailing kisses from the inside of her left knee all the way up to the edge of the neatly trimmed patch of brown curls before making his way back down the other leg.

With each touch of his lips to her skin, Caitlin mewled, whimpered, or openly begged for him to give her more.

"Oh, I intend to, luv. Hold on to somethin'."

She clutched the sheets as he pressed a firm kiss just above her clit, and when his tongue parted her slick folds, the swift jerk of her hips almost left him with a broken nose.

His laugh rumbled against her sensitive folds. "Easy, now. We heal quick, we do, but I don't fancy stoppin'."

"Please," she begged, and Liam angled one arm over her hips to keep her steady, then returned his attention to that sensitive bundle of nerves he knew he'd never get enough of.

Caitlin's element swirled around them. The drapes billowed, the scent of her—fig blossoms and arousal—filling the room, and time stretched out in endless moments of tasting, teasing, and pleasuring her. When she lost her words, he nipped at her inner thigh, bringing her back from the edge just so he could whisk her back to the precipice once more.

Time and time again, until he sensed she could take no more, and then he let her fly, drinking her in, watching her come apart in his hands.

He'd protect her with his life. No matter what. Because in that moment, she was a tornado. Wild, unafraid, powerful, and the most beautiful sight he'd ever seen. His mate. His love. Forever.

Caitlin

"My turn." How could she be even *more* desperate for him now? Still trembling from her release, her entire body felt like a live wire. "I want to see you, Liam."

He grimaced as he got to his feet, his rock hard length straining against his jeans, and yanked his flannel shirt over his head.

Shit. Muscles sculpted out of pure granite, a light dusting of reddish hair spread out across his chest, and a deep *v* that disappeared below his belt.

Caitlin reached for him, grabbing the buckle and fumbling twice before she managed to undo it and find the button on his jeans.

"In a rush now, are ya'?" he asked with a chuckle.

"I'm naked. You're not." The zipper gave her trouble as well, and Liam hissed out a breath when she caught it on his briefs.

Covering her hands with his, he leaned down and brushed a light kiss to her lips. "Let me, luv."

Flames crawled up her cheeks when he shucked his jeans and socks and stood in nothing but those dark blue briefs in front of her. The churning colors of his eyes captured her in a storm she never wanted to escape.

A fresh wave of desire washed over her as he slid those tight briefs down his hips, freeing his hard length. God. She wanted him inside of her.

Climbing onto the bed, he gathered her against him, and she ran her hands up his back, to his shoulders, and over an intricate tattoo of cliffs with the churning sea crashing on the rocks below. Whorls of gray—wind, if she had to guess—added a graceful movement to the piece, and in the center, a broken heart.

Her breath caught in her throat as she pressed a kiss to the ink. "Liam. Is this...?"

"You." He stretched out with her still held against him. "After I lost ya', I went through a bad spell. Nearly got myself kicked out of my pack. I took a leave from my job, forgot to pay my rent. Hell, I forgot to get out of bed for a couple of days."

Shame had her burying her face against his neck, but Liam hooked a finger under her chin and angled her head up to look at him again. "No guilt, luv. Ya' did what ya' had to survive. And ye're here now."

She was. And she'd promised not to run. "Tell me the rest."

"Tattoos don't last on us. On wolves. Shiftin' changes the skin and heals most of what might ail us. So I had to go to a witch. Tracked one down in San Francisco. Bren was her name. She didn't ask what I wanted. Just told me to think about why I was gettin' it, and this is what she left me with."

"It's beautiful. And sad." Caitlin trailed kisses over the cliffs, and Liam groaned when she straddled him, purposely grinding her hips against him. Fluttering breezes cooled her overheated skin as her wolf reached up and palmed her breast, flicking the hard nipple with his thumb.

His other hand delved between her thighs, two fingers playing with her clit, and her body threatened to implode again, but she wasn't going to come without him this time, and slapped her hand down on his tight stomach. "Inside me. Now."

He flipped her onto her back before she knew what was happening, leaned over, and snagged a condom from the pocket of his jeans. After a rustle of foil, he nudged at her entrance.

"Please," she begged, grabbing his hips to urge him deeper. When he finally, blessedly, seated himself fully, she wrapped her legs around him and focused on his eyes, seeing the truth she'd thrown away all those years ago.

Love.

Each thrust speared her with more force than the last. Clawing at his shoulder and pulling at his hair, she moaned his name, and as he clamped his mouth down on hers, she let go with a scream, flying apart and taking him with her.

HELD AGAINST HER BIG, strong wolf, she felt safe. Truly and completely safe. Yet darkness lingered in the far reaches of her mind, just out of sight.

Trailing her hand over his chest, she savored the feel of his skin. "What's this from?" she asked, her voice only a whisper as she kissed the span of a deep scar across his ribs.

Liam tensed, then wrapped a hand in her hair and tipped her head back. "Ya' don't want to know, luv. And it doesn't matter. Because ye're here with me now."

Guilt threatened to carry her away. Katerina had given him that injury. The memory of sending Cade's wolf flying against a curb, of whipping the flames into a frenzy, of watching as wolf after wolf succumbed to the depraved pairing of magic and Katerina's elemental charms.

"Liam, I didn't—I wasn't...me then."

"Shhh." He brushed his lips to hers, and the tender gesture only made her feel worse. "I know." With a deep sigh, he pushed up on an elbow. "We should go back to the pack house."

"N-no. I can't." She scrambled away and drew the sheets up to her chest. "Not after what I did."

"Yes, ya' can." Liam tugged on his briefs, then snagged his jeans. "Ye're the bravest woman I've ever met, Caitlin."

How could he say that? After all she'd done? After all the pain she'd caused him and his pack? After...giving away her air without a second thought. "I'm not. I gave up on us. On life. On ever being free. If that's not cowardice, I don't know what is."

"And ya' came back to Seattle, knowin' Cade probably wanted to kill ya'. Brought Mara back to us. and ye're goin' to fight. Once we find a way to get yer air back—"

"You say that like we're going to succeed."

Liam knelt on the mattress next to her, his flannel shirt unbuttoned, and she couldn't look away from the scar he'd carry for the rest of his life. Strong fingers cupped the back of her neck. "We will, luv. I swear it."

Silence, broken only by the pinging of the pipes in the wall and the low hum of a television in the room next to hers, filled the space, looming over them. His calloused fingers drew patterns on her skin, calming her frantic heartbeat.

"Ya' don't know him. He'll kill you without a shred of remorse or a moment's hesitation. And then...he'll own me again." She couldn't look at him, couldn't meet those stormy eyes and break his heart. Not a second time.

"He does *not* own ya'," Liam growled. "No one owns ya', Caitlin."

Her voice dropped to a whisper. "He does."

Liam sank down onto the bed next to her. "Tell me."

Through the tears clogging her throat, she fought to explain. "He found me only a few hours after I left ya'. For three years, I'd hoped...prayed...that he was dead. He'd changed so much. His eyes." She inhaled Liam's scent, and he pulled her close, his arm around her shoulders.

"Caitie, why did ya' leave me?" The sweet, singsong voice turned her stomach. She preferred it when he yelled. When he hit. The pain paled in comparison to the fear his barely contained rage could inspire. She backed into the dirty stone wall, trying to call on her element, but he smiled and used it against her, and she fought to even breathe.

"I needed ya'. Three years I spent locked away in that hospital. Drugged out of my mind. Ya' put me there, yeah?"

"No!" she gasped. "Please!"

He let go of his control just enough for her to draw in a single, wheezing breath.

"You disappeared. I thought...ya' died. Don't...punish me. Please."

"Oh, ye're goin' to pay for yer mistakes." Fergus wrapped his hand in her hair and dragged her deeper into the alley, popped the boot on his sleek, black car, and tossed her in. "And once ye've learned a proper lesson, ye're goin' to help me find water and fire!"

"Water and fire," Liam said, his deep voice rumbling against her back and pulling her out of her memories. "Which is why he'll want Mara."

"Y-yes. And why he won't ever let me go. He didn't tell me much about the practitioners," she said, clinging to her wolf like he really could protect her from anything. She wanted to believe that. So badly it hurt. "But right after Fergus took my air, he dragged me to Scotland. I don't know where." She shivered, remembering the cold, endless hours of darkness and fear. "He'd locked me in the trunk of the car with a thick canvas bag over my head. Then forbade me from taking it off."

Caitlin dragged her shaking fingers over her neck. "I couldn't resist him. Couldn't fight. And he knew it. Every time he'd *punish* me, he'd lock me in basements, closets...anywhere I couldn't see the sky or breathe fresh air."

"Luv, look at me." Liam shifted her and held her gaze. "Ye're safe here with me. Say it."

She shook her head. "I can't. I'm not safe anywhere, Liam. The practitioners? There were thirteen of them. And when he dragged me into their circle, they all started chanting. I couldn't move. Couldn't even blink. Fergus started screaming. And I could feel his pain. It was like they were tearing him in half. Everything went black, and the next thing I remember, he's begging me for help. We're in this dark room, and he's begging me. Telling me we need to get the other elements, or they'll kill us."

"I don't understand," Liam said, cupping her cheeks. His hands were so warm, and it felt like the temperature in the room had dropped twenty degrees since she'd started talking.

"The Thirteen are collecting the elements. But for some reason, they can't take Fergus's earth, and they only siphoned off a small bit of my air. They cocked up the spell." She managed a half smile. "Fergus and I are linked so strongly, if they transfer my air to anyone else, it'll kill him too. So they won't even try until they have all the elements together. And that's why they'll want Mara."

Liam shook his head and snagged Caitlin's sweatshirt from the floor. "It's been eleven years, luv. You really think they haven't found other elementals by now?"

"Even if they have, their plan isn't over. We'd...know." She sniffled softly, shrugged into her bra, and then pulled the sweatshirt over her head. "I can *feel* Fergus. The link between us. It's still there, and it's getting stronger."

"Then we'll break it."

He sounded so certain. And she wanted to believe him. So badly it hurt.

"I don't know if we can," she whispered. "The spell binding us together...the power behind it? I've never felt its equal. Not even from Katerina."

Despite her fear, the overwhelming despair, she'd made Liam a promise. And after failing him—and failing herself—eleven years ago, she'd keep it. As long as she could.

Trudging over to her duffel bag, she pulled out fresh panties and her favorite pair of jeans. "I'll go back with ya', Liam. But I need ya' to make me a promise as well."

"What?" He shoved his feet into his boots and snagged his jacket from the chair. "I'll do anything for ya', Caitlin. Ya' know I will."

"Fergus is going to call for me. He'll compel me, and I won't have any choice but to obey. I'll have to go to him. Please." She turned to him and took his big hands in hers. "When that happens, you have to let me go."

"No fuckin' way." Liam tugged, and when he had her flush against his body, he claimed her lips in a searing kiss she felt down to her toes. "Ye're mine, Caitlin. My mate. And I intend to prove that to ya' before the full moon. But ya' belong to no one. No one but yerself. And I'll fight for ya' until my last breath."

That was her greatest fear. That not only would she lose herself to Fergus, she'd lose Liam as well.

CHAPTER TEN

Liam

*W*hen he strode into the pack house with Caitlin at his side, it was quiet. Not surprising, as by the time they'd sated their need for one another, it was almost 3:00 a.m.

"Where is everyone?" Caitlin whispered, her gaze darting around the kitchen like she expected one of the wolves to pop out from behind a corner and tear her to pieces.

"Asleep, I'd wager. They were workin' on a plan to keep Mara safe when I left. But she was fadin' fast." He led her upstairs to the top floor. To his private space. He'd taken two rooms and turned them into one large suite, complete with bathroom. Along the far wall, a table held his leather working tools—a hobby he'd picked up after losing Caitlin—and on the opposite side of the room sat his bed and two tall bookcases.

Dropping her duffel bag next to his bed, he shoved his hands into his pockets. "Yer exhausted too, luv."

"I'm too nervous to sleep," she said, taking stock of the room before venturing to his work bench and running her fingers over a woven leather braid with an intricate design carved into each strand. "What is this?"

"Somethin' I do to pass the time when I'm not workin' on the house."

"It's beautiful." Her face held a mix of awe and respect, and she moved a stack of papers to the side, then gasped. "Liam."

Shite. He crossed the room in three steps and found her holding the one piece that meant more to him than any other.

Her face stared up at them from the flat piece of leather, and she traced over the gentle waves he'd carved for her hair. "This is...me?"

"I didn't think I'd ever see ya' again, Caitlin. And I'd begun to forget. It terrified me. So I started learnin' how to draw. Took lessons even." He chuffed out a tense laugh, then opened one of the drawers and pulled out the best of the thousands of sketches he'd done of her.

"I lost ya'. But I wouldn't let myself lose yer memory, Caitlin. Never."

She started to cry, silent tears streaming down her face.

"That wasn't supposed to make ya' sad." Dropping the sketch, he eased the leather portrait from her hand, scooped her into his arms, and carried her to his bed. "Talk to me, Caitlin."

"You did all that," she waved her hand towards his workbench, "and I *begged* Katerina to make me forget you."

"Ya' had a reason. And it kept ya' alive, so I'm grateful for it." Snorting, he shook his head. "Never thought I'd be grateful to that bitch, but I am."

"You're not angry?" His Caitlin cowered in his arms, and fuck. Despite how long they'd been apart, he could *feel* her shame and knew exactly why she was afraid. Raw fury prickled along the back of his neck, but he swallowed it down and pressed a gentle kiss to her lips.

"No, luv. I'm not him. I'll never hold yer choices against ya'."

She swiped the tears from her cheeks and shuddered in his

arms, the tension gradually leaving her the longer he held her and rubbed her back. Eventually, she fell asleep curled against his chest, and Liam didn't bother to undress, didn't even try to remove their shoes. Just stretched out on his bed with his mate in his arms and let himself drift off with her.

———

VOICES FLOATED UP FROM DOWNSTAIRS, a hint of light seeping through the curtains, and Liam gently eased Caitlin from his arms and stole from the room. His keen hearing picked up on two distinct tones: Cade and Livie.

"I don't know, bossman. Mara trusts Eleanor, but are you really sure taking her to a practitioner is a good idea?" Livie asked as Serena's happy, nonsensical babble floated up the stairs.

"No. I'm not. But these episodes are only getting worse. Driving all the way to Caitlin's hotel without knowing it? Hell, I want to take her down to Cannon Beach today in the hopes Eleanor can do *something*. Invited or not."

"No!" Liam bounded down the last few stairs three at a time and charged into the room.

"No?" Pushing off from where he'd been leaning against the counter, Cade straightened his shoulders, looking every bit the alpha, and Liam's wolf automatically started to back down. "Want to tell me why?"

"Because they want her to come alone. She didn't tell ya'?" Liam headed for the coffee pot to pour himself a cup. Like alcohol, he'd burn it off in minutes, but he'd take whatever he could get. It was barely eight, and he was still knackered. Plus, the motion helped him ignore Cade's stare for a minute longer.

"Apparently there are a lot of things she hasn't told me." The muttered words were filled with pain, and Liam turned to his alpha, reaching out and clapping a hand on the man's shoulder.

"Ya' know she loves ya', Cade. And she doesn't want ya' to worry."

"How am I supposed to not worry? She's not herself. She's losing time, and the only suggestion Eleanor came up with was to find a retired practitioner in Ireland. One who could just as easily try to *steal* Mara's power as cure her. I can't believe there isn't an elemental solution to this shit."

"You can't take Mara to Ireland."

The three of them whirled around at Caitlin's soft words, and Livie growled as she set Serena in her high chair. "Sneaking up on us isn't a good idea right now, *Bella*."

"You know I'm not Bella." Caitlin's blue eyes blazed with heat, and she didn't move from the threshold, even when Livie marched right up to her. "If you still think I am, then go ahead. Kill me. It'll be safer for everyone."

"Fuck me. Stand down. Both of ya'," Liam snarled. "No one's killin' anyone today." He draped his arm around Caitlin's shoulders and urged her into the room at his side.

"Ya' can't take Mara to Ireland," Caitlin said again. "Ya' can't bring her anywhere *near* Fergus."

"That's the last place we'd go. Trust me. But fuck. When Eleanor learned about Mara's elements months ago, she told us to come to Cannon Beach after things settled down. So Mara could learn how to work with her water and keep the fire from overwhelming her. And now...it's like the woman doesn't give a shit about her."

"Maybe she does." Caitlin nodded towards the coffee pot. "Can I have some of that?"

Liam poured her a full mug, and Caitlin cupped it between her hands and inhaled deeply.

"Explain," Cade said sharply. "You obviously know a hell of a lot more than you've let on, and I'm sick of having to pull every single secret out of you. If you expect us to trust you, we need to know everything. Right fucking now. No more air charms. No more running away. Got it?"

Liam bristled, the need to protect his mate flaring up and sending him two steps closer to Cade before he realized what he was doing. But his Caitlin set the coffee mug down hard enough a little liquid splashed over the rim, then squared her shoulders and met Cade's stare.

"Do you think I wanted to run? Really?" She huffed. "Maybe that first night. When you all were lookin' at me like ya' wanted to rip me apart. When I didn't remember—not really—who Liam was or why I was so drawn to him. And fine. Yes. I'd run now too if I thought I could actually end my own life before Fergus got to me. Because it would help keep ya' all safe. But I made a promise." She glanced up at Liam, her blue eyes shimmering. "No more runnin'."

"And the air charms?" Cade said on a low growl.

"I won't use them against ya'. Any of ya'."

Her voice had started to take on more of a lilt again, the musical brogue stirring up so many memories. Memories of her laughing. Of kissing her on Ha'penny Bridge, of all of their time together.

Shawn bounded down the stairs to join them, followed by Peter. The two males crowded close to Caitlin, trying to look intimidating, and though they pointedly didn't touch her, Liam's hackles went up.

"I still don't like it, bossman," Livie said as she pulled Serena from the high chair and gave her mate a withering look. "And Shawn? Get the hell away from her."

Liam stifled a laugh. He loved Livie like a sister, and he understood her place in this pack was as Cade's head of security. But that didn't mean he was going to stand for her—or anyone else—disrespecting Caitlin. "None of ya' have to like it, but ya' remember what Cade said before I left last night?"

He hadn't told Caitlin. And despite how much he ached to

reassure her, he didn't want to tell her now. That was his alpha's job. To remind everyone in the pack that Caitlin was just as much one of them as any other.

Cade cleared his throat. "She's family. She's Liam's mate, and we're not going to abandon her. Just like she's not going to abandon us. Right?" He arched a brow at Caitlin, and she swiped away a single tear gathered at the corner of her eye, then looked up at Liam, her expression an odd mix of accusation, awe, and disbelief.

"Cade had to be the one to tell ya', luv. It's how things work."

"I won't abandon you," she said. "Or Mara. Not by choice, anyway. But if Fergus calls to me—*when* Fergus calls to me—I won't be able to resist him for long. So we have to make sure Mara's safe before that happens. Otherwise...he'll kill all of us."

"Where is Mara?" Liam asked.

"Christine gave her a sedative." Cade headed for the coffee pot and poured himself another cup. "I installed a lock on the window last night, and Chrissy's sitting outside the bedroom door. If her fire takes over, we'll know." Despite his words, he turned instinctively towards the house next door, stifled a sigh, and then straightened his shoulders again. "So, Caitlin." He put a slight emphasis on her name, like he wasn't one hundred percent certain she wasn't still Bella, and Liam's low growl rumbled in his chest before Cade shot him a look that warned him to shut the fuck up. "Tell us why you think Eleanor wants to keep Mara away from Cannon Beach?"

Caitlin

She didn't want to sit down. Her nerves were on overdrive, and an invisible tether—the one she thought connected her to Fergus—was starting to tighten at the back of her neck.

Was he already searching for her? Or was this just her own worry rearing up to ruin things with Liam and his pack? She wished she knew, but those memories hovered just out of reach.

"Until I took off Katerina's crystal, I didn't remember anything about my past. But now, it's like every time I blink, there's something new."

Something bad.

Liam nodded with encouragement, and Caitlin stared out the large kitchen window. Sunlight sparkled along the water in a two-lane lap pool spanning their yard and the one next door.

"I told ya' earlier that the practitioners in Scotland—the ones who recruited Fergus—they think they can capture all the elements to combine them into the fifth element—Spirit."

"I don't understand what that has to do with keeping Mara out of Cannon Beach," Cade said.

"Mara's unstable." Caitlin took a quick step back when Cade growled and his chest puffed out. Liam angled his body between the two of them, and Caitlin blew out a breath. She could defend herself. Probably. But the more she used her element, the sooner Fergus would find her. If she could just stay hidden a little longer...

"Cade, ya' said ya' would listen," Liam warned, barely controlled anger lending a roughness to his voice.

A vein in the alpha's temple looked like it was ready to pop, but he gave them both a terse nod, and Caitlin eased out from behind Liam. "I didn't mean any offense to Mara. Her *elements* are unstable. If she's not careful, she's going to call on her water and cause a monsoon. Or worse. The fire will take over and she'll burn down the whole neighborhood. And it won't be her fault."

"Christine thinks she can keep her in check with herbal soothers and meditation," Cade said.

Caitlin almost couldn't stifle her snort in time. She hid behind her coffee mug for a moment, then swallowed hard. "She can try, but you don't understand what havin' two elements can do to a person. Fergus was sweet a long time ago. That's why I trusted him. I should have seen the warning signs, but even if I had...they weren't obvious, ya' know?"

"No. Explain," Liam said.

"His mean streak. The desperate need for power. But he was so earnest about his feelings for me. About why he wanted to be with me. At least...I thought he was." She darted a glance to Liam, and he was staring almost through her, his hands clenched into fists at his sides.

She could practically *feel* the wolf's claim on her. If only it were stronger than the tether binding her to Fergus, they might be able to survive this.

"Liam!" Cade said sharply. "Get your wolf under control. Right fucking now."

As if he'd been slapped, Liam sank down onto one of the dining room chairs and crossed his arms over his chest.

"Go on, Caitlin," Cade encouraged.

She didn't have much choice, even though she feared what the alpha would say and do when she finished.

"I don't know Mara," she said. "But water elementals are usually stable. Peaceful. Water is cool and calming. She's a peace-maker, yes?"

"She is." This, from a wolf with reddish ropes of scar tissue down the left side of his face. She thought his name might be Peter, but she didn't want to ask given that he was looking at her like she'd killed his best friend.

"Katerina wasn't. Even when she was happiest, she was volatile. That's why fire's the rarest element. So many of them can't control themselves and, either by accident or on purpose, end up killin' themselves or someone close to them." She hugged herself, the coffee suddenly souring her stomach, and met Cade's steely-eyed gaze. "Mara—on her own—is stable. But with Kateri-na's fire in her, she's...a powder keg."

"Watch how you talk about my mate," Cade snapped, and before Liam could defend her, Caitlin held up her hand.

"You see it," Caitlin said. "I know ya' do. Why else would ya' put a lock on her window? Station someone outside her bedroom door?"

The moment the wolf flashed in his eyes, her heartbeat spiked, and she dropped her arms. She wouldn't use an air charm on anyone in the room. She'd promised Cade that much. But she could protect herself if she had to.

But he didn't pounce, didn't start to shift, and dropped back down into the chair with a heavy sigh. "It's for her protection. So she doesn't end up wandering into the middle of the street unaware and get hit by a car."

"Ya' can tell yerself that all ya' want. But ya' know it isn't the truth. Not all of it. Katerina was an unstable, power-hungry, piece of shite," Liam said as he got to his feet. "And all ye're doin' denyin' the truth is puttin' Caitlin—and all of us—in more danger. Can ya' just let 'er finish?"

Everyone in the room held their breath. Though she'd never spent any time around wolves—other than Liam—she had a feeling him standing up to Cade was something that just wasn't done.

"Fine."

"Katerina was one of the most powerful elementals I've ever met. For Mara to be able to absorb her fire? Shit. I don't think anyone else in the world could have done what she did. If she *ever* loses control, it's going to be like a beacon lighting up the whole hemisphere. That amount of power doesn't go unnoticed."

"Unnoticed?" Cade asked. "What do you mean? How is anyone going to notice her power?"

"You really don't know anything about conjuring the elements, do you?"

Cade shook his head and for a moment, stared down at the

floor like he'd just realized how dangerous his lack of knowledge really was.

Though a part of her wanted to roll her eyes, she'd been that naive once too. And worse, she'd ignored all of her mother's warnings. All the admonishments to only use her charms in private, in the small town of Doolin where they were protected. Safely hidden by the mountains and a bit of magic freely given by one of the only practitioners to ever cleave from the mother coven.

"An elemental's power is unique in this world. And while most humans—even werewolves—would never know if I performed a small air charm, the kind of power Mara can command? No one's going to ignore that."

"And you don't think they've noticed already?" Cade scoffed. "That shit at Gasworks Park? Hell, it was in the fucking paper. They called it a gas leak that led to a minor explosion, but if anyone were searching for elementals with vast amounts of power, don't you think they would have come straight here?"

"No." Caitlin reached for the pendant she no longer wore, the one Katerina had enchanted with sigils and spells Caitlin had never given a second thought to. Until the woman's death. But it was gone now, and she found nothing at all. "Katerina hid our power. All of us. The small community of elementals in Phoenix? Protected. The elemental power at the park? The power she used when she...trapped you? Hidden from all prying eyes. At least magical ones."

"So, we hide it again," Cade said.

"It's not that simple." Frustration edged her tone, and along with it came a stronger pull on the tether binding her to Fergus. "Only a practitioner can create a spell like that, and they're finite." Cade and Liam both looked confused, and this time, she did roll her eyes. "They can only hide so much. Like...a parka can only keep you warm until the outside temperature gets too cold. Or earplugs can only block out so much sound. If I had to guess, I'd say the elementals in Oregon live protected. Like our small group in Phoenix. And they're scared that if they take Mara in, she'll be too powerful. She'll expose them. Draw the Thirteen directly to them."

"You're sure about this?" Livie asked from behind her. As Caitlin turned, her jaw dropped open. Livie sat in a chair in the corner, the baby latched on to her exposed breast, and no one else in the room had batted an eye.

Caitlin's cheeks flushed hot, and she stared down at the floor. "No. But it makes sense, doesn't it? Ya' said Eleanor was helpin' Mara before. Then, after she goes back to her community, she abandons Mara completely? Why? I'll bet she talked to the elders there and *they* were the ones who told her to cut you off."

"After she told us to find the practitioner in Ireland," Cade said, his shoulders practically vibrating in anger, "she stopped taking our calls."

"Shite." Liam shook his head and rose to pour himself another mug of coffee. Finding the pot empty, he set about adding beans and water to the machine, while Caitlin fidgeted with the hem of her sweater.

"I can try talking to her. Air to air. If she'll answer the phone."

"Good luck." Cade pulled a small slip of paper from his back pocket and slid it across the table. "But that still doesn't answer the most important question." He paused to run a hand through his rough-chopped hair. "If you're right and Christine can't keep Mara from losing control, what the hell do we do?"

Caitlin was about to tell him she didn't know when her chest suddenly felt like it was being crushed in a vise. She couldn't breathe, and the pain shot through her, all along her spine as Fergus's tether pulled, first hesitantly, then with violent conviction.

"Come to me, Caitie. I know ye're out there somewhere. Ya' belong to me, and I won't stand for yer hidin' from me any longer."

The harsh, bellowing words split her skull in two, and she

grabbed her head with her hands, collapsing to the floor with a moan.

"Caitlin!"

She was only dimly aware of Liam's voice. Of his strong hands wrapped around her shoulders. Of his warmth as he pulled her close.

"Look at me, luv!"

The house shook as the front door blew open, and the scent of fresh, loamy earth swirled around them, clogging Caitlin's throat, choking her, reminding her of all the times Fergus had locked her away underground. Weakened her. Worn her down until she couldn't even think of resisting him.

Tell me ya' hear me, Caitie. In her head, his voice took on a new tone, just as mean, just as vicious, but now, edged by a hint of fear. *Ya' know there's no escape. Not until we finish what we started.*

Could she risk it? Letting him into her mind just enough to send him a message? She had to try. Otherwise, there was only one option left.

No. I'm not yours any longer. Go to hell!

So ya' want me to punish ya' then. That can be arranged.

The tether snapped, like a string pulled too tight, and Caitlin drew in a wheezing breath, smelling only Liam, feeling only his strong arms around her as she struggled to focus on his eyes.

"I'm...okay," she managed. "He's...not here. Still far away. In Ireland. But he knows now." She was so damn tired. Not only the exhaustion of fighting off his spell, but the emotional and mental weariness from all the times she'd tried to run. All of her attempts to reclaim her life. Her element. Her freedom.

"Knows what, luv?" Liam smoothed a big, calloused palm over her cheek, and his soothing touch calmed her in a way nothing else ever could—ever had.

"That I'm alive. That I'm in the United States. Maybe even that I'm in Seattle."

"Then all ya' have to do is stay here, yeah? If he can't fly, and ya' stay with me—"

"It won't be enough." She buried her face in his neck for a long moment, savoring the delicious scent of him. The one she associated with safety. Comfort. Home.

If only she could hide away with him forever. But Fergus would never allow it. And if he managed to get here...no. She couldn't have all of their deaths on her conscience.

Easing herself from Liam's arms, she got to her feet, swayed for a minute, and then braced herself against the counter. "That air charm was only meant for me. So I don't expect ya' to truly understand. But his compulsion, his hold over me is so complete, I won't be able to resist him much longer. Even now... For a second, I wanted to go to him. So badly I would have fought you —all of you—and probably won to get away. I can hold him off for a time, but with every charm he uses, I'll get weaker. Soon, I won't be able to resist him."

"What if we run?" Liam asked. He reached for her, but she shrank away from him, and he let his arm fall with an expression of pure agony shadowing his handsome face.

"We can't. Not far enough or fast enough. I have to go to Ireland. To go to him. Or I have to die. Those are my only two choices. But if I go to Ireland now? Tonight?" She turned to Cade. "There's a chance I can hold him off long enough to get to this practitioner Eleanor told you about. There's no hope for me now," she said, refusing to look at Liam. "But maybe, we can still save Mara."

CHAPTER ELEVEN

Liam

"Ya' won't go to Ireland alone." He stopped her protests with a swift, hard kiss, and when she sagged against him, teasing her tongue along the seam of his lips, he assumed she'd yielded to his demand.

Until he tasted salt.

Pulling away, he found tears shining on her cheeks. "I have to," she said. "I'll help Mara as much as I can today. There are some sigils Katerina taught me that might keep her a bit more balanced. But Fergus won't wait long to try to compel me again."

"All the more reason for me to go with ya'."

Caitlin darted a gaze around the rest of his pack—save for Christine and Ollie—before wrapping her delicate fingers around his biceps and lowering her voice. "Please. Not here." She swallowed a sob, shame churning in the blue depths of her gaze.

"Cade, can ya' let us know when Mara's here? We'll be upstairs for a bit." Liam didn't bother to wait for his alpha's permission. Not for this. Not when his mate needed him.

With his arm around her waist, he half carried her up the two flights, and once they were alone in his room, he sat her down on the bed and knelt in front of her.

"Tell me. Whatever it is, luv, I won't judge ya'. Or be angry. Just don't keep secrets from me. That's all I ask."

"I need some air. Can ya' open that window?" The hem of her sweater would be twice its normal size soon if she didn't stop fiddling with it, and the tension radiating off her set Liam's wolf on high alert, but he nodded and raised the sash.

The early spring air swirled around the room, making the papers on his work bench flutter, but after a minute, Caitlin started to calm. She took a deep, shuddering breath, pushed to her feet, and started to pace.

"When he caught me the last time, I hadn't seen him in three years. Long enough for me to get sloppy. He had to be dead, I thought. I had my element, and I couldn't feel him. I thought maybe...he'd tried the spell without me. Or that he'd finally gone up against an elemental stronger than he was."

"That doesn't explain—"

She held up her hand. "This isn't easy for me, Liam. Let me get it all out."

He snapped his jaw shut, and she started pulling at the fraying hem of her sweater again. "When he found me—maybe an hour after I'd left ya', he could smell ya' on me. Air elementals...we can track by scent. It's how I knew Cade wasn't with Mara when we found her at her aunt's." Caitlin's cheeks flushed bright red, and she shoved her hands into her pockets before she flicked her gaze to Liam.

Anger flared, his wolf railing against his tight hold. His mate was still afraid. Not only of Fergus, but of the pack. Of what she'd done to them.

He gave her an encouraging nod, despite wishing he could pull her into his arms and make her forget everything but his love for her.

"He locked me in the trunk of his car." She beelined for the window, taking deep shuddering breaths. "We drove for hours, and I knew where we were goin'. He had a place near Doolin. A special place he only used when he needed to punish me. He dug out the basement not long after he first bound me. Twice as deep as it should have been. Maybe three times. He made me watch."

Her voice cracked, and though she had her back to him, he could see her shoulders shake with every sob she tried to hide.

"Ten meters down. Only big enough for a mattress, a toilet, and a sink. No light. No cracks in the door. He sealed it with resin so almost no air could get through. That's it. That's all I had."

Liam'd had enough of his mate crying alone. He wrapped his arms around her from behind and tucked her head under his chin. He wanted to promise Caitlin that he'd kill this Fergus bastard. That he'd pull his fucking arms off. That his wolf would rip out the man's throat. Tear him into pieces so small no one would ever find them. But she'd asked him to stay quiet, so he clenched his teeth and just offered her whatever strength he could.

"He kept me down there for almost three weeks. Only brought me food every other day. Nothing fresh. Crackers. Granola bars." She pressed her hand to her stomach, right over Liam's fingers. "I never want to see a granola bar again."

No granola bars. He filed that bit of information away, hoping to all that was holy he'd need it.

"Every time he came, he'd suffocate me until I passed out, then use a compulsion charm—one of *my* compulsion charms—to try to get me to tell him about ya'. Yer name. Where he could find ya'."

She turned in his embrace, tipping her head up to meet his gaze, and fuck. The anguish and abject terror in her eyes...his wolf growled, the sound rumbling through him before he could stop it.

"If ya' go back to Ireland with me and he gets a hold of me

again, he won't stop until he breaks me completely. I can't go back to that basement. I can't. And if I betrayed ya'..."

Liam leaned down and gently kissed her protests away. "Shhh, luv."

"He'll kill ya'," she whispered.

"Let him try."

Her eyes sparkled with tears, so beautiful but so sad. "He's destroyed everything I've ever loved, Liam. When I call on my air, I can feel him. But also...what he stole from me. It's this terrible, burning pain, this emptiness deep inside that I don't think will *ever* go away. And if he takes ya' too...even if he lets me live, I won't survive it. I won't. Not now. Not this time. Because now I know..." She cut herself off, burying her face against his shirt.

"Know what?"

She shook her head, refusing to look at him.

"Caitlin. What do you know? Tell me." His total and complete need to claim this woman warred with his desire to protect and soothe her.

"I know I loved ya'."

Caitlin

Liam held her until she stopped crying, then reluctantly let her go so she could shower—alone. Though the idea of fooling around under the hot water *did* sound appealing, she needed to think, and all she could do with the big, strong wolf's arms around her was *feel*.

And she felt *everything*. Her skin was almost electrified, anxiety holding her heart hostage while comfort and maybe even *love* tried to break through.

More than anything else, though, she needed to wash Liam's

scent off of her. If for no other reason than to let her focus if Fergus called for her again.

After pulling on a fresh pair of jeans and her favorite sweater —a deep green v-neck that always made her feel like she was wrapped in a warm embrace—she crept downstairs.

The scents of breakfast greeted her. Eggs, bacon, pancakes... and she gaped at the piles and piles of food on the big dining room table. Until she got a good look at Mara, who picked at her eggs, listless and groggy.

Cade had his arm draped over her shoulders, worry lines tightening around his eyes and lips.

"Mara? Are ya' all right?" Liam asked as he filled a mug with coffee and reached for a plate. She barely acknowledged him at all, and he glanced at Cade. "Mara?"

"What?" she asked when Cade squeezed her and nuzzled her neck.

Shit. Even her voice was weak and subdued.

"Liam asked if you were okay," Cade said in her ear.

"Oh. Sorry." Her green eyes were dull, and she struggled to focus on Liam. "Tired."

"We'll fix this, Mara. I promise ya' that," Liam said.

"I know." Leaning against Cade, she closed her eyes. "Not really hungry."

"You have to eat, honey." He added another two slices of bacon to her plate, but she pushed it away. "Mara."

"Don't 'Mara' me. If I eat anything, I'm going to throw up." She tried to stand, but her knees buckled and Cade caught her before she could hit the ground."

"Fuck me," Liam muttered and turned on his heel, almost running right into Caitlin.

"I know," she hissed at him as she rushed over to the water elemental. "Where's the crystal?" Staring Cade down, she tried to look as intimidating as possible. "The quartz I gave her. Where is it?"

"I took it off when she fell asleep. I didn't think it'd be very comfortable—"

Frustration lent a harsh edge to her tone. "It's not supposed to be *comfortable*. It's supposed to keep her balanced. She needs it. Now." He didn't move. Just stared at her like he couldn't believe she'd speak to him that way. Jamming her hands on her hips, she huffed. "Dammit. Go get it for her."

Silver and gold flecks glowed in his eyes, his wolf wrestling for control, and Caitlin desperately wanted to take a step back. Or hell. A lot of them. While running. Far, far away. But she'd made a promise, and Mara was holding on by a thread. Whatever sedative the healer had given her the previous night certainly hadn't helped.

Liam cursed under his breath. "Chrissy, go get the crystal." The order carried weight even Caitlin could feel, and the healer darted from the room.

Pulling out a chair next to Mara, Caitlin took a seat and held out her hands. "Mara? Remember last night? When you came to my hotel room? We're goin' to try that again, yeah?"

The woman didn't answer, and Caitlin linked their fingers. "Tell me what yer feelin' right now."

"Like I could float away." Mara's eyes fluttered, and her cheeks flushed before she gave a slow shake of her head. "Like a ghost."

"You need to ground yourself." Turning to Cade, she narrowed her eyes. "I'm going to use my air. Not against you. Or her. Or anyone in this room. But to help her. If you want this to work, you won't get in the way."

Cade slid his hand under Mara's shirt to rest against the skin of her back. "I won't. But it's easier for her to use her element if we're touching. She's stronger that way."

Nodding, Caitlin closed her eyes. "Mara, concentrate on pulling a few drops of water from the air. I want them between our palms, yeah?"

"I'll...try."

Another wolf approached, the healer. Caitlin could feel the stabilizing, healing energy of the quartz, and held out her free hand. As soon as Chrissy pressed the crystal into her palm, Mara drew in a steady breath.

"Let my air hold yer water close. Let it strengthen and protect you," Caitlin murmured, and a gentle breeze swirled around them. Where their hands touched, Mara's skin cooled, and a bead of water spread between their fingers. "That's it. Keep that focus."

Strengthening the charm, despite feeling the sharp tug of Fergus yanking on the tether that bound her to him, Caitlin touched the quartz to the hollow of Mara's throat.

For a split second, everything else fell away. All sound. All sensation. Then humid air tinged with coconut and almonds—a scent unique to Mara—filled the room.

Unsure she could risk holding the charm a second longer, Caitlin let her power fade away, then opened her eyes to meet Mara's clear, bright gaze.

"How...?" Mara asked.

Caitlin secured the clasp of the pendant behind Mara's neck. "The crystal isn't a cure. And it won't last forever. But ya' need somethin' to ground ya' to the earth."

"The earth?" Cade leapt up, his growl making the two elementals flinch. "You said a third element would be worse!"

Men. Overprotective, too quick to judge things they knew nothing about. Standing toe-to-toe with the alpha wolf, Caitlin forced strength into her tone. Despite his anger, he didn't scare her, because while she knew he could tear her apart without breaking a sweat, he had an honor to him. A code he wouldn't break unless he absolutely had to.

"Three would be worse. Except I'm givin' her a fourth. My air."

"Fuck me," Liam said from behind her, wrapping an arm around her waist in a not-so-subtle display of solidarity—and possibly a hint of challenge to the alpha. "Can Mara channel the fifth now? The spirit?"

"No. Because she can't *use* all four elements. My air isn't strong enough for her to take—even if she knew how to. And the small bit of earth she can access through the crystal? It's trapped *in* the crystal."

She leaned against Liam, needing his strength. Holding the focus she needed to ground Mara had taken more out of her than she'd realized—or perhaps Fergus was drawing on her power from afar.

"How do you feel, honey?" Cade asked her, cupping her cheek.

"Better."

An older wolf—one she hadn't formally met—came thundering down the hall from his room at the back of the house. "Turn on the TV," he said. "King 5 News."

The healer, who was closest to the large, open living room, grabbed the remote and flipped to the local news station.

On screen, the ocean churned angrily, and the thudding of a helicopter's engines was the only other sound. Horror threatened to drown Caitlin. "No. No, no, no." Icy fingers squeezed her heart, and she wheezed out a breath, hoping it wouldn't be her last.

"Caitlin? What is it, luv?" Liam asked, trying to turn her towards him, but she fought him, struggling free of his embrace and stumbling towards the television as Chrissy turned up the volume and an announcer's voice cut in over the chopper.

"A dozen people are unaccounted for, and search-and-rescue has been deployed to retrieve seven bodies at the foot of the cliffs. Ireland has very little history of earthquakes, and seismologists are baffled. A memorial plaque at the top of the cliffs, installed only a decade ago, cracked in two, one half crashing into the sea, the other tossed two hundred meters inland. We'll continue to update this story as it unfolds."

"Fergus...did...this." Caitlin sank to her knees, suddenly

unable to muster the energy to stay upright. "All those people... dead...because of me."

"We don't know that."

But the lack of conviction in Liam's words left her cold, and Caitlin shook her head. "The plaque. It's for me. He had it installed after I jumped."

Liam knelt next to her, confusion in the set of his strong brow. "I thought ya' hadn't been back there?"

"I found a photo of him online. Next to it. He called to me last night, and I fought him. He told me...he'd punish me." Tears brimmed in her eyes, and she didn't even try to stop them. "If I don't go to him..."

The reporter on screen suddenly yelped and started to hurry away from the edge of the cliff. "We're gettin' an aftershock," she cried as she ran, the picture shaking as her camera person rushed to keep pace beside her.

A great rumble filled the air, followed by more screams, and as the camera panned back to the cliffs, another huge slab fell away. The shot cut to the view from the air, where the massive landslide engulfed one of the search and rescue boats, carrying it down to the bottom of the sea.

CHAPTER TWELVE

Liam

*N*o one could look away from the destruction halfway across the world. In Ireland, the sun was starting to set, painting the sky in pinks and oranges and reds, a stark contrast to the horrors happening on land and the sea.

"Experts say the cliffs will be closed for at least the next three months. The BBC has obtained amateur video of the earthquake as it happened. We want to caution you that these images may be disturbing to sensitive viewers."

The slightly out-of-focus video was trained out over the water when a great rumble obscured the sound of the wind whipping across the landscape.

A twenty-foot section of the cliff sheared off and crashed into the sea below. Churning spray exploded in every direction, screams filled the air, and the tourists scattered like rats fleeing a sinking ship.

As the phone's owner pleaded for God's mercy and started to

back up slowly, the camera caught a lone man on the path that wound around the tallest of the majestic cliffs.

Arms raised to the sky, black hair whipping in the gales, he turned, an odd smile on his face. The plaque next to him cracked in two, one half flying in the direction of the camera, and then the video cut out.

On screen, the newswoman shook her head. "The bystander suffered minor injuries and was taken to hospital. The death toll has risen to seventeen confirmed, with six more missing."

Caitlin moaned, dropping her head into her hands, and Liam wrapped his arms around her. "Ye're safe, luv. I won't let him get to ya'."

"Safe?" She scoffed and tried to fight her way out of his embrace, but he held on tight. "He did all of that...killed seventeen people, probably more, all to punish me."

Livie muted the TV and turned to face Liam and Caitlin. "He called to you last night. And you refused to answer, right?" the petite blond wolf asked, head cocked and hands on her hips.

"Not exactly," Caitlin whispered. "I told him to go to hell. That I wasn't his anymore."

Livie snorted. "I just might like you, Caitlin. Didn't think that would ever happen."

Pride puffed out Liam's chest. He'd known the pack would eventually accept his mate. She was so strong, so brave, and so very much his. If only he could get *her* to believe that as well.

Starting to pace, Livie continued, "Fergus just destroyed a huge fucking piece of Ireland's biggest historical landmark. He knew there'd be a lot of people there. That anything he did would make the international news. That you'd see it, no matter where you were."

"That's Fergus for you. He's mad. Mental," she clarified. "Between what the Thirteen did to him and his own desperate need for power, he can't help it. He'll keep doin' shite like this until I give in." A tear raced down her cheek, and Caitlin swiped it away.

"He wants attention," Livie said. "So, give him some."

"Wh-what?" Caitlin sputtered.

"Can you call him? Or, um, use whatever charm he used on you to tell him you're coming?" Livie asked.

"She's *not* givin' herself up." Liam straightened, his voice taking on the growl of his wolf.

"I'm not suggesting that. Geez. Calm down." Livie rolled her eyes. "But if Caitlin can placate this asshole for a day or two, we'd have a chance to form a plan. It's not like it's easy to just show up at the airport and hop on an international flight."

"She has a point," Cade said.

Caitlin shuddered in Liam's arms. "I'm afraid if I try a charm to contact him, he'll use it against me. Compel me. I don't know that I'll be strong enough to resist him again."

"Could I help you?" Mara asked. "Like you helped me? Could I lend you some of my element? Or some of my sister's element, really."

Cade frowned. After the charm Caitlin had worked on her, she'd at least managed to force down two of the smaller pancakes and a couple of slices of bacon. She looked better. Not quite steady, but at least not about to pass out. "No, honey. You need to rest."

"That...could work." Everyone turned towards Caitlin, and she shrank back against Liam. "Mara's fire. I helped restore a bit of balance earlier, but it won't last. The fire she has in her? It's alive. It's only going to keep getting stronger. If I tapped into some of her fire, it might give her a little more time before the worst of the effects come back. But I still don't see how that does anythin' but delay the inevitable. I'll still have to go to him. Or end it all."

Liam tried, unsuccessfully, to stifle his growl. "You are *not* going to 'end it all.'"

"Do ya' think I *want* to?" She wriggled in his hold so she could meet his gaze. "I've never had a chance to live, Liam. To know what it is to be free. I want that more than anythin'."

His thoughts raced, a dozen possibilities running through his head while Shawn and Christine cleaned up from breakfast, Cade rubbed Mara's back, and Livie continued to pace.

"Farren can help." Why hadn't he thought of his childhood friend before? She knew the area, she had her own pack, and her mum used to work in law enforcement—and had come into contact with more than one practitioner in her time.

"Who's Farren?" Caitlin asked.

A smile tugged at Liam's lips. "My oldest friend, luv. And the only female alpha in the world." He dug his mobile out of his pocket, dialed, and put the call on speaker.

"Ya've reached Gray Eye Investigations. Please leave a brief message, and we'll return your call as soon as we can."

"Farren, I need your help—"

"Mailbox full." After a beep, the call disconnected, and Liam stared at the screen in disbelief.

"The fuck?" Scrolling through his contacts, he tapped a second number. The hair on the back of his neck prickled, and a vague sense of dread tightened in his gut.

"Who is this?" a young, male voice asked, and his worried tone did nothing to ease Liam's worry.

"Liam O'Sullivan. I need to speak to Farren. Now."

"She's, um...not here."

"Where the fuck is she, then?"

"Uh...missing. I think—we think—"

Cade snatched the phone off the coffee table. "Listen up. This is Cade Bowman, alpha of the Seattle pack. Where is she, and who the hell are you?"

The command in Cade's voice was unmistakable, and Liam sat up a little straighter. All the wolves in the room did.

"I'm Tierney, sir. Farren and our beta, Colin, went to Lahinch this mornin'. After the shite at the cliffs, we tried to reach 'em, but they're not answerin' their phones."

"Fuck me," Liam muttered, burying his face against Caitlin's neck.

"What were they doing in Lahinch?" Cade asked.

"One of the town elders was found dead two days ago. She was a water elemental, and rumors circulatin' say it was another elemental who killed 'er."

"Don't suppose the asshole's name is Fergus Tharp?" Cade asked.

"Yeah. That's him. Farren said her mum was huntin' him a decade ago, but then he disappeared. She told us to stay put. Not to leave the pack house, but we're gettin' ready to start searchin' for her."

Cade rubbed the back of his neck, and Mara reached for him, wrapping her arm around his waist. "You disobey your alpha, you're in for a world of hurt, Tierney. Call the Garda. Get them to look for Farren and Colin. The rest of you? Find out anything you can about the dead water elemental, but stay inside. And for fuck's sake, don't even breathe Fergus Tharp's name. Leave that to us."

"Beggin' yer pardon, sir, but ye're in Seattle. How are ya' goin' to stop the arse from there?"

"We're not. I'm sending help to Ireland. Make sure one of your pack stays by that phone. I'll be in touch."

Caitlin

Before she could even *try* to reach Fergus, Caitlin insisted on calling Eleanor. "I don't want to go anywhere near Fergus. Not even with a charm."

Peter let out a low growl. The scarred wolf with black hair

falling across the left side of his face was the only member of the pack who hadn't grudgingly agreed to trust Caitlin.

She held up her hand. "I will. Because I know it's the only way to keep Mara safe. To keep all of you safe."

She and Liam sat on the couch in the living room with Mara curled up in a recliner next to them holding Serena. The baby cooed and fiddled with a set of plastic keys on a large ring Mara shook for her every few minutes.

"I'm out of here," Peter said as he pulled on his coat. "Someone has to keep the business running. Because it's pretty damn clear Liam's going to Ireland by the end of the day." Serena's happy babble half-drowned out Peter's next word, but Caitlin thought it might have been "Stupid."

Cade stepped in front of Peter, drawing up to his full height. "Yes. He is. And I've had about enough of your attitude."

"My attitude?" Peter snorted. "Look at me, Cade." He swept his hair back, revealing corded, twisted scars from his jaw to his ear. "Some days, I can't even manage the stairs down to the basement. Did you know that?"

"And I can't feel my goddamn fingers," Cade growled back. "Do you think you're the only one who suffered here? Livie can't reach for anything above her head with her left arm. Christine has nightmares. Shawn doesn't want to let his mate out of his sight most days, and Ollie lost his career. He's on the night shift for fuck's sake."

Peter lifted his chin in challenge and jerked his thumb towards Caitlin. "And with all of that, you're just willing to accept her?"

"She's. Liam's. Mate." With each word, Peter flinched, but Cade wasn't done. "I'm not throwing her a fucking welcome party. But she's helped Mara more than once. She could have run. Did, even. And then she came back. Family sticks, remember?"

"Whatever." Peter turned and strode for the door, but Cade

barked out an order to stop, and the other wolf froze with his hand on the knob.

"Think good and hard before you come back here tonight, Peter," Cade said. "If you can't accept your beta's mate, then maybe this pack isn't where you belong."

Peter's shoulders jerked, and then he was gone, the door slamming behind him hard enough to shake the windows.

Liam pushed to his feet and stood in front of his alpha. "He's hurtin'."

"That doesn't mean he gets a free pass to disrespect Caitlin, and it sure as shit doesn't give him permission to defy his alpha. You should know that better than anyone."

"I do." Liam's voice dropped, and he glanced back at Caitlin for a moment, his green eyes dark and churning with emotion. "Ye're a good man, Cade. I didn't want to be yer beta when ya' asked me all those years ago. Didn't want to be anyone's beta."

"I'll be alpha one day."

Liam's declaration from their last day in Dublin echoed through her mind. His father had been an alpha. He'd been born to lead. And yet, here he was, Cade's beta. Why?

There was so much she didn't know about him. So much she still wanted to learn. If only they had more time.

"I'd tell you to start your own pack," Cade said as he clapped Liam on the shoulder. "But I need you here. At least...until we figure shit out. After that, you just have to ask. You'd have my blessing."

Liam swallowed hard. "This is where I belong." With a final nod at his alpha, he returned to Caitlin's side. "Let's get this over with."

Shawn and Christine slipped quietly out of the kitchen, while Livie, standing next to the recliner, held out her hands. "All right, little one. It's time for your nap." Pressing a kiss to the baby's soft, blond hair, Mara passed her over with a little sigh, and the baby snuggled against her mother. "You need us, bossman, just holler."

Cade grunted his acknowledgement as Mara scrolled through her phone's contacts and then tapped Eleanor's number.

The call went straight to voicemail, as they'd expected, and Liam pulled out his own cell and started to dial. "She won't recognize my number. Even if it is still a Seattle area code."

"Stop calling," came a quiet hiss when the call connected. "I can't help—"

"My name is Caitlin. Years ago, Fergus Tharp stole my air, and now, he's going to burn down the world to get to me. If he finds out about Mara, he'll never stop huntin' her. Please. Don't hang up."

For a few seconds, there was only silence, and then Eleanor whispered, "Not here. Not right now. Give me an hour, and I'll call you back at this number."

The call disconnected, and Caitlin sank against Liam's chest. The tether binding her and Fergus together was starting to tug once more. He wasn't calling for her yet, but he was using an air charm. Doing...*something*, and she didn't know how much longer she could hold on.

"Come on upstairs, luv," Liam said. "Let's find a flight to Dublin while we wait."

That was the last thing Caitlin wanted to do. Returning to Ireland was giving up *and* putting Liam in danger. But she didn't have a choice. And with him at her side, maybe...maybe she could fight back?

She didn't truly believe it, but she'd try. For him, she'd try.

CHAPTER THIRTEEN

Liam

*H*is Caitlin followed him up the stairs, and even though he couldn't see her face, he felt her fear. It was both strange and comforting to be able to sense her emotions. He'd never asked his alpha—or Livie—what it felt like to seal the bond, but he was starting to get an idea.

His mum and da' had always seemed like they knew what the other was thinking, especially if it involved punishing him for one of his many, *many* acts of teenage rebellion. But he'd chalked that up to them being together for so long.

Up in his room, he snagged his laptop and gestured to a futon next to his work bench. "Sit with me?"

She was back to fiddling with the hem of her sweater— though this one was bulkier. And softer. It molded to her curves, and the v-neck dipped just low enough he could see the swell of her breasts.

Fuck. His cock strained against his jeans. Not that it had completely stopped for more than a few minutes at a time since the previous night. But for most of the morning, he'd been able to keep himself under control. The seriousness of Mara's condition and the terrible destruction and loss of life on the Cliffs had tamed his wolf's desperate need to claim Caitlin, but now that they were alone?

"This is a bad idea," she said quietly as she sank down next to him.

"What? Sittin' here? Or goin' to Ireland?"

"Both." Her blue eyes shimmered slightly until she blinked hard to clear them. "I know I loved ya', Liam. And shite. I want to again. But I don't know ya'. It's—" Caitlin took a slow, deep breath, then shook her head. "You're so certain we're mates, and I *know* your wolf has already...what? Claimed me?"

"He has. I don't do casual, luv. After ya' died, I did my best to forget ya'. I'd get myself as drunk as I could—which took a hell of a lot of whiskey—and I'd find a woman in a bar. Chat her up. Take her somewhere if she were willin'. But half the time, I sobered up before we could get much past the gropin', and..."

"Oh, my God." Caitlin pushed to her feet and backed away until she was halfway across the room. "You haven't...hadn't...had sex since...I mean before last night?"

His cheeks blazed with heat. "Twice. The drink might have stolen a third time from me. All I remember was wakin' up in bed and smellin' a woman's perfume on me."

"Shite," she whispered.

Her shock sent a stark realization that hit him square in the chest. "Ya' weren't so...chaste, I take it?" His voice had taken on a gruff, guttural tone as jealousy flared. *She wasn't herself. Calm the fuck down before you say something you'll regret.*

"I..." Her fingers trembled as she ran them through her reddish brown locks. "I never wanted...not once in eleven years, Liam. I wasn't brave enough to go to a bar on my own or flirt with any of the customers at the shop. But Katerina set me up on dates a time or two. Usually when she needed somethin' from the men. I went. But—"

"If she weren't dead, I'd hunt her down and kill her right fuckin' now," he growled, crossing the room in three strides with the intent of taking his mate in his arms. But she held up her hands to stop him, shame and sorrow warring in her gaze.

"I couldn't say no to her, Liam. It wasn't just bein' grateful for what she'd done for me." At his snarl, she quickly continued, "I *was* grateful. I still am. Bad things happened to me in the days after I jumped. Things I don't remember. There was a ship. And pain. When she found me, I was nothin' but bruises and scrapes and broken bones..." Caitlin shook her head and swallowed hard. "She brought me to the hospital. Paid for everything. Took those terrible memories away from me. And hid me from Fergus. He would have found me, and I wouldn't be with ya' now if it weren't for her magic. She was *so* powerful. She studied with practition-ers, used what she learned to protect the little group of elemen-tals we had in Phoenix. Her spell, that crystal she gave me...it took everythin' from me. My name, my memories. I didn't even know how to use my element after I put it on. She taught me. Every day for months."

"Ye're talkin' like I should forgive her." He would do no such thing. Couldn't even think about the possibility. "Yeah, she kept ya' alive. But are ya' sayin' she made ya' have sex with men ya' didn't want to touch ya'? That's..." He couldn't say the word, but it slammed around in his thoughts like a battering ram.

"No!" Caitlin huffed and moved to his window, raising the sash and letting in the early spring air. "I went out on dates. Not many. Five, six over the years. Katerina would set them up and tell me what she needed. Information, usually. And I'd use my air to get it. I didn't sleep with any of them. Didn't get beyond kissin'. Sometimes, I'd make them think I had. Afterwards, I'd always feel so...so dirty. But one word from her and all my guilt would just...disappear."

She wouldn't look at him, just hugged herself tightly, her chest heaving and her cheeks bright red.

"Come here, Caitlin. Please. Let me hold ya'?"

Shaking her head, she turned away and stared out the window. "Not now. I can't. Just...find us a flight."

The desperation in her tone broke him in ways he'd never known a man could break. But they didn't have much more time alone before Eleanor called, so he returned to the futon, picked up the laptop, and started searching.

Caitlin

She sat on Liam's bed, watching him pack, lamenting the truly meager amount of clothing she'd brought with her from Phoenix. Not that most of her wardrobe was appropriate for Seattle. Or Ireland this time of year.

"Do ya' have a coat, luv?" he asked as he picked up her duffel bag, then frowned at how little it contained.

"No. I...um...left Phoenix in a hurry."

"Christine can go get ya' some clothes. Ya' need more than this."

"You ruined my best panties," she said. Until that moment, she hadn't realized she was actually a little bitter about the loss. She didn't have a lot of money, and she was *not* going to let him buy her a whole new wardrobe. "If there's a Target nearby, I can go there after we talk to Eleanor."

"Ye're not going anywhere without me." Liam tucked a fourth pair of jeans into his suitcase, then added a second pair of black leather boots.

"I promised ya' I wouldn't run," she snapped. He still didn't trust her. Her eyes prickled and started to burn, but she clenched her jaw. No. She would *not* let him know just how much that hurt.

Liam caught her wrist, and the heat in his fingers sent sparks racing up her arm, despite her frustration. "I'm not worried about ya' runnin', luv. But if Fergus calls to ya' and ye're alone? What's goin' to happen then?"

Shit. He was right. Deflating a little, she stared down at her mostly empty duffel bag. She'd paid her rent through the end of the month, but she'd known when she'd reached the bus station. She was never going back. Even if she wanted to—which she definitely did not—everything there was Bella's. Not hers.

"I'm sorry. I'm not used to this."

"What?" Liam asked as he tugged her closer.

A little laugh bubbled up as she realized how ridiculous her answer would sound. "Everything." Caitlin let him pull her down onto the bed next to him and leaned forward, her elbows on her knees. "I was Bella for so long, I don't remember what it was like to be Caitlin."

"But ya' said yer memories were comin' back."

"They are. Even the ones I don't want." She sighed and peered up at him. "But that's not the same thing as remembering how to *be* Caitlin. I'm not the same person I was back then, Liam."

"Do ya' think *I* am? We've all changed, luv." He reached over and tucked her hair behind her ear, then smiled and lightly touched her nose stud. "Ya' didn't have this eleven years ago."

"And you didn't have that tattoo. But it's more than that." How could she make him understand?

Liam turned her until they were face to face, and his eyes held more than a decade of pain, loneliness, and sorrow. "Caitlin, my wolf knows ye're my mate. Werewolves...we only get one. I love ya' with everything I am. I will for the rest of my life. But if ya' don't want me, once ye're safe, I'll let ya' go. I promise."

A single tear trailed down her cheek, and her heart threatened to break in half. She ached to love him. But how could she when she wasn't free?

"I want to know ya'. Or...at least I want the chance," she whispered.

"On my life," Liam said, brushing the tear away, "I'll make sure ya' have that chance."

———————

ELEANOR WAS PUNCTUAL. Down to the minute. Cade, Mara, Liam, and Caitlin gathered around the phone, and when Liam tapped the screen, the older air elemental started speaking immediately.

"I don't have long. This is Caitlin Brannigan?"

"Yes. You know me?" Caitlin reached for Liam's hand. She had no memory of this woman. But had they met?

"I know *of* you, my dear. Everyone in Cannon Beach has heard some story or another about Fergus Tharp. He's killed at least ten elementals—possibly more than a dozen—and if he's not stopped, he's going to continue to threaten us for the rest of his life."

"If ya' know all about him," Liam said, "why haven't ya' done somethin' to stop him?"

"Because he has magic on his side, wolf. You're that beta? The one who was so disagreeable?"

"I'm gettin' closer to ragin' by the minute, yeah."

"This little community has all of fourteen elementals. Most of us are well over sixty. We're safe here. Protected. The last time one of us went to Ireland—fifteen years ago—she didn't come back."

Nausea crawled up Caitlin's throat. "What was her name?" she asked.

"Tessa. She was water. Grew up somewhere near Doolin from what I remember. She only left to go to her mother's funeral. We got a single phone call from her when she arrived, and haven't heard from her since."

Caitlin's memories flooded back in a rush, and a sob escaped before she could stop it.

The slight woman trembled as she knelt in front of Fergus. Blond hair fell to her shoulders, and Fergus had bound her wrists in front of her with a thin leather cord.

"Please," Tessa begged. "I can't give you my element. I just want to go home."

Fergus tightened his fingers on the back of Caitlin's neck. "You know what to do."

"No. Don't make me," she whispered. "Not again."

He yanked her back against him, his breath hot on her cheek. "Do not test me, Caitie. Or ya' can spend another month underground when we're done."

Tears streamed down her cheeks as she met Tessa's gaze. "I'm so sorry." With the earth elemental's fingers gripping her so hard she feared he'd snap her neck without even meaning to, she called on her air.

"Ye'll listen now. No more cryin'. Ya' want to do everything Fergus asks of ya'. Ya' want us to have yer water. We'll be bound together forever." A gentle breeze slipped around them, the ruins of the ancient castle providing just enough privacy no one would ever see them. Fergus stood barefoot, drawing power from the earth and rocks around them. "Ya' want this, Tessa. Tell us ya' want this."

"I...want...this," she said. "I'll do whatever you ask."

"Give me yer hands," Fergus said. Under his breath, he started chanting, and Caitlin's thoughts dulled, like she'd tied on one too many at the pub.

Think!

She tried to concentrate, to remember the spell so she could write it down later. Maybe...if she could...she could find a way to break it.

But Fergus was too strong, and her air left her like a wave receding from the shore. "Join us, Caitie," he snapped, and she rested her hands over his.

Power punched her in the stomach, and Tessa screamed as the rain started to fall all around them.

Lightning arced across the sky, the thunder quickly following. Stones crumbled from the ruined walls, and then everything went quiet, dark, and still.

She came back to herself to find Cade arguing with Eleanor. "Mara can't go to Ireland. You *know* that. If she does, and Fergus finds out, he'll never stop looking for her."

Liam chimed in. "Caitlin and I can find the practitioner ya' told Mara about. If she can help Caitlin get her air back, then—"

"Then what, wolf? What'll you do then? Try to do battle with an army of magical beings who've had decades, centuries even, to perfect their defenses? You'll lose. And then you'll all die. I will not risk those I hold most dear on a chance so slim, it's practically transparent."

"He killed Tessa." Everyone in the room fell silent at Caitlin's words. "*We* killed Tessa. Please, Eleanor. He forced me to work the spell with him. At least five times that I remember. And if I can't find a way to stop him, to take back my element, he'll make me do it again."

"I should kill you myself," Eleanor hissed. "She was only twenty-four!"

"And I was only twenty-one. Fergus bound me at seventeen." Anger won out over shame, and she grabbed the phone. "I didn't understand what he was askin' of me, and by the time I did, it was too late. I never had a chance to live. He's callin' for me again. And I think he's even more unstable now than he was eleven years ago. Ya' think that mess at the Cliffs of Moher was terrible? He'll do a hundred times worse. A thousand even. Unless ya' help me stop him. And keep Mara safe while I do it."

For a full minute, Eleanor didn't say a word. "I didn't know all the details. There were rumors. That the air elemental with him wasn't there by choice."

"He told me he loved me. That we'd be together forever.

When yer first crush says that to ya'..." Next to her, Liam let loose with a feral growl, and Cade shot him a look that shut him up.

A heavy sigh carried over the connection. "With magic strengthening him, it wouldn't have mattered if you'd hated him. He'd have forced your hand."

"The practitioner ya' told Mara about?" Liam asked. "Will she help us?"

"She hates the Thirteen as much as anyone. If she can, she will."

"And what about Mara?" Cade leaned closer, his fingers twined with his mate's. "Can you help keep her grounded until Caitlin and Liam meet with the practitioner?"

Eleanor's voice took on a weary, resigned tone. "I can give you two days. That's it. Any longer, and I'll be missed. Two days from right now. As soon as I hang up, I'll get in the car."

Mara sat up a little straighter, and relief eased the furrow in her brow. "Thank you, Eleanor. You'll come to our house?"

"I'll be there in four hours."

The call ended, and Caitlin stared at the darkened screen until Liam touched her shoulder. "What do ya' say, luv? Do ya' feel strong enough to try reachin' out to Fergus?"

"No. But I don't think I ever will," Caitlin whispered. "I'll try. But Mara can't be anywhere around me. How long until our flight?"

"Five hours."

"I need to go somewhere close to the water. Lots of open air."

Liam nodded. "I know a place." He gathered her into his arms and kissed her so tenderly, tears burned her eyes. "And I won't let ya' go, luv. I swear it."

CHAPTER FOURTEEN

Caitlin

*T*he entire pack gathered in the living room—even Peter who'd begrudgingly left work for an hour to join the meeting. Caitlin positioned herself just behind Liam, fighting her urge to hide upstairs in his room.

Everyone focused on Cade when he cleared his throat. "Farren Denair from the Lahinch pack went missing. She was investigating the death of an elemental in her area, and it's highly likely that Fergus Tharp is responsible for that death and for her disappearance. Eleanor will be here in two hours to help us find a way to keep Mara off Fergus's radar, but Liam and Caitlin are going to Ireland to track down a practitioner who might be able to help her take back her air *and* keep Mara safe."

"Uh, look," Livie said. "Despite her being Liam's mate, despite her helping Mara, I won't lie. I can't say I'm ready to welcome Caitlin into this house. At least not yet. But is it really such a good idea for her to go to the one place she won't be able to escape Fergus?"

"I have to." Caitlin edged around Liam. "I can't have any more blood on my hands. My air is too weak for me to do much from here. I'll be able to reach out to Fergus because we're linked, but that's it. If I go to Ireland, I might be strong enough to find Farren. And if Fergus knows I'm close, if I can convince him that I'm comin' back to him, maybe he'll stop killin' innocent bystanders."

"Liam, this is insane," a tall, older werewolf—Ollie, she thought—said. "You're going to get yourself killed."

Silently, Caitlin agreed with him, but there was no way Liam would stay behind, and as much as she hated the idea of him risking himself, she had to admit...she needed his strength.

Before Liam could answer, Cade held up his hand to stop him. "If we don't do something, Fergus will keep killing. Hundreds. Thousands. This is the best option right now. So unless anyone else has a brilliant idea that doesn't involve sending Caitlin to her death alone, shut the fuck up and listen."

An hour later, she and Liam stood in Cade and Mara's living room, packed and ready to go. With one of Mara's older wool coats draped over her arm, Caitlin hugged the water elemental and whispered a quick blessing she'd learned from her mum years ago.

"May the rain fall lightly on your cheeks, the wind boost your spirit, the sun warm your days, and the earth bring you strength. May your burdens be eased by the blessings of the spirit until we meet again."

"Be safe," Mara said. "And come back."

Drawing away so she could meet Mara's tired gaze, Caitlin was surprised to find nothing but acceptance in the water elemental's eyes. "Are ya' sure?"

"Liam needs you." Mara smiled, and though it was obvious she was still tired, she looked better than she had in two days.

"And I think the rest of us do too. I'm not saying it'll be easy, but they'll accept you. If that's something you want."

"I'm not free. Wanting...*anything* is dangerous. But I want the chance to figure it out. Is that enough for now?" Caitlin desperately wanted to stay with Liam. To get to know him enough to decide what she wanted. A future with him? A mate? More?

"It's enough. Call us when you get to Dublin." Mara hugged her again, then trudged back to the couch where she curled up with a blanket.

Cade stared up at Liam—the beta wolf had a good three inches on his alpha—and clapped him on the shoulder. "Peter will be on the morning flight. Don't let your guard down for a fucking minute or I'll kick your ass into next week."

A wave of horror rolled over Caitlin, but she stared down at her boots until they made it outside and Liam slid behind the wheel of her old car.

"Peter's going with us?" she asked. Air swirled around them, carrying Liam's spicy, woodsy scent to her nose. "He hates me. And he should."

"We need him, luv." Liam reached over and cupped her cheek, and for a moment, she let herself savor his touch. "He knows Ireland almost as well as I do. Explored the whole of the west coast when we were hidin' out there after the fire. If anyone can help us find Farren—"

At the mention of the missing alpha, Caitlin pulled away and reached for her seatbelt.

"What's wrong?" He covered her hand with his, but Caitlin just shook her head. Something in the way he said the woman's name didn't sit well with her, and she couldn't understand why. "Caitlin, talk to me."

As he slid his hand into her hair, she deflated. "You talk about her like you love her."

His laugh was so deep and so sudden, she jerked back and glared at him.

"Oh, luv. Are ya' jealous?"

Refusing to dignify that with an answer, she dug into her small cross-body bag and double-checked her passport. Caitlin Brannigan wouldn't be flying to Ireland. No. Bella Pond was accompanying Liam. She hated even acknowledging the old name now, but she didn't have much of a choice.

"Caitlin. Look at me." The commanding tone, so forceful but also gentle, filled the silence between them, and she did as he asked. "I'd no sooner bed Farren than Peter. She and I have a history. Her da' led a pack outside of Dublin—one of two. The other was my own father's pack. I spent my childhood runnin' around the countryside with Farren and her beta, Colin. Thick as thieves, our folks would say. And about as much trouble. She's like my sister."

"Oh." A hint of shame crawled up her neck as Liam started the car, but he leaned over to brush a light kiss to her cheek before he pulled away from the curb.

"We're new, luv. Old and new, I suppose. But ya' feel somethin' with me, yeah?"

She sighed, wishing she had a better answer to give him. "I want to be able to love ya', Liam. I just don't know how with *him* still in my head." Old houses passed by outside the windows as they headed west, towards a park overlooking Puget Sound where Caitlin could try to reach out to Fergus.

Neither of them spoke the rest of the drive, and when Liam parked, Caitlin was out of the car before he'd even removed the key. She ran all the way to the edge of the cliff before sinking to her knees and staring out over the sparkling blue water. She felt like she was going to be sick. Even the possibility of hearing his voice, of feeling the tether between them tighten, had her heart racing.

Get it over with. If he's going to take you, best to be done with it.

Except now there was Liam. He knelt next to her and

wrapped his arm around her waist. "I've got ya', luv. Do yer thing."

God, she was terrified. Terrified Fergus would be too strong. That he'd somehow take Liam too.

"Two became one. Let my air find its home, its destiny, its other half."

A gust of wind swept over them, and Caitlin's muscles locked, her entire body rigid in Liam's hold. Without her air, she was nothing, and if Fergus wanted to, if he were strong enough, he might be able to simply end her life right here.

One minute. Two. Three. Would he answer at all?

"Caitlin? Say somethin'," Liam demanded, tightening his arm around her waist.

"He's not—"

"Where are ya', Caitie? Ya' belong with me. If ya' aren't here by mornin', so many more will suffer."

"I have a flight. But not until tomorrow. Ya' can give me two days, yeah?" Caitlin squeezed Liam's fingers, hoping he'd understand she had to focus, had to hold on with everything she was.

"Now, Caitie!"

His pull had her jerking in Liam's embrace, and for seconds that seemed to stretch out forever, her lungs wouldn't respond.

"No seats until then. Please. I can't breathe!"

"Ye're mine, Caitie. Stop fightin'."

The urge to just let go, to give up her control was so strong, until Liam shifted and rested his free hand on her cheek. Caitlin fought back, wrestling just a fraction of her element back from Fergus's iron grip. Enough to take a shuddering breath.

"Two...days. I swear it. Don't...hurt...anyone else."

He let go, severing the connection between them so violently, she collapsed, barely able to force her eyes open. Liam swept her up against his chest, and she settled with the heat of him, his strength, the way his voice rumbled through her. "Caitlin, say somethin'."

Through the shimmer of tears, she whispered, "I tried."

Liam

Caitlin didn't say a word on their way to the airport. Not until they'd passed through the TSA checkpoint and were at the gate did she come out of the slight fog that had plagued her since she'd reached out to Fergus.

"How long is the flight?" she asked, her voice flat.

"About nine hours." His stomach growled loudly, and he glanced across the terminal at a local hamburger joint. "I need a couple thousand calories. And ya' haven't eaten all day. What do ya' like?"

Caitlin stared at him like she didn't understand the question. "A cheeseburger? I guess?"

"Whatever ya' want, luv. What about a milkshake? Chocolate was always yer favorite."

She nodded, and when he returned with three bags and four milkshakes, her eyes widened. "I only needed one..."

"I only got ya' one. The rest are for me."

He was two bites into his double cheeseburger by the time Caitlin snapped her jaw shut. "How do you...? I'd be sick."

"Shifting takes a powerful lot of energy. This is nothin'."

Caitlin picked at her cheeseburger, but at the first sip of her milkshake, her lips twitched into what might have been a smile. "I haven't had one of these in...years."

"Why not?" He frowned as he polished off the second bag of fries. "They have milkshakes in Phoenix."

"I never had much extra money," she said, staring down at the floor. "Katerina didn't pay me most of the time. She just...took care of me. Bought my groceries, most of my clothes..."

Liam wanted to bring the woman back from the dead just so

he could kill her all over again. "She was just as bad as Fergus. Controlling ya'. When was the last time ya' made a decision for yerself?"

She straightened then, a bit of defiance blazing in her eyes. "When I came to Seattle."

"Before that."

Let it go before you say something you can't take back, dumbass.

"When she kidnapped Mara. And I helped keep her alive." Caitlin stalked over to the rubbish bin and chucked the rest of her milkshake. "I don't need ya' remindin' me just how stupid I was for lettin' her control me, Liam. I can beat myself up for that all on my own."

Fuck. She needed to eat, and he'd just killed her appetite because he couldn't leave well enough alone. Liam was so desperate to know everything about her, to find out who his mate was after eleven years, he'd pushed too hard.

She crossed her arms and stared out the large windows at the planes heading to and from the gates.

His own appetite gone, he stretched out his legs and stared up at the ceiling. After a few minutes, he hid his grin when Caitlin snuck a couple of french fries from the last bag on the table between them.

"I'm sorry, luv. I was an arse."

She sighed, but her words fell away when Peter strode up to them, a duffel bag slung over his shoulder and anger churning in his eyes.

"What the fuck are ya' doin' here?" Liam asked as he pushed to his feet.

"Tierney texted Cade. Another member of Farren's pack disappeared."

"Fuck, who?" Liam knew every one of them, though he'd only met the younger members briefly when he'd risked seeing her after he'd brought the pack to Ireland.

"Brian Duffy. The youngest. He was going stir crazy with the moon so close, and went out to run on her property this morning, or—fuck—I can't keep the time zones straight. Six hours ago? He hasn't come back. The rest of them are too scared to leave the house to look for him."

"Three left then. Tierney, Abagail, and Ewan, yeah?"

Caitlin pressed against Liam, shaking. "This is my fault. Obviously, I didn't convince him I was comin'."

"Duffy disappeared hours before you tried to contact Fergus," Peter said, and though he was clearly agitated, his voice had softened slightly. "If anything, this was Fergus making sure Farren and her pack got the message to leave him the fuck alone."

Liam ran a hand through his hair, his wolf pulsing under his skin, aching to run. "That doesn't explain why ye're here."

"Shawn worked some magic. Got me the last seat."

"How's Mara? Did Eleanor show up?" Liam asked.

Peter swore under his breath as he dropped his bag on the floor. "No. She called and asked them to meet her down in Tacoma. There's a practitioner there. Not one of the Thirteen, but someone who at least knows how to hide Mara's power from anyone looking for it."

"What aren't ya' tellin' me?"

"Something doesn't feel right. Ollie followed them. Just in case."

"Good. Give us a minute, luv." Liam jerked his head, and Peter followed him to the end of a long row of chairs. "I know ya' don't like any of this. And...if I were in yer shoes, I'd be just as angry."

"Don't, man. This isn't the time. Flight's about to board."

Fuck. Peter was right. When he returned to Caitlin's side, she was still trembling, and Liam wrapped her in his arms. "It's all right, luv."

"It's not. Fergus won't stop killin'. There's no logic in him now. When the magic takes hold of him, it's like...the boy I knew isn't there anymore. He won't care that I'm half a world away. He won't care that I promised to come back to him. Between the madness from havin' my element in him and the control the Thirteen has over him...how many more?"

The silence stretched between them like a raging river, drowning out everything but Caitlin's stuttered breaths and the scent of her fear. Liam ached to comfort her, but nothing he could say would fix this. She'd never be free as long as Fergus lived.

"Now boarding, Aer Lingus Flight 63, nonstop to Dublin, rows 10-20," the gate agent called.

"That's us, luv. Are ya' ready?"

Caitlin swiped at her cheek and dashed away a tear, then pulled out her passport. "Bella Pond is," she said sadly.

"When ye're free of him, luv, we'll find out who to talk to in Dublin to get new papers for ya'. I promise."

Caitlin

When I'm free...

She repeated the words over and over to herself as Liam dozed beside her, his long legs cramped in the tight seats. The rumble of the engines had put him to sleep within minutes of boarding—though she'd helped him along with a weak charm.

Across the aisle, Peter sipped a glass of whiskey and occasionally glared at them.

Fergus's hold on her strengthened with every passing hour, and the tension crackled against her raw nerves, eating away at any hope she'd found in Liam's arms.

Her element, at least, flourished in the skies, and between the rush of power and her racing mind, she knew she'd never be able to sleep. So she spent the time staring out the window and searching her fractured memories for anything that might help them.

Unable to keep still, she eased herself around Liam's bulk, brushing a kiss to his lips when he stirred. "Just stretchin' my legs," she murmured in his ear, then sent a charm whispering over his skin, urging him back to sleep.

On her third trip up the aisle, Peter blocked her path. "Back of the plane," he hissed and jerked his thumb towards the galley.

Everything in her wanted to refuse, but Peter was part of the pack, and if by some miracle she *did* manage to free herself from Fergus's control, she'd have it out with him eventually.

Leaning against the wall of the fuselage, arms crossed, she forced herself to meet his gaze.

"Does he really have a chance of living through any confrontation with Fergus?" the wolf demanded.

"None of us do." Lying wouldn't help them now, as much as she wanted to avoid raising Peter's hackles further. "Not unless the practitioner can help and I can find a way to take my element back. I'm defenseless against him. Truly. He'll call to me, and I'll resist for a few hours. Maybe even a day. But then he'll track me down and force me to go with him."

Every time she'd run, the scene played out like a script. Resistance. Capture. Pain. Fear. Surrender. Then, his insanity would pass for a time. He'd apologize. Disappear to track down another elemental. Or hide, ashamed of how he'd treated her. If he left for long enough, she'd build up the courage to flee, and the cycle would start all over again.

Peter grabbed her arm, his fingers digging into her bicep as he leaned close enough for her to smell the whiskey on his breath. "Then take it back."

"Do ya' really think I'm not tryin'? That I want to put Liam in danger? Mara? Cade? Any of ya'?"

Peter pushed her back against the wall, and his eyes flashed with the gold of his wolf. "I don't think Bella gives a shit about anyone but herself. I just don't know who you are anymore."

"I'm Caitlin," she spat, wrenching her arm free. "Whether ya' believe it or not. And I'll be makin' up for what Bella did for the rest of my life. But I'll be damned if I'm goin' to let ya' scare me into givin' up on the best man I've ever known."

"You're putting that man in danger."

"Don't ya' think I know that? Or are ya' too caught up in yer own pain to see anyone else's? If I thought it'd work, I'd charm Liam so he'd forget me and go after Fergus alone."

"Why can't you?"

"Because he loves me. Because I think he's my mate, and that bond can't be broken. I'll die before I'll let Fergus hurt him. And I'll do my best to take the arse with me. But if I can't, I'm dependin' on ya' to protect Liam."

His entire countenance changed as her words sank in. She didn't want to die, but unless they found some sort of miracle, she'd sacrifice herself to save the man she desperately wanted to love.

Peter let her go when one of the flight attendants approached. "Can I help you?" the young woman asked.

"Another two whiskeys," Peter said. "Please. For Seat 14-C."

"Of course, sir."

Peter gestured for Caitlin to head back up the aisle first, but he cleared his throat when she reached her row, and she stopped, but didn't turn around.

"He's my brother, Caitlin. I'll do my part. If you do yours."

CHAPTER FIFTEEN

Caitlin

The moment the plane landed, Liam pulled out his phone to check his messages, leaning close to her so she could listen too. Cade's strained voice immediately set them both on edge.

"Eleanor...fuck. She's dead. It was an ambush. They tried to *kill* Mara. We barely got out of there alive. Headed to the airport now. We're coming to you by way of New York. We'll get to Dublin at 5:00 pm. Don't trust anyone."

Before the message ended, Mara moaned softly and a car engine roared to life.

The beep made Liam flinch, and Caitlin gripped his arm so hard, her fingers ached.

"What's going on?" Peter hissed from across the aisle.

"Not here. When we get off the plane," Liam grunted and played the next message from Shawn recapping what he knew— which wasn't much. Livie had gone to meet them at the airport with a hastily packed bag, and she'd told him Mara had barely been able to form a coherent sentence.

Panic skittered up Caitlin's spine. She could sense Fergus now. Stronger than when they'd been in Seattle. At least he hadn't called to her yet. Darkness blanketed the country still, with only the lights from central Dublin lending a pale, ethereal glow to the sky.

By the time they got through customs and into the terminal, Liam's wolf was clawing his way to the surface. "Liam, look at me," Caitlin said as she took his hands, pulling him over to a quiet spot against the wall. "Your eyes are wild."

Crushing her against him, a desperate sound rumbling in his chest, Liam breathed in her scent. "I need ya', Caitlin. Naked," he said as he nuzzled her neck.

Peter stalked over to them, his gait slightly uneven. "Talk."

Liam just passed the man his phone. "Play the last two messages." He ushered them out into baggage claim while Peter listened, growing increasingly agitated with every passing minute.

"Why would anyone try to kill Mara?" Peter asked as he yanked his duffel bag free form a tangle of two other suitcases.

"Not here." Liam wrestled his own suitcase from the carousel and the three of them headed for the rental car counter. "We're going to get a room for a few hours, regroup, and try to piece together what happened. But until we're in the car, alone, away from humans, shut the fuck up about killin'."

Peter nodded, though the look on his face was anything but calm. Liam draped his arm around Caitlin's shoulders, steering her through a set of automatic doors. "Are ya all right, luv?"

No, she'd left "all right" back in Seattle. Or possibly in Phoenix. But she forced a weak smile. "I'm terrified, but he's not calling to me yet. Though he's probably still asleep. I doubt we have long. I can hide us for a short time once we're at the hotel. At least slow him down."

"How?"

"Not here, remember?"

The scent of Dublin in the pre-dawn stillness brought memories of college. Of the three years she spent thinking she might be free. Late nights studying, discovering the best coffee shops around the university, running on rain-slicked streets, unfettered and almost able to pretend the missing piece of her soul didn't matter. Freedom, though temporary, allowed her to find Caitlin— the woman who learned to play fiddle in a couple of local session bands, read romance novels, and found her voice on the school's debate team.

"I was Caitlin here," she said quietly once they reached the car. Not Caitie. Not Bella. This is where I first realized who *Caitlin* was."

"Ye'll find her again, luv," Liam said with a gentle kiss to her cheek before he opened her door.

Once he was maneuvering the small sedan through the roundabouts and narrow streets with ease, Caitlin dialed the pack house.

"Liam?" Livie answered, with Serena wailing close by. "The airline won't tell us whether Cade and Mara made the flight. Fuc —dging privacy laws or some...stuff like that. Take her," she said, presumably to someone else in the room, and the wailing faded away. "I had to meet them a mile from the airport at a rest stop, and Mara didn't look good. But if they made the flight, they'll land in an hour. Tierney's still at Farren's, and he's holding strong. The rest of them...they're terrified."

Liam checked the mirrors and pulled off onto a narrow, tree-lined street. "Farren's place is four hours from Dublin. But we're gettin' a room now. I don't want to leave until we hear from them."

"Shawn and I are taking the baby up to Vancouver for a while. We know the beta up there. Ollie and Christine are going to Bellingham."

"Good," Liam said. "Stay in touch, but keep yerself safe. We're almost to the hotel. As soon as we hear from Cade, I'll text ya'."

Caitlin ended the call, and silence filled the car until Liam parked in front of a fully restored castle, complete with multiple towers and a massive ivy-covered wall. A touch of modern architecture melded with the historical, a glass entryway lit with bright blue spotlights stark against the stone.

"What is this place?" Caitlin asked.

"Clontarf Castle Hotel," Liam said. "My parents owned it until they passed, and now it's one of the ways the O'Sullivan Foundation makes its money."

At the front desk, the clerk's eyes widened when she saw his passport. "Welcome, Mr. O'Sullivan, sir. What can I do for ya'?"

"A suite, if ya' have it. And the two rooms on either side of it. We could use some privacy."

Caitlin gawked as the woman tapped away on her computer for a few moments, then busied herself encoding keycards. "Seventh floor, sir. The suite is 704, and you also have 702 and 706. May I call someone for yer bags?"

"No, thank ya', Mary. We're quite fine on our own."

The moment the door shut, Peter lost his tenuous hold on his temper. "What the fuck is going on? Elementals turning on their own? Cade and Mara almost killed?"

Caitlin stifled a yelp. Peter's eyes glowed with his wolf, and his hands shook as he clenched them at his sides.

Liam drew up to his full height, and his voice took on the control and authority of an alpha. "I'm warnin' ya', mate. If ya' shift right now, I'm goin' to kick yer arse."

Peter yanked at the collar of his shirt, and a feral growl rumbled through his chest. "It's too close to the full moon," he managed.

"Get the fuck out of here, now." Liam nodded towards the door. "This hotel backs up to a preserve. Once ya' get past the tree line, ya' can shift and run for an hour. Ye're no help to anyone if ya' can't keep yerself together. We won't know anythin' about Cade and Mara for that long, and I won't have ya' threatenin' my...my Caitlin."

Peter didn't bother to reply, and the slam of the door echoed like a shot.

"Caitlin, luv. Come here."

She relaxed into his embrace, needing the steady, solid weight of his arms around her. While they'd talked to Livie, Caitlin had used her phone to check the news for any more horrors Fergus might have unleashed while they'd been in the air. But other than a single story confirming all of the missing from the "earthquake" at the cliffs had died, there'd been nothing.

He brought her to the bedroom, eased the jacket from her shoulders, and sat her down on the bed. "Ye're exhausted, Caitlin. I could pack a week's worth of clothes in those bags under your eyes. He's not lookin' for ya' yet. Rest. I'm goin' to call Tierney and see if anyone's heard from Farren, and then I'll join ya'."

If only a little rest could solve her problems. But Liam had a point. Once Fergus called to her, they'd have no choice but to fight. And without sleep, she'd be no good to anyone.

"Don't be long. Please," she whispered. Liam's eyes hadn't returned to their calm moss green since they'd landed, and she wanted him with her. Needed it.

But despite her exhaustion, she was too frightened, too on edge to sleep, so she crept out into the suite's main room to find Liam standing at the window, staring out at the back lawn of the old castle's grounds.

"And ya' haven't heard anythin'?"

Caitlin smoothed her hands over his shoulders, massaging the tight muscles, working her fingers into his hair, and he tipped his head back to allow her better access. With a stifled groan, he dropped into a chair. She called a bit of her element to enhance the conversation on the other end of the line and continued to work out the tension gathered in his neck.

"Nothin'. Called the local Garda, the barrister whose office is next to Farren's, and...fuck."

Liam sat up, instantly on alert. "What is it?"

"The Hen and Boar," Tierney said, his voice full of uncertainty. "It...collapsed last night. They're sayin' it was a gas leak. The whole buildin' came down."

"Fergus," Caitlin whispered, her fingers stilling on Liam's shoulders. "It has to be."

"Farren. Shite. What if she and Colin are buried under the rubble?" Liam asked.

"Accordin' to the local paper, the search dogs didn't find anythin'." Tierney blew out a shaky breath, and someone else muttered words Caitlin couldn't hear over the line. "But that's the last place we knew they were goin'."

"We'll be there soon, mate. See if ya' can find out anythin' more about the buildin', and stay inside."

With another groan, Liam let Caitlin take the full weight of his head in her hands. She alternated light, soothing touches with firm pressure along the base of his skull, the sides of his neck, and behind his ears.

"How many more?" Caitlin whispered. "If Farren and Colin are dead too..."

"Don't talk like that, luv." Liam tipped his head back to meet her gaze for a brief moment. "Farren's not an easy one to kill. And Colin's an ornery son of a bitch. We'll find them."

If only his tone hadn't carried the same uncertainty and pain that weighed on her heart. The longer Farren and Colin were missing, the less likely they were to find the two wolves—at least alive. If Fergus had them, he'd either kill them or use them to get to her.

She ground her knuckle into a particularly hard knot at the curve of Liam's shoulder, held the pressure for a count of three, then smoothed the flat of her hand over his back. "Come to bed. I can do more if you lie down."

Leading him to a mattress large enough to lose herself in, she removed his vest, the travel-weary blue button-down shirt, and his belt. "On your stomach."

While he shed his pants and wrapped his arms around one of the thick pillows, Caitlin shut the bedroom door. "I've known Farren since we were six years old," he said when she straddled him and started pressing the heels of her hands into his back. "We lost touch after...after ya' died. Hell, I only called her once the whole time we were in Ireland last year. I shoulda' been a better friend."

Despite how much she *needed* reassurance, hearing Liam was as worried as she was helped, in a way. She spread the flats of her hands along his shoulder blades and whispered a quick, soothing charm.

"Oh God," he murmured into the pillow. "What are ya' doin' to me?"

"It's one of the few charms I'm good at even when my air's at its weakest. It eases yer mind a bit and loosens yer muscles." She savored the feel of his sculpted body under her fingers, the coiled strength, the soft silk of his hair, and the low, appreciative rumbles and groans as she worked on his shoulders.

If only she could reassure him. Farren would have to be a strong wolf to lead a pack, but Caitlin had seen Fergus break too many elementals—including her—to force any confidence into her tone.

"I can feel yer pain, luv." Liam turned under her, pulling her to his chest. "Talk to me."

"Just...memories. Nothin' that can help us."

A woman's scream echoed in her mind, and horror washed over her. How Fergus had been so mad the first time she'd run that he'd tracked her back to her childhood home where her mum had tried to protect her. Until Fergus had used his element to open a sinkhole under their home. Her own air wielded against her, she'd followed him outside while her mum had been trapped in the small cottage as it sank deep into the earth.

Grief threatened to choke her, and she rolled off the bed and yanked open the window. Her heart pounded, and the drapes billowed as her emotions let loose a storm within her.

Liam wrapped his arms around her waist, nuzzling her neck and whispering her name. "*Is breá liom tú.*"

If only love could erase the past.

Tears streamed down her face, and huge, choking sobs wracked her body. "He killed my mum, Liam. I remember now. He...buried her alive because I ran from him."

"Shite."

"Ya' shouldn't love me. He made me help him kill at least three elementals I can remember, and maybe more. How can ya' possibly forgive me for what I've done?"

Liam turned her to face him and cupped her cheeks. A gentle kiss brought a promise of everything she'd longed for: acceptance, respect, and protection. "Answer me this, luv. Did ya' ever choose to kill?"

"It doesn't matter. I chose to give him my element."

"At seventeen. And he lied to ya'. Used magic and a teenage crush to force yer hand. So I'll ask ya' again. Did ya' ever choose to kill?"

"No. I fought him every minute I had the strength to do so. Even that final day when I threw myself off the cliffs. I 'died' fighting him."

"That's how I can love ya'."

CHAPTER SIXTEEN

Caitlin

"*L*et me in," he whispered, and a gentle hand skimmed over her hip, raising goosebumps along her spine. "I need ya'."

Fingers danced lower, teasing towards her center, and a burst of warmth turned into a tremble, then a cascading waterfall of emotion, churning and sending her flying over the edge. Her element caught her—caught them both—and wrapped around them, a hauntingly beautiful melody accompanying the sounds of their pleasure.

"Liam," she moaned, arching her back, the thick sheets rustling beneath her. He scored his teeth along her collarbone, then feathered his lips to the spot behind her ear he seemed to love so much.

Still riding the high of her release, she needed more, but when she tried to open her eyes, off-key notes echoed in her ears.

The first stirrings of panic rose inside her, but his teeth closed around her nipple and she cried out, desperate, aching for him until the strident, grating sounds obscured everything.

"Ya' fuckin' whore! Givin' yerself to that wolf! Ye're mine, Caitie, and when ye're back at my side, I'm goin' to make ya' end him yerself!"

"No! Please, no!" Behind her shuttered lids, Fergus loomed over her. Another kiss to her neck wrenched a scream from her throat, and she clawed at the hands that skimmed down her arms, shoved at the chest pressed to hers. "No! Stop!" she wailed.

"Can't ya' feel the power we could command together, Caitie? Once ya' see the error of yer ways and destroy him, we can be happy. Ya' want that, yeah? Together? Bound by magic and air for an eternity. Come to me. Come now!"

"Caitlin!"

She crashed to the floor, the impact singing along her left shoulder, hip, and the side of her head. Dazed, she blinked back the stars floating in her vision.

Liam landed next to her in a crouch, his eyes wild with amber flames, and angry red trails oozed blood across his chest.

"Look at me, Caitlin. Now." The rough, commanding tone snapped her out of her panic just enough to focus on him, on his hands braced on either side of her shoulders, on the scratches along his forearms. "Where are ya'? I need ya' to answer me."

"Liam," she gasped. "Oh, God. No."

The door slammed open, sending her skittering back against the wall by the window where she wrapped her arms around her knees and trembled so violently, she could hear the lamp on the table next to her shake.

"What the hell is going on?" Peter stood in the doorway wearing only his jeans, the scars on his chest so much worse than she'd imagined. They covered the entire left side of his body, disappearing below his belt, and Caitlin dropped her head into her hands with a moan.

"Leave. Now," Liam ordered. "We're fine. Or we will be." His words carried a physical weight even Caitlin could feel, and the door closed with a quiet *snick* two seconds later.

If she didn't move, would Liam go away? Leave her to her misery? She almost snorted as she realized how ridiculous that was.

"Caitlin, luv? I'm goin' to touch ya' now, all right?"

"No, no, no," she moaned, pressing the heels of her hands to her temples. She had to drive Fergus from her thoughts, close herself off from him completely, find some way to stop him from sending his influence even deeper. "F-Fergus...in my h-head. He knew...I was w-with ya'."

"I'm goin' to take yer hand. Help ya' up." Like he was tending to a wounded animal, he announced his movements, easing her inch by inch into his arms, then lifting her up and bringing her back to the bed.

His tenderness warred with the memories of Fergus's threats, and when he started to stroke her hair, she forced a deep breath, inhaling the scent of her and Liam together. It centered her, and she snuggled closer as he drew the blankets up around them.

"Tell me what happened. All of it."

Shivering, she stared out the window. "We were...you woke me up...and I wanted more."

Liam pressed a kiss to her temple. "I'm sorry for that. My wolf knows the full moon's comin'."

"My air—I gave in to it, used it. I wanted to protect us, to just live in that moment." She sniffled and swiped at a single tear balanced on her lashes. "But then *he* came for me. Fergus must have felt me usin' my element."

"He *came* for ya'? Like when we were at the pack house?"

"Worse." She didn't want to meet his gaze, but he tipped her chin up.

"How could it be worse?" Love churned in his glowing irises, the amber streaks still just as bright and intense as ever.

If she thought she could run away, if she could find a way to keep him safe, no matter how much pain she had to endure, she'd do it.

"He said he'd make me kill ya'." Caitlin forced the words out in a rush, hating herself more and more with each one. "He called me a whore. Said I belonged to him. Only to him. That no wolf could give me what he could."

"How does he know me?" Liam asked, his muscles coiling with tension, ready to spring. "Is he here? Do we need to run?"

"N-no. He's still...still far away. I think." She closed her eyes and tried to sense the missing piece of her soul, the other half of her element.

Whispering the location charm, she let it flutter over her skin, seep through the walls, over the landscape, all the way to the farthest reaches of the continent. For several long moments, she sensed nothing, until a hint of Fergus's loamy, dank scent reached her nose, and she shuddered.

"He's in the west. Far away. Probably close to the cliffs." She stiffened as Fergus turned her element against her, and buried her face against Liam's chest. "Don't let him take me," she whimpered.

"I've got ya', luv." One arm banded tightly around her waist, and the other hand rubbed rhythmic circles over her back. She breathed in his scent. The woodsy aftershave, the freshly laundered sheets, and the strength that *was* Liam. "Ye're okay. He won't touch ya' when I'm around."

That's what she was scared of. Terrified even. Nothing was okay in the least, and she feared it never would be again.

Liam grunted as he adjusted his arm around her. The coppery tang of blood was harsh on her tongue, and she drew in a sharp breath. "I hurt you."

"I'm a werewolf, luv. All I have to do is shift, and I'll be fine."

He started to release her, but the ringing phone made them both jump. Liam jabbed the screen, sending the call to speaker. "Cade. Thank fuck."

"We're about to board the flight to Dublin. Mara lost her phone, and mine ran out of juice right after I left you that message. Had to buy a charger as soon as we landed."

"What happened to ya'?" Liam asked.

"We don't have much time. Eleanor...she tried to protect Mara, but shit. They killed her." His voice cracked and he swore under his breath before he continued. "I don't even think they cared."

"And Mara?" Caitlin asked, taking Liam's free hand and holding on for all she was worth.

"Sick. She needs you. Whatever you did for us at the house— the sigils, the quartz—she needs it again. They took the crystal you gave her." The alpha wolf sounded so lost.

"Put her on."

"Caitlin?" The single word slurred, and in the background, Cade begged her to focus. "Are...you and Liam...?"

"We're fine, Mara. Listen to me. To my voice. Concentrate on it. Take a deep breath in and hold it until I tell you. Four. Three. Two. One. Release. Again."

Caitlin talked her through half a dozen slow breaths before instructing her to make sure Cade could hear too.

"Lay your hand over Cade's heart. Skin to skin if you can. You can use him to center your water element. Focus on his heartbeat and try to match yours to his. Liam, count for them. Another six breaths."

As Liam took over, Caitlin pulled open the nightstand drawer and found a pen and paper. The sigil flowed across the page, three lines, almost like the letter T and a sideways question mark, then rummaged in her bag for her cell phone to snap a picture.

"Mara, are ya' feelin' steadier?" Caitlin asked after she'd texted the photo to Cade.

"Little bit."

Shite. Her voice was still too weak. "I just sent a picture to Cade's phone. Have him trace it over your forehead, then over your heart. It won't be as good as what I did back in Seattle, but it'll keep ya' grounded until ya' get here. Any time ya' start to wander, even a little bit."

"Now boarding, Aer Lingus Flight 63 to Dublin."

"Honey, let me talk to Liam again," Cade said. "I'll use the sigil in just a minute for you."

"'Kay."

"We land a little after five. Stay in Dublin. Mara's going to need Caitlin."

Liam met her gaze, his brow arched in question. "Can ya' hide us if Fergus tries to get to ya'?"

She saw the determination in his eyes. If she said no, he'd do whatever he could to protect her, even if that meant not being here when Cade and Mara landed.

"I think so. For a short time."

A muscle in her wolf's jaw ticked, and he adjusted his grip on the phone. "We're at Clontarf Castle Hotel. But we have to leave for Farren's as quick as we can."

"Call the pack and let them know we're all right," Cade said. "Boarding now."

The call disconnected, and Liam leaned back against the headboard with a heavy sigh. "I hope to all that's holy we haven't just killed Farren."

"Send Peter to Lahinch?" Caitlin suggested. "You said he's familiar with the area. Fergus won't know anythin' about him. He'll be safer than either of us."

Liam's brows knit for a moment. "Yeah. Okay. I'll go talk to him. Ya'll be okay?"

Nodding, despite feeling anything but okay, she watched him pull on his briefs and stride from the room.

Fergus's threat echoed in her ears.

Once ya' see the error of yer ways and ya' destroy him, we can be happy.

She'd never hurt Liam. She'd destroy herself first.

After washing away the hours of travel, Caitlin dressed quickly. She needed air and, more than anything, needed to get away from Liam for even an hour.

Every time he touched her, kissed her, even said her name, she felt Fergus tugging on her element. She wanted to love Liam. Or, at least let herself relax around him enough to get to know him, but between his worry over Farren and her unease—what if she kissed him again and all she heard was Fergus's voice?

She wouldn't let the earth elemental ruin whatever they had building between them. But he would if she couldn't find some way to get clear.

Liam paced the suite's main room, the tension doing nothing for her nerves. When she shrugged into the borrowed coat, he narrowed his eyes. "Where do ya' think ye're goin'?"

"I need to get quartz and sage for Mara."

Liam reached for her, but she jerked back.

"Don't touch me. Please," she whispered. "I can't. Not right now. Not after what Fergus did."

"Caitlin, I promised ya' I'd stay by yer side." He positioned himself between her and the door, his eyes dark and dangerous.

No. She wouldn't back down. "I know ya' want to protect me. And I'm sorry. But I have to do this alone. He's still far away. I'm not in any real danger from him." The lie didn't sit well with her. Fergus was twice as strong as she was—if not more—and he could try to compel her. But she thought she could resist him for at least another few hours.

A breeze ruffled his hair, and she focused all of her energy on the charm to drive him back one step, then two.

Clutching her bag to her chest, she edged around him. "Two hours. Maybe three. I'll be back. I promise, Liam."

Turning, she fled, trying to ignore Liam calling after her.

Aided by her element, she flew down the stairs and burst out of the hotel like a drowning woman clawing her way onto land.

A taxi pulled up less than a minute later. She tried to calm her turbulent emotions. "Grafton Street, please," she said as her phone buzzed in her bag.

Caitlin, please don't do this.

A minute later, a second message flashed across the screen.

Don't let him drive a wedge between us.

That stung. Even if he were right. But she couldn't reply. If she did, she'd give in and go back to him.

Fergus's charm had done more than put her on edge. More than sully the new—and old—love she was finding with Liam. No. It had done something she hadn't known she needed, and wouldn't he be angry if he ever realized the truth?

The magic he'd used to try to divide her and Liam, to try to turn her to his side had reminded her that once, she'd been free. She hadn't been Fergus Tharp's punching bag or his unwilling slave. She hadn't been bound by magic and air to a man who thought suffocating her was just punishment for daring to speak her mind.

She'd been Caitlin Brannigan. And dammit, she was going to find that woman again before it was too late.

As the taxi turned onto Grafton Street and pulled over to the curb, Liam sent her one final text.

I love you. Be safe.

Throwing some money at the driver, she fled into the crowds. As she lost herself amid tourists and locals alike, she tapped out a quick reply.

I will. I promise.

GRAFTON STREET WAS home to hundreds of shops: jewelry stores, mobile phone kiosks, upscale boutiques, bookstores, and banks.

Caitlin hoped the area's seedier end hadn't changed much in the years she'd been gone.

Wandering among the shoppers, she could almost pretend she lived here again.

A coffee at Baker's. A scone at Nola's. She window-shopped at some of the city's more expensive clothing meccas as she headed for her destination, and every step, every choice she made on her own strengthened her.

"He doesn't get to take this from me. Not again. This is *my* life," she said to no one as she wandered into an alley, praying she'd find the occult shop quickly. Their website had been woefully out of date, but if they still existed, they'd have what she needed.

The sun dipped behind the tall, gray stone buildings, leaving only a thin slice of sky above her. A chill crept into her bones, and she pulled the borrowed coat tighter around her.

Cloch Anam.

The sign's creaky hinges lent an air of the *other* to the alley, and Caitlin stopped, her fingers trembling on the door handle.

Mara needs this.

A wall of incense threatened to choke her, but she sucked in a breath through her teeth and let the magic and mystery surround her.

Floor-to-ceiling shelves held every manner of glass jar filled with herbs, dried animal parts, and baubles, along with weathered tomes and ornamental athames, Celtic crosses, and engraved ceremonial bowls.

"Hello?" she called. "Blessings be."

After a few tense moments, a crackling response no louder than a whisper came from behind her. "Blessings be, child. What can I do for you?"

Turning, Caitlin forced a nervous smile for the elderly woman leaning on a cane. White hair fell in soft waves around her haggard face, and a black shawl wrapped thin shoulders.

"I need five smoky quartz stones, cleansed if you have them; a quartz or jasper worry stone with a carry bag, smudge sticks of white sage and rosemary, and both essential oils."

"Ya' have an eye for the craft, do ya'?" The old woman reached around Caitlin and plucked a leather pouch from a high shelf, then side-stepped her with more speed and grace than she should have possessed to withdraw a small glass jar filled with gray stones.

"No, but I had a good teacher in America."

The woman's laugh riled Caitlin's anger. "There are no good practitioners in the States, lass. Ye're mistaken, and ye're goin' to get yerself in a bad way if ye're not careful."

Plucking one of the smoky quartz stones from the woman's hand, she closed her eyes and let its vibrations wash over her. "This stone hasn't been cleansed. There's so much negative energy here it's making me sick."

The shopkeeper nodded, respect shining in her eyes. "Ya' passed the first test. Can ya' identify the sage?"

With a snort, Caitlin snatched the smudge stick from the shelf behind her. "Ye'll have to try harder than that."

One by one, the elderly practitioner arranged Caitlin's purchases on the counter, finally adding the red jasper worry stone. "Ya' know this, I expect. But red jasper is a talisman for warriors. Are ya' a warrior?"

"None of these are for me."

The woman's pale hazel eyes narrowed. "Are ya' sure? Give me yer hands."

Bony fingers reached for hers, and a subtle current of energy flowed between them.

"Air. Muddy. Tainted. Weak. But somethin' pure as well. Ye're strong, lass. The red jasper will lend power to yer will and allow ya' to escape what hunts ya'."

Caitlin yanked her hands away. "No. I can't. Nothin' hunts me. I don't need—"

"Ya' do. There'll be no arguin' with Shayla. And ya' did nothing wrong. The guilt in ya' weighs heavy. Release what burdens ya' so ya' can be free."

The ache to be truly and completely free settled in her heart as Shayla wrapped each item in paper, tucked them all in a large sack, and retrieved a second, smaller pouch from under the counter, then pressed it into Caitlin's hand. "This is a second red jasper, and I'll not take it back—or charge ya' for it. Wear this around yer neck, and ya' will find strength ya' didn't know ya' had."

Caitlin tucked the sack in her messenger bag, then reluctantly draped the pouch around her neck. No talisman, crystal, sigil, or rune would save her when she faced what she feared most. But jasper carried power, and the quartz *had* worked for Mara.

If she were going to take back her life, she needed all the help she could get. Her guilt and pain were too much for even a hundred stones, but still, she thanked Shalya and slipped out the door, intent on heading back to Liam.

STEPS FROM GRAFTON STREET, the magic and air hit her in the chest.

She couldn't hear him, but his dark, insidious magic wormed its way through her, locking her muscles and muddling her thoughts.

West. I have to go west.

The urge to find a bus, a taxi, any means possible weighed her down. One foot, then the other obeyed his command, and she fought with everything she had in her to break his hold.

He'd never been this strong before. His air tasted *wrong*. Tainted with the salty, bitter flavor of magic. The Thirteen were helping him. Strengthening him.

With every halting step, she fought, and finally managed to

send out her own charm. It was weak and sapped her will even more, but she had to know.

Distance still separated them. Hours and hundreds of miles, but when the charm came back to her, it hit her harder than anything she'd ever felt before.

The sun washed over her as she emerged onto Grafton Street, and every muscle strained, her attempts to fight him growing weaker by the moment.

Crowds passed by, and though she managed to grab the arm of one strong-looking young man and whisper, "Help me," he stared at her like she was speaking a foreign language.

She was on her own. One, anonymous woman in a sea of people she didn't know, couldn't trust.

"Ya will find strength ya' didn't know ya' had."

Repeating Shayla's words over and over again, she fought against his hold, and with every step closer to the bus station, hairline cracks formed in his control.

Caitlin fumbled for the leather pouch around her neck, but couldn't close her fingers over it. Another turn, another street, and she found herself at the banks of the River Liffey with Ha'penny Bridge a block away.

A bus rumbled by, the deep vibrations jarring her out of her mental fog, and reminding her of Liam. His arms around her. His warmth.

Fight. You're Caitlin Brannigan, dammit. He can't have you.

The bridge stood watch, tall and proud over the river. Families, lovers, and college students wandered, lingered, and the sunlight sparkled like hundreds of precious jewels scattered over the water.

"Let the air bend to my will. Let it protect me. Surround me. Comfort me. It is mine, and always will be."

A memory flashed through her. She'd been on this bridge once before.

"I have something for us, luv."

Liam held out his hand. An old-fashioned padlock rested in his palm. On her first night in Dublin, Caitlin had walked along Ha'penny Bridge, and the love surrounding the span had staggered her. She'd shared the memory with him, and the twinkle in his eye now pulled a laugh from her lips.

The physical presence of so many promises wrapped her in a warm blanket against the chill of her past, and she gently plucked the heavy lock from Liam's hand to read the etching on the back.

Liam and Caitlin

"I have the key." He offered his other hand, and the long antique key caught the light, glowing in the waxing moon.

"Shall we?" she asked. He nodded, turned the key in the lock, and wrapped his fingers around hers. They closed the lock together, and with their hands still joined, he brushed a tender kiss to her lips, then threw the key into the river.

"Now, no one will ever be able to keep us apart," he said, and for at least that night, she believed him.

Fergus's hold on her shattered as she reached the center of the bridge. His anger and shock punched her in the stomach, and she doubled over with a hand on one of the bridge supports.

"No. Ya' can't have me, ya' bastard. No one can *have* me."

Whoever she'd been this morning—whoever she'd been under his control, she wasn't that weak, terrified woman now.

Everything she'd done while *his*, that guilt belonged to *him*, to the Thirteen who'd bound him as much as he'd bound her.

Free from his compulsion, she took an easy breath as she trailed her hand over the padlocks. City officials cleared the older ones away from time to time, but an ornately carved design caught her eye.

Leaning half over the barrier, she brushed her fingers along the back of the lock. Even without being able to see the etching, she knew. If she turned it over, she'd find *Liam and Caitlin*.

Her phone buzzed, and she pulled it out of her pocket.

Are you safe?

The guilt and fear that had stopped her from admitting the truth fell away, and she accepted what she'd hoped for all along.

She *could* love Liam. She *wanted* to love Liam. And now...she had to tell him.

CHAPTER SEVENTEEN

Liam

*H*e'd paced for an hour, had almost gone after her twice—not that he knew where his mate was—and finally, he'd retreated to the shower, hoping that washing her scent off of him would let him think clearly.

It hadn't helped. The pull of moon was getting stronger. Only two more days until it was full, and then...the mating call would be impossible to ignore.

He'd been so close to claiming her eleven years ago, and now...if he couldn't...if she rejected him, he didn't know if he'd survive.

Liam tugged on a pair of jeans, then stared out the window as he rubbed a towel over his hair. The back lawn of the hotel stretched out for a hundred yards, and the woods behind it called to his wolf.

The lock on the suite door beeped, and he whirled around as she practically flew into his arms. "Liam."

"I was worried," he said, the words hard to force out over the lump in his throat.

"I'm sorry. I needed some time."

"I don't want ya' alone with Fergus so close. What if he'd compelled ya' and taken ya' away? I can't lose ya', Caitlin."

He breathed in her scent, all fig blossoms and fresh air, and she shuddered once before meeting his gaze. The storm in her eyes troubled him, and he dragged a knuckle along her cheek as she whispered, "He tried."

"What?" Stepping back so quickly, she almost toppled over, he corrected in the next breath and steadied her again. "I'm goin' to find the bastard and tear him apart. Tell me what happened. Now."

Caitlin pressed her lips together, her turbulent gaze even darker as she straightened her shoulders. "He called to me. Had me headin' for the bus station, but I broke free. I fought him."

"Shite. Ye're not leavin' my side again," he growled, his beast threatening to take over.

"That's not practical and ya' know it," she shot back. "And did ya' not hear the part where I fought him?"

With a huff, she turned on a heel and headed for the couch, dropping down and waiting for him to join her. When he did, she took his hand, and the touch calmed his wolf enough that he no longer felt like he was about to come out of his skin.

"His charms, along with the magic he has from the Thirteen, they can control my body. But before...before today, he could also affect my mind. I think because I felt so guilty over what I'd done, over what he'd made me do, I didn't think I deserved to be free. I hurt so many people, Liam. Not directly...not until Katerina...but still... My mum, all the elementals whose elements he tried to steal after mine. I blamed myself for all of them."

"It wasn't yer fault—"

"I know that now." She stared up at him, and for the first time since she'd come back into his life, her gaze wasn't filled with guilt. At least…not entirely. "I understand why I let Katerina bind me. But also why I helped Mara." Caitlin ran a hand through her reddish locks, then shook her head. "Katerina infused the fire agate crystal with a bit of my own power. I gave it to her willingly, because I was so desperate to escape Fergus I would have done anything. But my air…it worked against me. She compelled me with my own element. I'd thought every choice I'd made was my own, but I was wrong. My only decision was trusting her in the first place. And with Fergus…I never had a chance."

"I still don't understand what's so different now," he said.

"I am. *I'm* different. And I won't let him ruin what we're building. What we *could* build. Together."

Hope warmed his heart, but his Caitlin was shaking, and he slid closer so he could wrap an arm around her waist. "Then why are ya' tremblin' so?"

"I let him come between us this morning. I'm sorry for that." Slipping a finger through one of the belt loops on his jeans, she rose and tugged him towards the bedroom.

He followed willingly, but refused to let her pull him down onto the mattress. Running his hands along her back, he cupped her arse and held her flush against him. "I need ya', Caitlin. Like I need my next breath."

Her fingers carded through his hair, and she angled his head down so she could capture his lips in a searing kiss.

A low rumbling moan vibrated through his chest as his tongue sought entrance, and she yielded to him. Light touches along his jaw, down his shoulders, all the way to the button on his jeans, and he broke off the kiss.

"Naked, luv. Now."

Two quick steps took her out of his reach, and she pulled the green sweater over her head, then toed off her boots and let her pants fall to the floor. Before he could slide his arms around her, she shook her head. "No. This time? This is for me. Hands at your side, wolf. No touching."

He growled, a low warning that he couldn't go much longer without being inside of her, but when she stripped off his jeans and palmed his cock through his briefs, her wicked smile almost made him come right then and there.

Caitlin rained kisses over his chest, grinding her lace-clad mound against him as she hooked her fingers along the waistband of his briefs.

"Fuck, Caitlin. I won't last," he managed. "Not with ya' doin' that."

Her arousal perfumed the room, and he fumbled for her panties until she captured his wrists. "I thought I told you 'no touching'?"

"We're too close to the moon. I can't keep my hands off of ya'."

"Yes. You can. At least for another few minutes." Caitlin grabbed a pillow from the bed and prodded him over to a chair, stripping him of his briefs before she pushed him down and sank to her knees. With her gaze locked on his, she wrapped cool fingers around his length, then tasted him.

He groaned, gripping the arms of the chair so hard, he feared they'd crack. The first tentative stroke of her tongue made him see stars, and when she took him deeper, hollowing out her cheeks until the heat of her mouth was enough to brand him, he panted. "Shite, luv. Let me—"

Fingers digging into his thigh shut him up, and she ran her tongue along the underside of his cock. He couldn't help thrusting his hips, but Caitlin simply shifted and took him deeper. A hum, almost a keening sound vibrated from her throat, and he tightened his hand in her hair.

"Gonna...come," he ground out, and she cupped his balls as she took one last hard pull and he let himself go.

When his tremors subsided and she'd gently pulled away, he brushed a thumb over her swollen lips. "Fuck me, luv. That was..."

"Did I do it right?" she asked, her voice husky with her own need. "That was my first time."

"Right? That was brilliant." He tugged her up and into his lap. "The moon rises in two days. I want ya' more and more every minute."

"So take me."

Under the lace bra, her nipples pebbled, and he reached up to roll one between his fingers. "Oh, I plan on doin' just that."

Liam ravaged her mouth like his very life depended on the kiss, and she writhed under his touch, her little moans and whimpers spurring him on. When he lifted her, she wrapped her legs around his waist, and he carried her to the bed, laying her down so he could memorize every curve of her body.

The white lace bra and panties had to go. Right now. Sliding a hand under her back, he flicked open the catch on the bra and she wriggled free, but stopped him when he reached for her hips.

"Ya' already destroyed one pair, and I'll not have ya' buyin' me more." Despite her words, she grinned as she shimmied out of the last barrier between them, and Liam growled, his wolf asserting his claim as a fresh wave of her arousal hit him.

Positioning himself between her thighs, he splayed his hand over her stomach as he nuzzled her. "Ya' smell like the wind. And yer taste..." The first flick of his tongue made her moan, and she tilted her hips, desperate to get closer to him.

He felt the tremors start deep within her and plunged two fingers into her slick heat as he lapped at the singular spot that would send her flying.

Caitlin cried out as she came, and Liam held her hips as she rode out her climax. He couldn't wait any longer to be inside of his love, and yanked a condom from the nightstand drawer, thought twice, and went back for a second—and a third.

"Ya' have a high opinion of yerself," she said with a laugh as he knelt over her and ripped one of the wrappers with his teeth.

"My wolf...he's claimed ya' already, and we're so close to the moon... This might be the last time I can touch ya' until it's no longer full." He didn't know how the hell he'd manage to be close to her without taking her. But until she accepted him, he wouldn't risk it. She was too important. Her choice, her freedom was too important.

His Caitlin's eyes darkened, and she cupped his cheek. "Why? Because ya'd mate with me? Because there'd be no goin' back?"

"Yeah."

"What if I wanted that?"

Shock stole his breath as she stroked her hand over the tattoo on his shoulder, traced the crashing waves inked on his skin—all in memory of her. They were older now. Both of them wiser and sadder too, but the connection between them, the one reforged the moment Liam had seen her at his construction site, had only strengthened.

"I went to Ha'penny Bridge, Liam," she said softly as she guided him to her entrance. "Our lock is still there."

"Ya' remembered." Slowly, one throbbing inch at a time, he slid deeper, and Caitlin shivered, raw need churning in her eyes.

"I love ya', Liam. I loved ya' eleven years ago, but I might love ya' more now. Because ya' never gave up on me or forced me to do a single thing I wasn't ready for. I'm still terrified of facin'...*him*, but now that I know I can fight him, I'm not afraid of us."

Liam started to rock his hips into her, slowly at first, then faster as she wrapped delicate fingers around the back of his neck and pulled him down to slant her mouth to his.

He lost himself to her, man and wolf coming together to claim her with a possessive growl.

Not. Yet.

Starting at the corner of her lips, he kissed all along her jaw and back to her ear. He loved the way she shuddered when he scored his teeth over the tender flesh, and her air surrounded them, ruffling the drapes, then the bedsheets as their emotions flared, bright and hot and overwhelming.

"Liam!" she cried out as he thrust harder and bit down on the curve of her neck.

His wolf roared, and he came with a shout, man and beast united in their love for her, and when Caitlin's body tensed, stilled, and then imploded in endless waves of pleasure, he found a peace he'd never known possible.

"Oh God," she whimpered as he held her close and smoothed his hand over her hair. "That was..."

"Did ya' mean it, luv?" He had to be sure. Had to know she didn't regret her words.

Caitlin smiled, her blue eyes bright and clear, even though her chest still heaved and he could feel her heart racing. "I love ya', Liam. I want to be yer mate."

He rolled onto his back and settled her on top of him. "Never in my life have I wanted somethin' more than to hear those words. I know we've a battle ahead. And shite. I'd give anythin' to be able to just run away with you and never look back. But for now, I'd just like to hear ya' tell me again."

Caitlin linked their fingers and brought their joined hands to her lips. "Ye're mine, Liam. And I'm yours."

BETWEEN THE MOON'S approach and worry for his alpha, Liam's shoulders felt like granite—that someone was chipping away at with a sledgehammer.

Whether her own nerves or a reaction to his mood, Caitlin couldn't sit still either. She'd stretched out the hem of yet another sweater, and he'd worn a pattern in the thick carpet with his pacing.

Mara had made it through the flight, according to Cade's text, but she couldn't keep food down, and he'd even had trouble getting her to drink anything.

Several different stones and two bundles of herbs were laid

out on the coffee table, ready and waiting, though Liam didn't understand how they could possibly help.

"Ye're goin' to exhaust yerself," Caitlin said, peering up at him with tired, bloodshot eyes. The hours they'd passed in bed hadn't been restful, and though he regretted nothing, he wished she'd been able to nap.

"A mite late for that."

The knock made Caitlin yelp, and Liam threw open the door of the suite to find Mara clinging to Cade, her normally pale skin almost bone white, her hair dull, and her eyes half-lidded.

A single duffel was slung over Cade's shoulder, and Liam caught the scent of blood.

"Give her here," Liam said and lifted Mara in his arms, carrying her to the sofa where Caitlin waited. It felt wrong to touch a woman other than his mate, but Cade looked like he was about to fall over himself.

"Water," Caitlin demanded as she took Mara's hands and called for a rush of air to surround them.

"Just tired," Mara slurred. "Hard to focus."

"She's been in and out of it for hours." Cade sank down next to her with a grunt. "When she's...gone," his voice fell almost to a whisper, "she keeps trying to use her fire. We're lucky they didn't turn the plane around and arrest us."

"Get her to drink a little." Caitlin picked up one of the milky stones, traced a pattern in the air with her fingers, and then ripped open the top two buttons on Mara's shirt. Pressing the stone over Mara's heart, she drew on more of her air, and almost immediately, Mara's cheeks pinked slightly.

"How did you do that?" Mara asked, blinking hard. She took a deep breath and the humidity in the room rose almost immediately.

"I wish I could take credit for it, but that's the quartz. This, however, is me." Caitlin lit one of the herb sticks and sent her element winding around Mara. Drawing a complex pattern of lines and swirls over the water elemental, concentrating on Mara's head and heart, she whispered words Liam couldn't quite make out, then handed him the smoking bundle to extinguish so she could spread a drop of essential oil between Mara's eyes.

"Put this on," she said, handing Mara a leather pouch on a long strap. "Don't take it off except to shower. Finish off that water and you should feel better."

Caitlin sank back against the cushions and reached for Liam's hand. Shite. She looked tired and weak herself now, though Mara was improving by the second.

"I'm better," the water elemental said once she'd drained the bottle. "And really hungry."

"Luv, can ya' see to Cade? I think he's hurt. I'll order room service," Liam said.

In truth, Liam didn't want Caitlin's hands on his alpha any more than he wanted to touch Mara, but she could relieve Cade's pain, and he couldn't deny the man aid. Not after all he'd done for the two of them.

"I shifted," Cade said. "After we parked at the airport. We had a few minutes. I'm hungry and exhausted, but I'm not injured."

"They're sendin' up enough food for an army." Liam sank down next to his mate and finally relaxed when she fit herself to his side. "Ten minutes or so. Tell us what happened?"

"Where's Fergus?" Cade asked. "Are we safe here for a while?"

"He hasn't come after us. Well, not directly, anyway." Caitlin explained how the bastard had invaded her dreams and tried to charm her when she'd been alone on the streets of Dublin, and Liam filled them in on Peter's absence.

The arrival of food brought all questions to a halt. Liam and Cade put away two steaks each. Caitlin only managed half of hers, but Mara, surprisingly, cleaned her plate, kicked off her shoes, and curled against Cade, fiddling with the leather pouch Caitlin had given her.

"Will the quartz keep working?" she asked, a hint of worry in her voice. "Even if I...get worse?"

"For a time, yeah. Cleansed stones absorb negative energy. I can cleanse them for ya' every few weeks, or—" Caitlin peered up at Liam for a moment, a hint of fear in her eyes, "—I can teach ya' how to cleanse them on your own."

Cade arched a brow and leaned forward. "You're not planning on sticking around after this mess is done?"

She stopped Liam before he could say a word. "I need to ask your permission...uh...to join the pack as Liam's mate."

A storm loosed inside him, and his wolf pulsed under his skin, desperate to break free. He hadn't known how much he'd needed to hear those words from her—or needed his alpha to agree she could stay.

He held his breath. As accepting as Cade had been back in Seattle, the elemental attack could have changed everything for him—and for Mara.

Mara slid her hand along Cade's thigh, a gentle smile on her face. He met her gaze, held it for one long, meaningful moment, and nodded.

"I told you before we left. You're family. I can't say the rest of the pack will welcome you with open arms, but they'll respect you or they'll have to deal with me."

CHAPTER EIGHTEEN

Caitlin

"Mara's too tired to go to Lahinch tonight," Cade said as he rubbed the back of his mate's neck. "We won't be any good to anyone until we get some rest."

"Luv, is Fergus still in County Clare?" Liam reached for her hand, and the contact steadied her enough to try to locate the man she feared most in this world.

The charm billowed the drapes, and Caitlin drew in a sharp breath through her teeth. "He's still there. Or...far enough away we should be safe for the night. If he gets close, I think...I'll feel it."

"What happened when ya' got to Tacoma to meet Eleanor?" Liam asked.

With how bad off Mara had been when they arrived, it must have been terrible, and a part of Caitlin wished she could hide away in the bedroom. She had too many horrors playing on a loop in her memories to add more, but Cade and Mara were family now—or would be soon, and she'd do anything she could to help them.

Cade ran a hand through his hair, wincing with the movement, and Mara rubbed slow circles over his shoulder. "When we met Eleanor at the park, she was sitting on a bench under an umbrella. It was spitting rain, and we couldn't see her face until it was too late."

"She didn't turn on us," Mara said softly. Tears shimmered in her eyes. "She was forced to lie to us. Her eyes...when we got close enough, I could see how scared she was."

"There were six of them." Cade swore under his breath. "Shit, Liam. They surrounded us. Earth and air, mainly. They knocked me back fifty feet. Broke my fucking arm. Tried to bury me and take Mara away. They're convinced she's going to fall victim to the Thirteen and end up destroying the whole world or something."

"I will." Mara's voice broke, and she shied away from Cade when he reached for her. "Every time the fire flares up, I lose myself even more. I don't remember *anything* after they separated us. Not until we got to the airport. Not Livie, not you shifting. Nothing."

"Honey, please. Don't give up. You can't leave me."

"I don't know that I'll have a choice." She stared at Cade's hands clenched on his thighs. "Tell them the rest of it."

"The air elementals compelled her. All working together. I shifted, but there was this huge wall of earth and rocks all around her. By the time I could see her again, they were forcing her to drink something. Then...everything went to shit." Cade's eyes darkened, and a shadow passed over his features, like he was trying to decide how much to tell them. "I had to shift back to get her out of there. She was too weak to hold on to my wolf, and when I did, I found a bottle of pills on the ground. Clozapine."

Caitlin gasped. The memory was so vivid, she could taste the blood from the split lip Fergus had given her.

"I'm so sorry, Caitie. Ya' have to forgive me, yeah?" He pulled a

bottle from his pocket and fumbled for the lid. "I need my pills. I'm not a bastard with them. Ya' know I'm not."

The label was so clear in her mind. During one of his lucid moments, Fergus had checked himself into a mental hospital and claimed he'd been possessed by powerful magic. The doctors had treated him with Clozapine, and when he took the pills, his madness ebbed, and he almost reminded her of the boy he'd been. The one she'd trusted.

"Caitlin, luv? What is it?" Liam cupped her cheek and turned her to meet his gaze. "Ya' look like ya've seen a ghost."

"Fergus. He took Clozapine. The Thirteen...in order to enhance his elemental power, they bound him with a sigil burned into his side. It channels their magic." She shuddered, remembering how *wrong* it had felt. Every time she'd been close to him, she'd sensed it. Like a beacon. Liam wrapped his arm around her shoulders and pulled her closer. The heat of him helped her focus. Helped her realize she was here in this fancy hotel with the man she loved. "When the magic flared, he was so much meaner. But sometimes, he'd come back down and he'd realize what he'd done. How he'd hurt me. He'd remember the elementals he'd killed."

Shite. She couldn't do this. Pushing up, she stumbled to the window, but she couldn't get it open. "Liam, please!"

He was at her side in a heartbeat, flipping the lock and lifting the sash so the fresh spring air rushed into the room. "Ye're safe, luv. I won't let anythin' happen to ya'."

"Ya' can't promise that. If the practitioners come after us, none of us will survive."

"Caitlin?" Cade's voice broke through her panic. "When I got to Mara, she could barely stand. The drug knocked her out in under five minutes. But it stopped her from using her fire."

"What?" Mara's shock had Caitlin turning around, and the look on her face was pure agony. "I used my—Katerina's—fire? Oh, God. Did I kill anyone?"

Cade embraced her, protective, like he wanted to protect her from the entire world, and she shrank against him. "Three." Tears welled in her eyes, and he nuzzled her neck. "Honey, if you hadn't, we wouldn't have gotten out of there alive."

"I can't...don't let me hurt anyone else, please," she begged.

"Ya' won't as long as I'm here," Caitlin said. "As long as ye're wearing the quartz and lettin' me help ya'."

"But all it took..." Mara shook her head. "I remember one of them. A woman. Brown hair. Gray eyes. Shit. She tore your necklace off of me. I couldn't move. The air charm, it was like my body wasn't mine anymore, and then she had the quartz in her hand and everything went dark."

"I could hear them," Cade said. "Even over the rumble of the earth. They sensed magic in the quartz. That's why they took it. Then, someone yelled, 'fire.' After that, it was a lot of chanting, smoke. Screaming 'Get the pills.' And 'hold her down.' That's when I finally reached the top of the berm they raised all around them and saw Mara pinned, one of the men holding a bottle of water to her lips. Her hands were still on fire, but by the time I reached her side, the flames were gone, and—" his voice cracked and he tightened his arms around her, "—so was she. Still conscious, mostly, but everything *Mara* wasn't there anymore."

The two held on to one another like they were the only things anchoring them to this world and, Caitlin realized, they likely were. Bonded. Mated. They grounded one another. Like Liam did for her.

The breeze from the open window helped calm her, and she nodded up at Liam. "I'm better now." He led her back to the couch, and she blew out a slow, deep breath. "Clozapine is an anti-psychotic. It helps people suffering from bipolar and schizophrenia to regulate themselves. For Fergus, it couldn't really touch the practitioners' magic, but it stopped my air from affecting him so terribly."

"Would it work on me, too?" Mara asked, her voice trembling.

"No, honey. We're not going there. If all it had done was stop your fire, then sure." Cade traced a knuckle along her cheek. "But it stole everything from you."

Caitlin took Liam's hand, hating what she was about to say. "It will work. But," she added when Cade's eyes glowed with his wolf, "it's a last resort only. And a temporary one. Because just like the quartz and the runes and sigils? She'll fight it. Even if she doesn't realize she's doing so. That's why it never worked on Fergus for long. He'd take one pill, maybe two. And then the madness would flare up worse than before."

"So there's no hope for me." Mara swallowed a sob and tried to extricate herself from Cade's arms. "We can't keep taking chances like this, Cade. Next time, I could hurt you. Or Caitlin and Liam. Or anyone around me. I can't ever go home. What if I hurt Serena? Or Aunt Lil? I can't…"

She pushed up and ran for the bedroom, the door slamming behind her with a finality that made the rest of them flinch.

Cade's expression made her heart ache. His world, his life, slipping through his fingers like water. "We have to find the practitioner Eleanor told us about," he said, the words flat and almost devoid of emotion. "If we don't, I'm not sure she'll survive this. And if she doesn't, I won't either."

"The practitioner—Diedre, wasn't it?—isn't far from Farren's place." Liam's eyes flashed with his wolf, and he tightened his fingers on Caitlin's. "Not far from Fergus either, I'm afraid."

Cade leaned forward, holding Caitlin with a piercing stare. "Can you stop him if he comes after you?"

Liam practically growled. "She doesn't have to. I'll protect her."

If only he could. He'd never seen the evil inside the earth elemental. Not close up. "No, Liam. If he gets anywhere near us, ya' have to run. All of ya'."

"Ye're talking to a werewolf, luv. We don't back down. Not when someone's threatenin' our mates."

"Dammit!" Anger gave her a burst of strength, and she jerked her hand from his hold. "Ya' don't know him. And I'm fuckin' sick and tired of ya' tryin' to 'save me.' I'll save myself."

"No, Caitlin—"

"No? Ya' don't get to tell me no. I'm not yer little damsel-in-distress-porcelain-doll-about-to-shatter, and growlin' at the problem won't solve a damn thing. Fergus is goin' to come for me —for all of us—unless I stop him. *Me*. The one whose element he stole. The one he's convinced can fix him. Don't misunderstand. I need yer help. Yer strength. But ya' can't be the one to fight him. That's on me."

For several tense moments, Cade and Liam just stared at her, two wolves united in their intense need to protect. To save their mates. She understood. Truly she did. But understanding and accepting were two very different things, and she couldn't let either of them face a man so unbalanced, he'd kill anyone who opposed him.

"We'll be talkin' about this," Liam said. Caitlin rolled her eyes as her wolf turned his attention to Cade. "Mara needs ya'. And ya' both have to rest. We'll start out first thing in the mornin'."

With a nod, Cade grabbed the duffel bag and disappeared into the bedroom. The rumble of his deep voice, along with Mara's sobs, came from behind the closed door, and Caitlin's heart ached for them. So much, the anger and frustration at Liam's overprotective nature faded into the background.

"I should have paid more attention to Katerina when she was usin' the magic she'd learned," she said as Liam stood and offered her his hand. "Maybe then..."

"Hush, luv. Ya' can't change the past. All we can do now is try to change the future. Come to bed. We'll both be shattered tomorrow if we don't get some rest."

She knew he was right. She was so tired, her eyes hurt. With one last look at the closed bedroom door, she whispered a simple charm, hoping to ease Cade and Mara's pain, even if only a fraction.

A light breeze swirled through the room, visible only to her, before slipping under the door and finding its target in the wolf and elemental who'd accepted her, even after all she'd done, and given her the possibility of a family and a future with the man she loved.

Liam

Caitlin disappeared into the bathroom, and Liam sat on the bed, unsure how to get through to her. He didn't want her facing Fergus on her own. She had to understand he was a werewolf. One who should have been an alpha, but chose a different path.

He had all the possessiveness and protectiveness of a caveman—but Caitlin was a strong woman. Stronger now than she'd ever been. How could he keep her safe without driving her away?

After a few minutes, she emerged wearing the flannel shirt he'd left hanging on the back of the door. She didn't look at him, just climbed into bed, her back to him.

"Talk to me, luv," he said as he stripped out of his jeans and shirt and slid between the sheets. "I don't want ya' goin' anywhere near him. Let me kill the bastard."

"I could say the same thing to you. Pretty sure I did, actually." She huffed, then reached up and turned off the light. "And I don't want to kill him. He's sick, Liam. Insane. Tortured and trapped. He can't help himself. If I can take back my air, and the practitioner we're goin' to see can help break the Thirteen's hold over him, maybe he can find some peace."

He'd been about to touch her, to skim his hand down her arm, but he jerked back at her words. "Do ya' still love him?"

Caitlin rolled over, and even in the darkness, he could see her eyes widen. "No. I love you."

"Did ya' ever...?"

"Not like that. I cared for him, yes. I had a teenage crush on him. A fondness. Because he was kind and protective and I thought he'd take me away from all those things you want to escape when ye're seventeen. I never loved him. But don't I have a responsibility to try to save him?"

"And what if that responsibility kills ya'? What then? I'm a werewolf—"

"That's not goin' to save ya', Liam. I stopped ya' and half yer pack with one of my charms a few days ago. Not for long. But long enough. I'm weak compared to him. So very weak. If he sets his sights on ya', he'll make ya' slit yer own throat as easy as *that*." She snapped her fingers, then stared up at the darkened antique light hanging from the ceiling. "Don't ya' see how foolish it would be to fight him? He knows I was with ya' all those years ago, and he knows I'm with ya' now. When he caught me before, he was ready to kill ya', and we'd only kissed! What do ya' think he'd do now that we're lovers?"

"Mates." He wasn't going to let her forget it. Not when every single moment brought them closer to the moon.

"Even worse." She cringed, then reached out and cupped his cheek. "I didn't mean it that way."

"I won't let ya' face him alone." Nothing she could say would ever change his mind. Caitlin was his mate, and he'd defend her until his last breath.

The utter anguish in her expression sliced through his heart, and he wrapped his arms around her and nuzzled her neck, kissing all along the delicate skin until she shuddered against him. How could he possibly let her risk her life alone?

CHAPTER NINETEEN

Caitlin

*T*he drive across the country passed in blurs of blues, greens, and grays, vast rolling hills, clear skies, and the occasional rambling stone wall in stark opposition to the tense mood filling the car.

With every passing kilometer, the tether between her and Fergus pulled tighter. Her missing element was a constant burning pain in her heart, threatening to leave her nothing but a hollow shell by the time they arrived at Farren's.

Resisting his call in Dublin had almost made her believe she could break free, but the constant pull, the weakening of her element, and her fight with Liam the night before left her doubting herself yet again.

The only chance they possibly had? The bottle of Clozapine tucked in Caitlin's cross-body bag. Before throwing Mara over his shoulder and running—naked—from the elementals who'd attacked them in Tacoma, Cade had grabbed the bottle, and the ten little off-white pills might be their only chance to keep Fergus calm. Of course, she'd have to get close enough to him to convince him to take one. Or four.

Cade's phone rang half an hour from Farren's, and when he put it on speaker, Peter's tense voice filled the car.

"Colin's dead."

"What?" Cade and Liam said at once.

"Tierney, Ewan, and Abagail were going batshit, so we all shifted and ran together this morning," Peter said. Cade's expression hardened, and a low growl came from his throat, but Peter quickly continued, "You weren't here. It was either that or one of them would have snuck out on their own. This was safer."

"You're walking a thin line with me," Cade muttered. "What the fuck happened?"

"No idea. He was in human form. Naked. Beaten all to hell. With a brand carved into his shoulder."

Ice shot through Caitlin's veins, and her voice shook. "A brand? What kind of brand?"

"I'm sending you a photo. Looked at least thirty-six hours old."

Cade tapped the screen, and Caitlin sucked in a sharp breath. Colin's entire back was bruised and bloodied. And just above his shoulder blade, a series of lines and curves had been carved into his skin. A vague representation of a person with a head, a body made of two straight lines, and curved arms stood inside a wide *U* and stared back at her.

"No. No, no, no," Caitlin said as she shrank back against the seat and buried her head in her hands. "That's...it's like the brand Fergus has. It's a variation of an old Scottish sigil, twisted for their purposes. It's how the Thirteen control him. It lets them channel their magic through him."

"So the Thirteen did this to him?" Cade asked.

Peter cleared his throat over the line. "Do we need to worry about bringing his body back to the house? We're almost there."

"No. The magic won't be able to work on a dead body. Some

things are beyond even practitioners." Caitlin shuddered. Even as powerful as the Thirteen were, they couldn't control the dead. Something about the sigil bothered her, though, and she held out her hand for the phone.

"Let me see it again?" She didn't want to look. Not at the obvious torment Colin had suffered, nor the symbol that had brought her nothing but pain through Fergus.

Cade passed her the phone, and she enlarged the photo. "The lines and curves are unsteady. Rough. Fergus's mark is a burn. A brand. These are cuts." Narrowing her eyes, she frowned. "Peter, it almost looks like there's a second set of lines offset from the first. Is that right?"

He grunted and didn't reply until after some shuffling carried over the line. "Yeah. Kind of like there are two full images here. One slightly behind the other. But the second one's almost healed over."

Liam spared her a quick glance. "Weres heal quickly, luv. Even if we don't shift."

Her mind raced as Cade told Peter they'd be at Farren's within the hour and then hung up. Two symbols. One behind the other. A memory hovered at the back of her mind, but she couldn't coax it forward. This meant something.

"Farren has to be dead," Liam said quietly, his knuckles white as he gripped the steering wheel. Caitlin reached over to rest her hand on his thigh, and when he flicked his gaze to hers, his eyes shone. "She'd never abandon Colin if she had a choice."

"You don't know that. If Fergus had them and he lost control, he could have dumped Colin's body just to get it out of the way." Cade's words made Liam flinch, and the beta wolf shook his head.

"If so, that means he's still torturin' Farren."

Silence filled the car for the rest of the journey, Mara leaning against Cade in the back seat, Caitlin staring out the cracked window, trying not to focus on the ever-tightening connection between her and the earth elemental. He was close. Less than fifty miles, she thought. Close enough that if he called to her now, she feared she wouldn't be strong enough to fight him for long.

You're not his. No one owns you. Not now. Not ever.

TURNING off the main highway onto a narrow, two-lane road, Liam navigated the tight turns with ease, despite low stone walls that looked to Caitlin like they were pissed off the road dared to part them.

"We're here," he said as an old castle, restored to the glory of a long-forgotten time, came into view, towering against the graying skies.

Peter met them at the door, and the next few minutes passed in a cacophony of protests, pleading, and sharp words. Cade wasted no time taking control, ordering Farren's wolves to stand down, find rooms for them to stay in, then gather in the living room.

Tierney and Abagail carried in mugs of coffee and tea for the group, and when they were all seated on well-worn leather couches gathered around an ornately carved and darkened hearth, Cade stood in front of everyone.

"Until we find Farren, you don't have an alpha or a beta. You're not officially my pack. I can't order you to do a damn thing. But I'm asking you to trust me and Liam—and by extension, Caitlin. She knows this Fergus asshole, and she has more to lose if he remains free than any of us."

"Beggin' yer pardon," Abagail, a female wolf with curly red hair said. "But we've heard of her before. She used to run with this Fergus bloke, and at least two elementals from Doolin lost their lives because of her."

Liam growled a warning, and Abagail backed down, shrinking against the sofa cushions. "She didn't have a choice. Ya' think Colin wanted to be carved up and beaten to death? Caitlin had no more choice in what she did than Colin, and ya'd do well to remember that."

"Liam's right," Cade said. "There's a lot you don't know."

Tierney, a tall, lanky boy who couldn't be far into his twenties stood and approached Cade. He had at least four inches on the alpha, and Cade stared up at him, glacier blue eyes blazing until Tierney took a knee.

"Until we get Farren back, I'll pledge my loyalty to ya', Cade. And to Liam. Farren spoke highly of ya' a time or two, and I know she'd want us to listen."

Ewan, the only other male in the room, bowed his head. "I'm with Tierney, sir. Tell us what ya' need us to do, and we'll do it." Giving Abagail a pointed stare, he arched a brow.

The female wolf was older. Mid-thirties, maybe, with a wild look in her eyes Caitlin didn't understand.

"Fine. I'll listen," she said sharply. "But Colin was my oldest friend, and I'm not goin' to just sit here and let his death go unavenged. Not for long."

"No one wants to see Fergus pay more than I do," Liam said, taking his place next to Cade, alpha and beta united in their anger. "But we're goin' to be smart about it. He's powerful strong, can wield both air and earth, and he's got magic on his side. I knew Colin as a lad, and he mattered to me too. Understand?"

One by one, the last three wolves in Farren's pack nodded, and Cade started to tell them what they needed to know.

CAITLIN STOOD outside Farren's home, one of the female alpha's leather jackets clutched in her hand. The woman owned four of them, and her unique scent enveloped Caitlin—an odd combination of watermelon, the sea air, and fresh rain.

PATRICIA D. EDDY

"Are you sure this is going to work?" Mara asked as she came up behind Caitlin.

"No. Even if it does, I'll only get a general sense of what direction she might be in. Fergus is usin' too much of my air. I can feel it." The back of her neck prickled, and she grabbed Mara's hand, needing to hold onto something. "Shite. He's...angry. Really angry."

"I'll get Liam—"

"No. It's all right. He's not callin' to me. This is a side effect of the magic, I think. The spell that binds us together? Sometimes, I know what he's feelin'. If we're close enough. Just...don't let go." A cold ball of fear sank like a stone in her stomach, but Mara's presence helped calm her.

"I'm right here."

"I call upon my air. Send it far and wide, in search of Farren Denair. Guide us and shield us from harm."

The charm flowed from her outstretched hand, rustling the grass and sending gravel tumbling along the driveway.

The charm wouldn't return to her immediately. Not as weak as she was. So Caitlin led Mara back inside where Cade, Liam, and the rest of Farren's pack were huddled around a laptop.

"Why do you always say the words?" Mara asked.

"They help me focus," Caitlin said. "Because Fergus commands so much of my air, I need all the help I can get. And... it's what my mum taught me to do. I feel closer to her when I use them."

"That's sweet."

Liam slammed his fist down on the table, then jerked to his feet.

"Ye're sure that's her?" Tierney asked

"I am. Ciara Murphy was the name on her first fake ID. Remember it as clear as my own. Michael Walsh. We got 'em together in Dublin on a school trip."

"There could be a dozen Ciara Murphys in this county alone," Ewan said.

"And how many of 'em would put an ad in the local paper sayin' *that*?"

"What?" Caitlin asked. "What is it?"

Liam turned, stress and strain battling in his eyes. "I think Farren's tryin' to send us a message. 'Someone took out an ad in the Lahinch Online Journal."

Tierney turned the laptop so Caitlin could see the screen. "For the best soaps in County Clare, contact Ciara Murphy," she read. "Are ya' sure this Ciara isn't actually sellin' soaps?"

"If she is," Liam said, "she's doin' it out of O'Connor's Pub. Because that's the phone number listed here."

"Can you tell when the ad was placed?" Cade asked.

"No. But I can call 'em." Tierney pulled out his phone, dialed, and was immediately put on hold.

"We're wastin' time." Liam turned to Cade and grabbed his arm. "The address Eleanor gave ya' for the practitioner is forty minutes away. O'Connor's Pub is between here and there. We can stop, see if anyone knows Farren—or this Ciara Murphy—and if not, we'll be that much closer to findin' answers for Mara—and maybe findin' a way to best Fergus."

A muscle in Cade's jaw ticked, and he stared hard at his beta. "You're sure about this?"

"As sure as I am about anythin' at the moment. And what's the alternative? Abandonin' Farren to that bastard after he killed Colin? And what about Brian? This way, we're not sittin' here wastin' time. Peter can stay with Farren's pack and search for Brian, and the four of us will find the practitioner. What was her name?"

"Diedre McKean," Mara said, still clutching Caitlin's fingers. The water elemental's hand was warm and dry, and Caitlin was starting to worry about her again. But her voice still held its usual clarity, and her green eyes had only lost a small bit of their brightness since they'd left Dublin this morning.

"We leave in fifteen minutes," Cade said. "I need a few minutes with my mate first. Alone."

CAITLIN SPLASHED cool water on her cheeks while Liam paced the bedroom they'd been given on the second floor.

When she emerged, Liam stared at her, his gaze roving slowly up and down her body. "Are ya' all right, luv? Ya' haven't said much since we got here."

She shivered, hugging herself tightly. "I feel him. All the time now. Like he's under my skin. His emotions. Anger. Rage. Desperation."

With every word, Liam's eyes darkened, and she cursed herself silently for not keeping her thoughts to herself. He was under enough stress, and he couldn't do anything about Fergus's hold on her. Not yet anyway. She tried to brush past him on her way to the door, but he grabbed her, spun her around, and pressed her back against the wall.

The heat of his lips seared her neck, and he scraped his teeth along the delicate curve until a wave of arousal hit her so hard, she thought she just might drown. "I won't lose ya'," he whispered against her ear, then nipped at her throat.

When his hand pressed firmly between her legs, she barely held herself together as raw need consumed her.

"Liam. God. We...can't."

He pulled back, his eyes dark and dangerous, and traced her jaw with his knuckle. "I know, luv. But the moon rises in less than ten hours. The mating...shite, Caitlin. I can't think straight. All I want to do is lose myself in ya'."

Cupping his neck, she urged his mouth to hers and poured

her soul into their kiss. Heat thrummed deep in her core, and his hard length pressed against her stomach.

"Listen to me, Liam," she panted when they came up for air. "Ya' have to trust me now. He's so close, and I wouldn't put it past him to have taken Farren because he found out she meant something to ya'."

Her words registered like a slap to his face, and he sobered almost immediately.

"Cade has half the Clozapine. I have the rest. If Fergus shows up, if he comes after me—or God forbid, comes after you, I can shield ya' for a short time. Long enough for Cade to try to drug him. He'll try to hurt me, but he *needs* me. He won't kill me, not even if we fail."

"Caitlin, ya' better not be askin' me to let him take ya'," Liam growled.

"I am. Because I know ya' won't rest until ya' find me again." She cupped his cheek, and he leaned into her touch. "I have somethin' now I didn't have eleven years ago."

"What's that?"

"A reason to fight." She brushed her lips to his. "I know what it is to love ya', and I won't let him take that away from me."

CHAPTER TWENTY

Liam

$\mathcal{T}$he car bounced along unpaved roads on the way to Doolin. With every kilometer, Caitlin withdrew further, curling into herself, occasionally opening the window and sucking in air like she thought she was about to drown.

The humidity rose steadily the closer they got to the sea, and Mara spun droplets of water from palm to palm, trying to keep herself balanced and suppress the fire she said she could feel lurking just under her skin.

No one spoke until they passed by an old castle, and Caitlin sat up with a jerk. "Stop the car, Liam. Please."

He pulled over, though strictly speaking, there wasn't any sort of shoulder to the road. Only a thinning of the bushes. His mate rolled down the window and inhaled deeply.

"I call upon the air, return with the answers I seek," she murmured, holding her hand out, palm up. Her scent—fig blossoms and the sea—filled the car, and she frowned.

"That's the castle where Fergus took my element." Her voice shook, and Liam reached over and cupped her cheek.

"Ye're safe, luv. He's not here."

"He's close," she whispered. "I can feel him." Her hand went to her neck, and she tugged at the collar of her long-sleeved T-shirt. "It's like he's strangling me so slowly, I'm terrified I won't notice until I run out of air."

"Come here." Liam wrapped his arms around her, and damn the gear shift. He wanted to pull her into his lap and comfort her, but he couldn't.

A car passed them and honked loudly, and Caitlin drew back. "I'm all right. He's not there, but I think Colin was. And Farren. Not now, though. Farren... She's that way."

Caitlin pointed straight ahead, and Liam started the car again. At the top of the hill, Mara gasped. The view was stunning, he'd give her that. They could see all the way down to the sea a good three kilometers away, and for a moment, it seemed like they were on top of the world.

"It's beautiful," Mara said and rolled down her window to inhale the sea air. "And, shit. I feel so much better here."

"Doolin's at the bottom of this hill," Liam said, pointing to a small gathering of buildings.

"*That's* a town?" Cade asked. "I count ten buildings."

"So many of the towns around here are like that," Caitlin said, a hint of melancholy and longing in her voice. "I grew up in Doolin. We had a dozen families, maybe? After Fergus took my air, the elementals fled, leavin' only the humans behind."

"Last time I talked to Farren, she said it was comin' back. They have a grocery store now." Liam chuckled, though the action felt strained and out of place given the mood in the car.

"My mum used to joke that Doolin didn't put on airs like Lahinch. *They* had the only grocery store when I lived here."

"It's peaceful." Mara leaned against Cade in the back seat, and he draped his arm around her shoulders. "Maybe...if we can find a way to fix me, we can stay here for a few weeks."

"Anything you want, honey. And we'll figure this out. I promise."

Cade met Liam's gaze in the rearview mirror, and the desperation in his alpha's eyes, mixed with the steely determination that had allowed him to survive being trapped as his wolf for the better part of a year, blazed in the amber and silver streaks amid the blue of his irises.

The tiny town spread out over less than a hundred acres, with one stoplight and four hotels along the main road, two pubs, a bookstore, bank, grocery, and petrol station.

The sun shone brightly, lending a happy, welcoming glow to the buildings, and only the faintest of white clouds dotted the horizon.

"The Old Peculiar is one block south," Liam said, and Caitlin sent out a charm, closed her eyes, and shook her head.

"No. She's north. And close. O'Connor's if I had to guess."

"Liam, take Caitlin to O'Connor's," Cade said. "Mara and I will check out the Old Peculiar. Meet back here in ten minutes."

Liam offered Caitlin his arm, and she tucked her hand in the crook of his elbow. "Something's...off. There's magic around here."

He tensed, peering down at her and letting his wolf edge closer to the surface. "Fergus's magic?"

"No. The brand, the magic he could wield, it always sickened me. This is somethin' different."

With one last glance back at Cade and Mara, who'd reached the Old Peculiar, Liam set his shoulders and opened the pub door. "Don't leave my side, luv. Not for anythin'."

Caitlin

O'Connor's had opened just ten minutes earlier, and only three patrons graced the scattered tables in the dimly lit rooms. Two with scruffy beards, and a third wearing a hood and staring into a pint glass.

Dozens of bottles in every shape, size, and color stood gleaming behind the bar, with a handful of taps off to one side.

A beefy man with a polished, bald head and bushy white brows eyed them. "Kitchen opens in an hour. Session band starts not long after that."

Caitlin scanned the back room while Liam rested an elbow on the counter. "We're lookin' for Farren Denair. Ya' know her, mate?"

"Nope. If ya' want a pint, though, I can pour ya' one."

An elderly man, frail, with the look of one who'd lost most of his teeth to age, fixed his pale blue eyes on Caitlin, touched his cheek, and nodded with a half-smile.

Pulled by a force she didn't understand, she approached as he withdrew a pair of spoons from his pocket and slapped them on his thigh in time with the reel playing on the sound system.

"Paddy knows ya'," he said, his voice as frail as his body. "He's been waitin'."

"For me?" Her stomach flipped, and she looked around, but none of the other patrons met her gaze.

"Aye. Ya' need answers, ya' do. Tryin' to save them. And yerself."

"What the hell? How did you...?"

Paddy grinned, confirming his distinct lack of teeth, before he touched the tip of his nose. "Right I was." The spoons rapped on the table. Four knocks, a beat, three more, and he stared over her shoulder at the bartender.

Caitlin turned in time to see the man gesture to one of the

male patrons who rose, locked the door, and went back to his pint without a word.

"What the fuck is the meanin' of this?" Liam lunged over the counter and grabbed the bartender by his shirt to pull him closer.

"Took ya' long enough," a distinctly feminine voice said. Shoving back the dark gray hood of her cloak, the solitary drinker revealed long, silver-blond hair, sharp cheekbones, and plump, bow lips that curved into a half smile under deep blue, bloodshot eyes. "Good to see ya' again, Liam."

Releasing the bartender, Liam staggered back. "Shite. Farren."

Caitlin watched as Liam pulled the slight woman up by her arms and crushed her against him, both touched and a little jealous at another woman locked in an intimate embrace with the man she loved.

A soft touch to her hand made her turn to find Paddy grinning at her. "Sit. Old Paddy has lots to say."

"Put me down, ya' oaf," Farren said with a wince. "Ye're crushin' me."

Liam set her on her feet. "Farren, this is Caitlin. My mate."

The female wolf's fingers trembled slightly as she shook Caitlin's hand. "I've heard of ya'. Came back to set Liam to rights, have ya'?"

Her words stung, and Caitlin dropped her gaze to Paddy rapping his spoons against the table once more. "I guess so."

"Farren," Liam wrapped his arm around Caitlin's waist and lowered his voice. "Colin—"

"I know." Her blue eyes shone, and she kicked one of the chairs halfway across the room. "Sorry, Mickey," she muttered as the bartender glared at her. "I couldn't save him."

As Farren passed her to retrieve the chair, scents of blood, earth, and magic reached her nose. A second later, someone pounded on the pub's locked door hard enough to shake the walls.

"Fuck me," Liam muttered. "Cade and Mara." With a raised

brow at the bartender, he asked, "Ya' mind? That's my...my brother out there."

Mickey grunted, but ambled over to the door and admitted Cade and Mara. "Don't look much like yer brother to me."

"Farren?" Cade asked. "Thank God."

"Never thought I'd see you this side of the world," she said. "And mated."

After everyone had been introduced, Farren twisted a chair around and threw a leg over the seat, resting her folded arms along the back.

"Where have ya' been?" Liam asked.

Farren sighed, her voice weary. "Paddy saved my life."

"All we know is that you went looking for Fergus," Cade said. "Something about a dead elemental in Lahinch?"

"Aye. Colin and I went to the Hen and Boar in Lahinch. That's the last place anyone reported seein' the bastard. Stayed there half the day, tryin' to get anyone to talk to us, but ya' know how it is."

"Afraid I don't," Cade said as Mara settled closer to him in the booth.

"I've worked among the supernatural community for six years now, but they still consider me an outsider." Farren lifted her pint and took a deep swig. "Ya'd think we'd stick together, but werewolves don't trust practitioners, practitioners don't trust elementals, and elementals don't trust anyone. So when a water elemental knocked on my office door three days ago, well, ya' can imagine my shock. Clearly she wasn't from around here."

"What'd she want?" Liam asked.

"Her aunt was killed last week. Suffocated, but not a scratch on her. No bruises. Just lyin' on the floor of an abandoned castle at the top of the hill outside of town."

Caitlin sucked in a sharp breath. "The one off of Ballyellery?"

"That'd be the one. Not the first body to show up there in the past fifteen years," Farren said.

Snapshots of memories, each more horrible than the last, flashed through Caitlin's mind. Water. Air. Fire. All dead. All because of her.

No. Fergus killed them. Not you.

"Caitlin?" Liam ran his nose along the curve of her neck, and she shivered. "Ya' all right, luv?"

"That's where he used to bring all of them," she said. "It's where he'd take their elements. Or try to. Where he took mine."

"The niece was a sweet one. Not more than twenty-two. Had a bit of water herself, but said she couldn't use it like her aunt could. I did some askin' around, and no one wanted to say much, but the few rumors I heard were that Fergus Tharp had returned to County Clare and was up to his old habits. Huntin' down elementals and killin'. Right before Colin and I went to the Hen and Boar, I called the lass and told her to get the hell out of town."

Draining the last of her pint, she signaled Mickey for another, and he brought a round for everyone along with a shot of whiskey for Paddy, who was still tapping his spoons on the table from time to time and staring at Caitlin like she held the secrets of the universe itself.

Farren called after him, "Bring us a bottle, Mickey. We're goin' to need it."

"Farren," Liam leaned forward, his hand still wrapped around Caitlin's. "Ya' need to tell us what happened. And someone needs to check ya' for...a brand."

The female wolf let out a low growl, threw back her cloak, and lifted her bloodstained gray flannel. "Like this?"

Her toned stomach was a mass of bruises, and on her side, two vertical lines sat over a half circle. They were faint, like they'd been made a week ago.

"Fuck me," Liam muttered. "Ya' shifted?"

"Eventually," she spat as Mickey returned with a bottle of Irish whiskey and five more glasses. "We were about to leave the

Hen and Boar. Give up for the night. The ground started rumblin' like Mother Earth herself was ready to blow a gasket. Somethin' hit me in the back of the head, and that's all I remember until I woke up underground somewhere." She reached up to touch her neck, her fingers trembling, "I couldn't move or even breathe. And Fergus was carvin' me up."

"How'd ya' get away?" Liam asked.

After a snort, Farren drained the first shot of whiskey and poured herself another. "After the first couple o' cuts, he started poppin' pills. Kept mutterin' to himself about how he just needed his air. He'd be steady if he found her, but he had to kill her wolf first."

Fear chilled Caitlin down to her toes, and she pressed closer to Liam. He rubbed her back in slow, gentle circles, trying to calm her.

"Once he took those pills, I could breathe again. Move a little. Still couldn't shift." Farren shuddered. "I kept tryin'. The bastard would come back every couple of hours and make another cut or two, and all the while, it was like my wolf was locked inside a cage, and she was about the eat the head off me."

Cade's glass fell to the table, whiskey racing across the old, worn wood, and Mara whispered something to him Caitlin couldn't—and didn't want to—hear. "I need a minute," he said as he got to his feet, his mate's hand clutched in his.

"Never will be whole," Paddy mused. "Not that one. Not unless evil leaves this world."

"What do you mean?" Caitlin asked.

"That's not for ya' to know yet." He shook his spoons and took another sip of his drink. "Old Paddy sees what's hidden."

"Paddy saved me," Farren said. She reached across the table to squeeze the old man's gnarled fingers. "Fergus left me—he'd started a second set of cuts on my arm, but his hands were shakin' too much—and after a few hours of howlin' and fightin', my wolf fought her way free. But he'd broken two of my ribs and my arm. Couldn't heal everythin' fully. I ran until I couldn't anymore, and passed out not more than fifty meters from Paddy's old shack."

"Hid ya' well, I did." The old man smiled a toothless grin. "No more, though. The end comes."

Mickey strode to the table and crossed his arms over his broad chest. He had to be pushing seventy, but he was built like a bear. "Kitchen opens in twenty minutes, and it's goin' to be a busy night. If ya' want to stay hidden, might be best to leave."

Digging into his wallet, Liam came up with two hundred euro and passed it to the man, but Mickey waved him off. "Farren's money's no good here. Neither is yers."

"Ye're a good man, Mickey," Farren replied, her gaze softening. "We'll be gone soon enough." Turning back to the rest of them, including Cade and Mara, who'd taken their seats again, her shoulders slumped. "I put the ad online because I knew ya' would come, Liam. Fergus's rantin' and ravin', goin' on and on about Caitlin and how she'd run off with ya' years ago, makin' him suffer…I figured she had to be alive. And if she were, she'd be with ya' now."

"That's a powerful big chance ya' took." Liam still kept a hold of Caitlin's hands, but his gaze was completely focused on Farren, and a spark of jealousy caught deep inside of her.

They're friends. Nothing more.

"Paddy sees ya', lass," the old man said as he leaned closer to Caitlin. "Hears ya' too. Paddy knows lots o' things. Listens. No one pays Paddy any mind." He smiled along to a joke only he seemed to know, and a gleam crept into his eyes. "The one ya' seek hides in plain sight."

"The one we seek?" Caitlin asked. "You mean Diedre?"

Paddy tapped the side of his nose and chuckled. "A smart one. Keeps her wits about her, she does. Even though she knows nothin' of the world. Paddy hears whispers from all around. Ghosts." Turning to Caitlin, he drew a complex pattern in the air with two fingers, a rune or a sigil she couldn't tell, but it wasn't one she knew.

"Paddy? What was that?"

His eyes paled, clouding over, and his voice lowered, the haunting, raspy tone sending chills down Caitlin's spine. "Promise lives on this soft auld day. Legends warn, but they can't know one's heart. Strength finds the silver wolf when all is lost, and one kept in the dark can bring light to all."

The spoons fell from his hand, and Liam retrieved them from the floor. "What are ya' goin' on about?" he asked.

The old man's eyes returned to their normal color, and he touched Caitlin's cheek with a wrinkled finger. "Go now. Mickey's openin' soon. Paddy can't stay with ya'. When darkness comes, he'll see ya' again. After the storm."

Farren leaned over and kissed Paddy's wrinkled cheek. "I can't repay ya' for savin' my life."

"Ya' will one day."

Before Farren could pull away, Paddy grabbed her arm, moving faster than he had any right to at his advanced age. "Earth denied. But earth remains. Yer help will aid what once was slain. Storms rage on, here and there, ne're calmed by earth nor air. One will come but few can go. Yer wolves don't know, and nay do you. Two become three, but three can't do. One with magic now ya' seek; be wary of one who appears so meek. A man's eyes can never know what lies far away below."

He let his words sink in for just a moment, his hand still wrapped around Farren's arm, then smiled. "Beautiful. And brave." Rising, he patted Caitlin's shoulder. "Find yer strength bonny one." And then he shuffled off towards the stage, slapping his spoons against his thigh with each step.

"What in the bloody hell was that shite?" Liam called after him. But Paddy just shook his head and kept walking. "Farren, I don't mean to disrespect ya', but he's as daft as a brush."

Farren gave a small shake of her head. "Paddy's been around

Doolin so long, no one remembers him comin'. Always been that way. Soothsayer, prophet, crazy loon...he's been called it all. And I've never been able to figure him out. But I trust him. Even if I can't understand a word he says sometimes." She swept a glance around the table. "Where's yer car? Do ya' have room for one more? I'm goin' with ya' to find this practitioner, and I don't fancy runnin' the whole way. My wolf's still too skittish after my time with that arse."

"We're parked just out front. Are ya' sure ya' don't want to go home and rest? I can call Abagail and Ewan. They went to Lahinch with one of ours," Liam said.

"I wouldn't miss this for anythin'." Farren smiled, her blue eyes bright, despite the exhaustion she carried in the bags underneath. "I've been wantin' a bit of excitement for years."

"Be careful what you wish for," Caitlin muttered as Liam wrapped his arm around her waist and led her from the pub, Cade and Mara following them, with Farren bringing up the rear. Excitement was the last thing she wanted, and the sick, churning feeling in the pit of her stomach told her it was coming soon— and it would be worse than any of them could imagine.

CHAPTER TWENTY-ONE

Caitlin

*A*s the car turned off of Doolin's main street and headed up a hill, a vague sense of unease crept over Caitlin's skin, settling at the back of her neck. "Liam—"

Her entire body bucked, and her head slammed into the seat. Fergus's glee—almost child-like—raised goosebumps along her arms and obliterated her thoughts, taking control and pulling a scream from her throat.

Air swirled violently through the car, Fergus's charm stripping her bare until she couldn't fight any longer. He stole the breath from her lungs, and the world darkened around her.

No. I am not yours!

"Caitlin!" The car swerved, and a horn blared from somewhere far away. Cool fingers grasped her from behind, and she was dimly aware of Mara's voice telling her to fight.

She couldn't. Fergus was everywhere. All around her. In her thoughts. Her memories.

Liam. She could feel Liam. His hands on her arms, his lips

against her ear. His voice. Urging her to say something. His wolf. The bright amber streaks glowing in his green eyes.

A string of Gaelic drowned out her wail, and fresh air billowed over her.

After another minute, the sickening sensation passed, and she could focus on Liam's concerned face.

"Caitlin, say somethin'."

His hands on her cheeks brought her back, and she swallowed hard. "Fergus. Callin' to me again. I've never felt him so... desperate. Or afraid. He's in pain, and he's close."

Liam cradled Caitlin against him, lifting her from the passenger seat. "Cade can drive, luv. I've got ya'."

They crammed into the back seat with Farren, and she started to settle, his warmth, his strength, even his scent calming her in a way she'd never thought possible.

The phone rang, but she didn't pay the conversation any mind. Keeping her hold on reality was hard enough, and she rested her hand over Liam's heart to help tether her to the here and now.

"Well, shite," Farren muttered. "I knew I shoulda' sent them all off somewhere."

"What's going on?" Caitlin asked, blinking hard as she stared up at Liam.

"Farren's wolves are gettin' a mite stir crazy."

"Tell 'em they can shift, but not run. No leavin' the property." Farren shook her head and stared out the window. "They're all young. Less control over their wolves than the rest of us. I'd send them all to Scotland for a week, but at this point, they're safer at the house."

"Peter will look out for them," Cade said and hung up the call. "But, are you sure they're trustworthy? You told them you and Colin were going to the Hen and Boar, right?"

"I did. And I'm not sure of anythin' at the moment. I didn't even want to trust Paddy, but I didn't have much choice," she said, a weariness to her tone blending with an edge of frustration. "Though I could do without his endless riddles."

"I wrote down as much as I could remember." Mara passed a small notepad to Caitlin, the Clontarf Castle logo decorating the upper right corner. "Did I get it right?"

"Earth denied. But earth remains. Your help will aid what once was slain. Storms rage on, here and there, ne're calmed by earth nor air. One will come but few can go. Your wolves don't know, and nay do you. Two become three, but three can't do. One with magic now you seek; be wary of one who appears so meek. A man's eyes can never know what lies far away below."

"I think so. Not that I know what it means. Earth denied? I guess that could be Fergus not getting what he wants. And the storms? Could those be from the practitioners? Since my air and Fergus's earth weren't enough for them?" Caitlin closed her eyes against the headache still threatening, playing the words over and over again in her mind.

She was so tired of fighting. So was Fergus. She could sense his exhaustion even as his mania strengthened. The magic pouring through him—along with the earth and air elements— were wearing him out. Physically. Emotionally.

He was so desperate, and desperate men were the most dangerous of all.

Liam

The car pulled onto a long, winding road so narrow, Liam had Cade check the GPS a second and a third time, fearing they'd taken a wrong turn.

Shrubs closed in on them from both sides with creeping vines that looked like they'd grab the small car and toss it down the belly of a lush, green beast.

No one said a word. Mara huddled in the front seat, her hands curled around the leather pouch Caitlin had given her.

Farren's gaze remained fixed out the window, even when there was nothing to look at. Whatever she'd been through—and Liam would bet she'd only told them half of it—had changed her, and she wasn't the confident, take-no-crap-soon-to-be alpha wolf he'd remembered growing up. Not even the reluctant one she'd been the last time he'd seen her.

Born to lead—like him—but never comfortable with the role, she'd tried to refuse the mantle, but Colin, Ewan, and Tierney had been insistent.

"We're here," Cade said.

A single-story farmhouse hid behind a stone wall that had seen better days. Paint peeled from the eaves, and moss had devoured the northern side of the structure.

Languishing to the west, a small garden offered half-rotted cabbages and winter squash, and crows fed on the remains.

"I don't like this." Liam helped Caitlin to her feet, and Cade took Mara's hand. "We're in the middle of nowhere. Are ya' sure Eleanor was truly on our side?"

"She died trying to protect me," Mara said quietly. "If that's not 'on our side,' I don't know what is."

Farren lingered by the car, drawing her cloak closer around her body. Liam was about to call for her to join them when the door flew open, revealing an elderly woman leaning heavily on a cane.

"Who the hell are ya'?"

"Eleanor Nathem sent us," Mara rushed to explain. "She said you could help us fight the Thirteen. That you knew about elementals and practitioners and—"

"Air." Diedre hissed out a breath and pointed at Caitlin. "Ya' gave it away, and now ye're lookin' for a way to fix what's broken." A string of Gaelic words Liam couldn't understand flowed from the woman's lips, and all four of them stumbled back, the sudden, percussive force almost enough to knock Liam onto his arse.

Caitlin got her bearings first, and she took two steps forward, her blue eyes blazing. "I do want answers. But I'm not the one who broke Fergus. The Thirteen did that, and ya' used to be one of them."

Liam and Cade stood together, their wolves at the ready, while Mara took her place at Caitlin's side. "Please, Diedre," the water elemental said. "We need a way to separate two elements. Both to help Fergus and to save me."

She held out her hands, and above one palm, a droplet of water tumbled and spun over and over again. The other hand started to glow red hot, and Mara clenched her fingers tightly, then sent the water crashing over them. "My fire's taking over, and I'm a danger to everyone if I lose control."

"I'm older than all of ya' put together, ya' know." Diedre huffed out a breath. "So no tryin' anything daft like charmin' me or havin' those three wolves shift and try to intimidate me. I could end the lot of you with a snap of my fingers."

Turning, she limped down a narrow hallway, and the five of them trailed after her until they reached a large, airy room that looked like it hadn't changed in fifty years.

Gauzy curtains hung from the large picture windows, and the pink couch was covered with white lace. The distinct scent of liniment hung in the air, mixing with the spicy incense burning in the western corner of the room.

"You'll get no coffee or tea here. The longer ya' stay, the greater the risk, so say yer piece, then get out."

Mara and Caitlin sat on the couch across from Diedre with the three wolves standing behind them.

"Did you help the Thirteen trap Fergus?" Caitlin asked.

"What do ya' know about them, lass?" Diedre narrowed her watery green eyes at Caitlin, as if she couldn't quite figure her out.

"I saw them. Once. Met them. In a way." Caitlin's voice

cracked, and she cleared her throat. "Fergus brought me to the Thirteen not long after he bound me. But I don't remember much of it. They tried to separate my air—the part of it he'd stolen anyway—from him, but I don't think it worked. At least not the way they wanted it to. They tortured him. Locked us both underground, and I can't recall anythin' after that."

"I left them when they started talkin' about commanding the spirit," the old woman said. "No one being can control that much power. I vowed I'd never go against them—otherwise they woulda killed me before seein' me leave. I try not to work with the craft at all if I can help it. Not anymore."

Mara seemed to shrink before Liam's eyes. "So, you can't help us? We were hoping you could teach Caitlin how to separate elements."

"It's started then," Diedre said, her harsh gaze fixed on Mara.

"I...yes. I'm losing myself. When my fire takes over, well...the last time, I killed several elementals who were trying to kill me." Cade rested his hand on Mara's shoulder, and she seemed to take strength from the touch. The humidity in the room doubled in the space of a single breath.

"I suppose I should tell ya' all of it." The elderly practitioner rose and shuffled over to a bookcase behind Liam. Her bony fingers trailed over the spines, the occasional muttered word passing her lips.

After what felt like an eternity, Diedre withdrew a single volume with faded golden text inscribed on the dark blue cover. "The practice of magic is not for the faint of heart. Few can wield the power without succumbing to its whispered promises of mystical wonders. It is how things have always been."

Clutching the book to her chest, she returned to the sofa and pinned Caitlin with her stare. "I sense great strength in ya', daughter of air. And a talent for the craft too. But it will not be enough—"

Liam growled, the low, feral sound rumbling through him and waking his wolf. "So ya' won't help?"

"I said nothin' of the sort. But ye're battling the might of thirteen of the world's most powerful. Do ya' really think any *one* of ya' could survive?"

When no one responded, Diedre gave them a curt nod. "The young have hubris on their side, but not much wisdom. Ye'll need a bit of foolish pride, ya' will, but also the knowledge that only comes from decades spent walkin' the earth. Listenin' to the wind. Hearin' the song of the sea and the crackles of the flames. I shouldn't even be talkin' to ya'. But my time will soon be over, and I cannot bear to see my greatest fears come to pass."

Sliding the book across the table, Diedre's wrinkled lips smoothed into what might have been a grin and her eyes paled. "The answers ya' seek are here. But readin' and understandin' are not the same. One requires sight, the other...patience. In the end, only if ye're willin' to sacrifice everythin' will ya' succeed. Ya' can only take what is freely given, and ye'll need a key to unlock what ya' seek."

"A key?" Liam asked. An uncomfortable pressure settled around him, and he tried to reach for Caitlin, but found he couldn't move. The old woman's low, haunting words seeped into his mind. "Leave this place and forget ya' ever met me. I'm no one. A senile old woman. Ya' found the book in an old library, and none of ya' will remember any different. The key will come to ya'. When ye're ready. As is my will, so mote it—"

Farren keened, a high-pitched wild cry, and the ground rumbled as a great gust of wind and shards of glass pelted them. Mara and Diedre screamed, while Caitlin cried, "Not here! Not now!"

Bits of lace flew through the air, and a lamp hit the wall. Cade shoved Mara to the floor and flung himself over her as Farren tumbled back into a glass cabinet.

Diedre murmured words Liam couldn't understand, and her

body turned almost translucent. Like she was fading away before his eyes. *What the fuck?*

He lunged for Caitlin, hauling her back behind the sofa. Shards of glass rained down in a violent storm, slicing her cheek. The coppery scent of her blood riled Liam's wolf.

Plates crashed in the kitchen, and she strained in his hold. "Fergus. He's...here. I have to go to him. He's too strong...Liam, please..."

And then, Liam saw him. Black hair. Wild hazel eyes. Arms outstretched, he stood outside the broken picture window, a crazed grin splitting his face. "Caitie!" he called. "Come to me now, and maybe I'll let yer wolf live."

"No!" she wailed and struggled even harder to free herself from Liam's arms. In his periphery, Cade's wolf shook off his clothes, howled, and nudged Farren, who was still crumpled against the bookcase. Mara crawled over to them as the ground rumbled again and one whole wall of the house fell away.

"No one invited me to the party." The sing-song voice was strangely compelling, and Liam shook his head as hard as he could. The urge to let go of Caitlin was almost overwhelming—at least to his human side, but the wolf had no intention of listening and made himself known with another growl. Fergus spared him only a quick glance. "Come now, Caitie. Ya' know ya' want to."

Mara, alone and unprotected as Farren came to and started to shift, flung a torrent of water at Fergus, drenching him and driving him back to where the wall had been moments ago.

"A water elemental. How convenient," Fergus said. His glee carried over the loud cracks of wood, Cade's desperate lupine vocalizations, and Liam's pleas in Caitlin's ear.

"Fight for me, *mo ghrá*. Don't let him win."

He released his mate long enough to get to his feet, then drew her against him, his arm secure around her waist. "Ya' have one chance, fuckwit. Leave Caitlin alone and walk away or I'll rip your head clean off."

"No." The single, snarled word escaped as he hurled another air charm at them.

Liam whirled around, his back taking the brunt of the force, and the two of them tumbled over the sofa, landing next to where Diedre had once been, but now...only her sweater, long skirt, and cane were left behind.

Flames burst from Mara's outstretched hand, and Fergus's shirttails caught fire. "Fire as well? This is everything I have been searching for. Come to me, lass. With fire, water, and air, I'll finally be free!"

A second fiery plume arced towards Fergus, but he was ready this time, shouting in Gaelic for the air to be at his beck and call.

Cade's wolf whined weakly, his chest heaving, and collapsed to the floor, his silvery blue eyes pleading for Caitlin to help him.

"Try another fire charm, lovey, and I'll kill yer wolf." Fergus's voice lowered, his words smooth and reassuring. "Let go of my Caitie, wolf. Now. Air, water, and fire. Come to me."

Liam's arm fell away, and he crumpled with a groan as all the air left his lungs. Helplessly, he had to watch as Caitlin took one step. Then another. And another. In one desperate move, he wrapped his fingers around her ankle.

"Help me," Mara whispered. Her green eyes clouded, and she stepped over Cade's struggling wolf. The veins in her neck throbbed against Fergus's hold, and tears fell in tiny rivers from her eyes.

Caitlin sobbed and begged. "If ya' ever cared for me, Fergus, please..." She sucked in a deep breath, then flung her own weak charm towards Liam.

For a moment, he could breathe again, and he yanked Caitlin's ankle as hard as he could, sending her tumbling back over the piles of books, broken bits of plaster, and ruined furniture.

Fergus got his hand around Mara's neck and hauled her

against him, squeezing hard enough her eyes widened and she clawed at his fingers, scratching until she drew blood.

"Fuck...you..." she croaked, and an intense wave of thick, wet heat drove them all to the floor. Blood vessels popped in the whites of Cade's eyes, and he tried to get up, his paws scrambling on the hard wooden floors.

Fergus's arm burst into flames, and Caitlin sent a gust of air towards the earth elemental. The blast dislodged his hand from Mara's throat and drove her to her knees.

Freed from the earth elemental's compulsion, Liam surged forward and rammed his shoulder into Fergus's solar plexus. "Protect the book!" he shouted.

"Get. Away. From. My. Family!" Mara shouted, and a tidal wave of water washed Liam and Fergus down the hall, and almost to the door. "Liam, shift!" Flames roared towards them, and Liam landed a punch to Fergus's jaw.

The house shuddered, and half the roof caved in, burying the two of them, battering and bruising Liam's ribs, his hip, and his back. A fiery lance of pain shot through his leg, and he let out a howl.

And then, as quickly as the rubble had covered them, it lifted into the air and Liam caught sight of his Caitlin. Her blue eyes were wild and bright, and behind her, Cade dragged Farren free from the rapidly collapsing and shifting house, his jaws clamped around her wolf's scruff.

Mara helped Caitlin climb over a pile of wooden planks, and the two stumbled free from the rubble. Thank God. Mara would protect his mate, leaving him to tear this fucker limb from limb.

Fergus rose behind him, and before Liam could release his wolf, the earth elemental whispered a string of words in his ear. His body stilled, his arms and legs suddenly made of lead.

A pocket knife appeared in the man's hand, and he ripped open Liam's shirt, then carved something into his flesh. It burned, and he wanted to scream, but he couldn't make a sound.

Caitlin!

When Fergus straightened, he hauled Liam up.

Fuck! Pure agony shot from his toes all the way to his hip, and he still couldn't move. Couldn't run. Couldn't fight.

"How could ya' fuck this piece of shite, Caitie? Did ya' really think he could give ya' what I couldn't? Ya' want one of my lessons, don't ya'? Ya' remember how I'd teach ya', yeah?"

"Fergus, please!" she cried. "Let him go."

Blood plastered Liam's shirt to his chest, and he struggled for each shallow, wheezing breath. He could barely form a coherent thought. "Run," he mouthed. "Caitlin. Run."

More quiet words in his ear, a sour, bitter taste in his mouth, and he was floating. The pain in his leg faded away, and he let Fergus pull him down the driveway.

"You're going to burn." Mara's voice had turned harsh and deep. Red locks of hair rose around her like a fiery halo as her hands glowed white hot. Waves of heat shimmered, burning the water from the asphalt.

Fire and water twisted together like ribbons, and Fergus spun, slinging Liam over his shoulder like he weighed nothing at all.

An oppressive darkness settled over him, and he landed on something hard before everything faded into silence.

CHAPTER TWENTY-TWO

Caitlin

a strong hand wrapped around her arm and tugged her to her feet. "Stand up, Caitlin. We have to get the fuck out of here and find Liam." Cade's deep voice shook her out of her panic-induced haze.

She blinked. More than six feet of solid muscle interrupted only by scars stood in front of her, naked. Mara leaned against him, her eyes dull and red-rimmed. Strain tightened her lips, and she was drenched.

A silvery white wolf howled as bones popped and cracked, fur rippled and disappeared, and Farren's white hair sprouted from her head. When the shift had completed, a very naked Farren Denair lay panting on the ground until she swore viciously. "Bastard broke my ribs. I'm goin' to rip his fuckin' intestines out through his throat."

Caitlin's heart stuttered, and she sank against the car. "Liam's...gone. Fergus will kill him."

"Look at me, Caitlin," Cade said sharply. "Fergus ran because he couldn't fight all of us together. So what does that tell you?"

"That he's going to kill Liam. He'll use him to hurt me as much as he can, and then he'll kill him." Tears spilled over, and she tried to swallow her sobs.

"No." Cade started to pace, still unabashedly naked, while Mara leaned against the car door next to Caitlin. "Fergus might be insane, but he's also a fucking bully. Just like Katerina. And bullies are cowards at heart. If we find him, we can end him and get Liam back."

"How?" Caitlin sniffled and swiped her hand over her cheeks.

"You're an air elemental with an unbreakable link to Fergus. You tell me." Cade tried the car door, then kicked the tire with his bare foot. "Fuck. The keys are somewhere in that mess." Gesturing to the ruins of Diedre's house, he shook his head. "Caitlin, I hope your phone still works. Otherwise, Farren's going to have a hell of a long run home."

Her bag was still slung across her torso, and she dug inside. Everything was damp, but not completely soaked through, and she passed Cade her phone as Mara slipped an arm around her shoulders.

"You have to try, Caitlin. Please. I used so much power back there...it'll be a miracle if the Thirteen haven't sensed me by now." The water elemental's eyes were still dull, but at least her words were clear. "I lost myself for a while. The fire...I could feel it taking over, and I let it. I had to. It was the only way I could fight him."

Shame heated her cheeks as she realized the truth. Mara had succumbed to Katerina's element willingly—knowing she might not come back from it. She'd done all of that for Cade. For Liam. For Farren. And for her.

If Mara could be that brave, so could she.

Caitlin nodded. "I'll try." Taking a few steps away from the car, she closed her eyes and let the soft melody of her element wrap her in a gentle embrace. Magic lingered, the taste of it oily and bitter on her tongue.

"I call upon my air. Help me find my mate. Lead me to him."

Blades of grass, dirt, and small pieces of debris tumbled down the driveway with her charm, and a few seconds later, a gentle breeze came back, bringing hints of Liam's scent, then Fergus's, along with blood, burning wood, and rain.

Where is he?

Nothing made sense. Her locator charms had always been rubbish—except when she'd been with Katerina—but now...it was like Liam was everywhere and nowhere at the same time.

"If Liam's still alive," Caitlin said softly, her knees landing in mud, "Fergus—or magic—is hiding him. They could be anywhere." Hope faded just as quickly as it had sparked, and she buried her face in her hands.

"No. They're somewhere. If your element can't find them, then *you* can." Mara knelt next to her, and the water elemental's eyes were clearer now. She held on to the leather pouch with the red jasper like it was the only thing keeping her sane.

And then she unzipped her jacket. The black leather book with gold lettering was tucked against her green sweater. "We can do this. Fergus took Liam because we're stronger together than he is. He tried to compel both of us and we fought him. We need to see what's in this book and then find a way to take him down. We'll get Liam back. Fergus isn't going to kill him until he has you. He'll hurt him, but he won't kill him."

Mara's clarity and confidence bolstered Caitlin. The water elemental was right. Liam would suffer, and it would be all Caitlin's fault. But Fergus wouldn't end his life until Caitlin gave up everything. Her freedom. Her life. All of it.

Fergus wanted her. The Thirteen wanted her. But Liam needed her more, and she'd fight until her last breath to find him. No matter what.

After a tense phone call with the rental car company—who thankfully could unlock the car remotely—Cade used Caitlin's phone to call Peter.

"Where the fuck have you been?" Peter asked. "I've been calling you for an hour. I need you back at Farren's. Now."

Cade bristled at Peter's tone. "Shut up and listen. Fergus showed up at the practitioner's. She's gone—I watched her fade away before my eyes—and that earth asshole took Liam. I had to shift, and my clothes are buried somewhere in the rubble. Along with my phone. Farren's too. I need you to meet us in Doolin at the back of O'Connor's Pub with fresh clothes, cash, and a new phone. Diedre gave us a book, but we haven't even opened it yet. We were too busy trying to get out of there alive."

Caitlin ran her fingers over the faded gold lettering. She couldn't remember much Gaelic from her youth, and the words were familiar, but only just.

"Liam? Oh, fuck. I think...I might know how Fergus found you. Abagail's gone. She was in the room when you called and told me you were going to Lisdoonvarna. Tierney saw her leave. He said she was angry about Colin's death, that she couldn't believe we weren't out looking for Brian. If she went to Fergus or if he found her..."

"Fuckin' hell," Farren muttered as she ran her hand through her white hair. She wore only her cloak, her bare legs covered in gooseflesh. "If I ever find her, I'm goin' to break every bone in her body. She always hated my job. Said I was puttin' us all in danger because I wouldn't turn away practitioners or elementals."

Peter choked out another apology, but Cade cut him off. "Unless you called Fergus himself and told him where we'd be, I don't want to hear it. Not until we get Liam back. Get clothes for all of us and meet us in Doolin. Go. Now."

Reaching under the dash, Cade yanked a few wires free. "I've only done this once," he muttered and started fiddling with the multi-colored strands. After several seconds, the car purred to life.

Caitlin opened the book's cover as they pulled out onto the main road. Symbols and runes she'd never seen covered the pages, along with scribbled words in Gaelic, Scottish Gaelic, and Latin.

Think. Mum taught you how to read all of these when you were young. You can do this. Liam's life depends on it.

Liam

Pain. Darkness. He tasted copper, tried to suck in a breath, but everything faded into an agonized howl. When the beat of his heart in his ears faded, he tried to raise his head, but didn't make it more than an inch before collapsing again.

Grit scraped against his eyelids, and whatever he was lying on bounced, his forehead slamming into metal.

Fuck. He was in the trunk of a car. That bastard had cut him, compelled him, tossed him in the boot, and now they were headed to God-knew-where.

He'd stood in front of Fergus like a trained dog waiting for a treat. How the fuck was the man that strong? The mark. Whatever the arse had carved into his chest. It had to be the same sigil he'd used on Colin.

With a groan, he tried flexing his hands and feet, assessing his injuries. His shirt stuck to his chest, the cuts deep and burning with a pain he'd never felt the likes of before. His right arm wouldn't move at all. Tingling and numbness spread down his arm. Dislocated, he'd bet.

Feeling along his chest with his left hand, he found the mark, still bleeding. Fuck. When he tried to move his legs, he howled, the agony sending him hurtling towards unconsciousness once more.

He remembered now. The cracking of his left femur. A roof support slamming into him.

An intense fit of nausea washed over him, and he struggled not to vomit in the confined space. He had to shift. His injuries would heal, and he'd rip the earth elemental's head off. Or maybe tear out his throat.

All he had to do was relax and call upon his wolf. But the shuddering, bumpy ride made that difficult.

Focus.

He reached for his wolf, his constant companion just under his skin, ready to break free at a moment's notice. The animal railed for freedom, clawing and fighting his way to the surface, then shrank away, almost whimpering.

No, that noise had come from the man.

What the bloody fuck?

Fergus's words came back to him. Whispered in his ear.

"The power of the Thirteen flows through me. I can command ya'. Control ya'. End ya' with a single word. Yer wolf will obey. Ya' will not shift. We forbid it. Ye'll remain a man for all the pain I have in store for ya'."

No! If he couldn't heal his broken bones and his dislocated shoulder, not to mention that fucking mark, he'd never be able to fight the daft bastard. And where was Caitlin? Had she escaped? He remembered her screaming his name, but then everything had gone dark.

"Caitlin!" he roared, banging on the lid of the boot until his knuckles bled. "Ya' fuckin' arse, what did ya' do to her?" The car lurched, tires squealing, and Liam rolled forward until his broken leg twisted and white-hot pain drove him out of his mind.

His wolf howled inside of him. The moon approached—less than twelve hours away, and the beast yearned to be free. Liam tried to hold on to the vision of Caitlin smiling, the memory of her touch, but as the motion of the car aggravated his injuries, he drifted in and out of consciousness. The pitch of the engine lowered, and the bouncing intensified. Occasional plinks of rocks and branches hit the undercarriage, and every time he jerked, the pain would send him sinking into unconsciousness once more.

Broken bones—and the agony they caused—could be ignored. Mostly. Every bone in his body shattered when he shifted, but they healed almost immediately. But the blood loss and the magic burning through him...those could be fatal.

He was too weak to do much more than raise his head. If he couldn't heal those damn cuts soon, he'd bleed out and die.

Time and time again he tried to shift, and once, he felt his skin ripple before his wolf ran away and hid deep inside.

They lurched to a stop, and Liam rolled and slammed into the front of the small enclosure. Muffled footsteps approached, and light blinded him as the trunk popped open.

Fergus laughed, a thin, rasping sound. "She's mine, wolf. And ye're goin' to help me teach her a lesson."

Fergus's punch knocked his head back, dimming his awareness for just long enough for the man to yank him up by his arms and throw him over his shoulder.

Dark spots obscured Liam's vision, and Fergus chuckled as a set of keys jingled. "Ya' touched what's mine. Made her think she could fight me."

"She...can," Liam managed. "She already...has. And she'll do it...again."

Down a set of stairs, the air turning staler with each step, and Liam fought to breathe. When Fergus slammed him down onto hard-packed earth, he gave up fighting and let the comfort of unconsciousness take him.

CHAPTER TWENTY-THREE

Caitlin

*H*er head ached, and her clothes smelled like burnt wood, mud, and Diedre's magic. She'd tried to make sense of the shaky scrawls, but between the bumpy ride, her lack of experience with runes and sigils, and worry for Liam, she couldn't decipher any of it.

"We should see if Paddy's still at O'Connor's," Farren said from beside her. "If anyone knows what those markings mean, it'll be him."

As Cade eased the car into the narrow alley behind the pub, Caitlin focused on Peter stalking towards them.

"Clothes," Cade said when he'd shoved the door open. He'd found a blanket in the trunk that he'd wrapped around his waist before getting into the car, but he tossed it at Peter before he yanked on his pants, a long-sleeved black shirt, and a pair of Keds.

Mara stripped off her sopping wet sweater and donned a dry

sweatshirt, then grimaced when Cade handed her a fresh pair of jeans.

"Stripping in a back alley in Ireland. I guess I can cross that off my bucket list." Mara almost glowed—a tall, red flame in the half-light of dusk—and Cade reached for her hand.

"Are you all right, honey? You look different."

She did. Caitlin elbowed Farren, and the female wolf focused on Mara. "Shite. Ya' look like yer hair's on fire."

"Whatever happened back there," she said, her voice taking on a hint of confusion, "it's like it helped me balance the two elements. A little. I'm not about to lose myself. At least not yet."

Peter continued to pace and mutter to himself quietly. "We have to do something. Liam's out there—"

"Stop." Cade took Peter by the shoulders and pushed him up against the wall. "We're no good to Liam if we fall apart. Once we get somewhere safe, we'll figure out what to do. You can feel guilty later."

Anxiety tugged at Caitlin's mind. Along with anger. The emotions weren't hers, though. Fergus was practically in a rage, and she feared he'd only keep Liam alive long enough to come after her. Because if he compelled her again, she didn't think she'd be strong enough to fight him.

"Hey," Mara said. "We have the book." Her cool touch on Caitlin's wrist and her gentle tone helped Caitlin take a steady breath and pull herself out of her own dark thoughts.

"Where can we go?" She forced a nod. "I need time. The internet. And a gallon of coffee."

"Mickey has a back room," Farren said. The female alpha had changed into a pair of black leather pants and a tight black sweater. "A shot of whiskey will clear ya' right up. Then coffee."

Farren ducked into the pub to see if Paddy lingered—and make sure Mickey would give them the space. A few tense moments later, she propped open the back door. "Come on, then."

The back room of O'Connor's carried the scent of stale cigars, fried fish, and whiskey. An old card table bore nicks and scars from decades of gambling, and along the back wall, boxes of vodka, gin, and whiskey sat on wooden pallets.

Paddy sat at the far end of the room, slouched in one of the hard wooden chairs. He'd removed his tweed cap to reveal a messy head of white hair, and he whispered to himself, rocking side to side every few words.

"Mickey's makin' coffee," Farren said. She slammed a bottle of Jameson in the center of the table, and six glasses waited for them. "We're safe here for at least an hour or two."

"Old Paddy isn't safe anywhere," the old man said and turned his watery stare to Farren. "They aren't either. Balance too far gone."

"What balance?" Farren asked, but Paddy just shook his head and poured himself a shot of whiskey.

"Can't say."

A hard tug on her element made Caitlin gasp, and the book slid from her hands. Pain and a bone-deep sadness swamped her. Her knees buckled, and she would have hit the ground if it weren't for Farren's arm around her waist.

"Easy now. Ya' need to eat," the wolf said. "I'll have Mickey—"

"It's Fergus." Caitlin pressed the heels of her hands against her temples, trying to focus through muddled thoughts and the emotions that weren't her own.

Jealousy.

Rage.

Desperate need.

"He's using my element. Help me."

Mara linked her fingers with Caitlin's, and the rising humidity in the room calmed her ragged breathing. The two women held on to one another, and after a few minutes, Caitlin started to feel better.

"What did you just do?" Mara asked.

Leaning against the back of the chair as her head pounded, Caitlin sighed. "When Fergus uses my air, I can't fight him. My element isn't...*mine* anymore. He controls it. That fuckin' spell made him the earth to my moon. I'm bound to him like gravity to the planet. This time, when he started taking my air, I tried...to give it to you."

"Is that smart?" Mara caught her lower lip under her teeth. "If I'm like him, won't giving me your air make me worse?"

Cade reached for her hand, bringing her wrist to his nose and inhaling deeply. "How do you feel, honey?"

"I'm fine, Cade. Really. Using my sister's fire at Diedre's *hurt*. More than ever before, but somehow, I didn't lose myself completely. I still had my water. I was still...*me*. I'm just a little queasy. I need coffee. And some fries. And an ice pack." She rubbed her neck, where deep purple bruises from Fergus's hand darkened her pale skin.

"I don't think ya' can *use* my air," Caitlin said. "More like...I'm channelin' it through ya'."

No one spoke for a moment, until Farren ran a hand through her white hair. "So who's left at the house? Tierney and Ewan?" Her voice took on a rough edge, and her face betrayed the strength she'd forced into her words.

Cade shot Peter a look, and the scarred wolf nodded and dropped down into the chair next to Paddy.

"Why didn't ya' warn me?" Farren demanded, giving Paddy a gentle prod to his shoulder. "I was with ya' for almost three days! Ya' can't tell me ya' didn't know. Brian turned twenty-two a week ago. He'd started courtin' a lass in Dublin. Had his whole life ahead of him." Tears spilled over her long lashes and glistened on the bruise healing along her jaw.

Paddy's blue eyes darkened, and he sat up straighter. "Paddy warned ya'. Best he could. Told ya' no one would survive this, he did. Ya' chose not to listen."

Farren slammed her glass of whiskey on the table and it

tipped over, the drink coming perilously close to the book before Caitlin snatched it up and cradled it to her chest. "Ya' told me there was danger about. That magic would destroy all I held dear. Ya' never told me *Fergus* had magic in him. And what good is anythin' ya' say if ya' don't tell me how to stop it?"

"Quiet," Paddy spat, and the whole room gaped until his voice softened again. "Much of this world remains hidden from ya'. From all of us. Paddy sees bits and pieces when he's meant to. Find comfort, despite yer anger. Fire burns all, and the answer is but a feather on the wind."

Farren swiped at her cheeks and poured herself another shot of whiskey. "Will ya' tall me one thing? One straight answer?"

"Paddy'll try."

"Will we be safe if we go back to my home?"

"Safety comes from family."

"Fuck me," she muttered and reached for the bottle again.

Caitlin turned her attention to the book, but before she could open it, Paddy touched her arm, then ran his wrinkled fingers over the cover. "Bonny words for a dark day. Twistin' and weavin' until two become three and three become four."

"Again with the riddles." Farren pushed to her feet and started to pace. "What the hell does that mean?"

"The world balances under a rare moon."

"Fuck me, Paddy. *One* straight answer. I've put up with ya' for more than a decade. Let ya' guide me with those daft words. But if ya' can't give us anythin' that makes any sense, what good are ya'?"

"Far'n, ya' do not listen." Paddy's lips pressed together, his wrinkles even more pronounced, and he turned to Caitlin. "Ya' understand Paddy, lass?"

"No."

"The old one is gone. Ya' will."

THEY HEADED BACK to Farren's, but only five minutes outside of Lahinch, Caitlin suddenly sat up straight. "Wait. I know this road."

Cade slowed and pulled over, scraggly bushes scraping against the car doors. "How?"

"There's a house, a shack, really, where he'd take me—" her voice cracked, "—when he wanted to punish me. It's not far."

"You think he'd take Liam there?" Farren asked.

"I don't know." She tried to sense the other half of her element, the man who'd bound her, and the wolf who loved her. But where back at O'Connor's there'd been rage and desperation, now...she felt nothing. "I don't think he's close. But we should go, yeah? Maybe Fergus left somethin' behind we could use."

"Tell me where to go," Cade said.

She directed him down a one-lane road, past a farm with grazing goats, an abandoned shack missing a wall.

Lowering the window, she inhaled deeply. Fresh grass, a recent rain shower. And the rich leather of Liam's jacket around her shoulders.

"There." Ahead on the right, the fence still stood, though the paint was peeling off in long ribbons. Up on the rise, a burned-out shell of the home stood sentry over the countryside, a single support beam and a handful of planks all that remained. The walls—thick knotty pine that had warded off the worst of Ireland's damp chill once he'd sealed them to be almost airtight —had disintegrated into ash.

Cade passed the home and rounded a bend, finding a narrow pullout next to a hedgerow of blackberries. "We stick together. Farren and I will shift. Mara, you're with Caitlin. If Fergus is there, the two of you have to stick together. And fight."

"We will."

As Cade stripped off his sweatshirt, Mara gave him an appreciative look, just for a moment, and he cupped her cheek. "Are you sure you're up for this?"

Leaning forward, she kissed him gently. "Liam's my brother. I won't give up on him, and I won't let his mate be taken by that fucking asshole who tried to kill all of us. Stop treating me like I'm broken. I'm not. Sick, maybe. Troubled. But not broken."

Despite the strength of Mara's words, Caitlin thought the word really did fit her. Something about Katerina's element *had* broken Mara, just like Caitlin's air had broken Fergus.

As the wolves dropped to their hands and knees, Caitlin couldn't look away. Bones popped and cracked, their skin rippled. Farren's small, firm breasts shrank back into her body, and a magnificent white tail sprouted from her arse. Her face changed shape, muzzle lengthening, and sharp teeth glistened as she growled. She was magnificent. Pale, almost silvery fur with the barest hint of gray stripes, and luminous gray eyes.

Next to her, Cade's steel and flaxen fur ruffled in the breeze, and Caitlin couldn't close her mouth fast enough. "Wow."

Farren's vocalization was almost pride, and she tossed her head back, curving her dark lips into what Caitlin thought had to be a smile. With Cade next to her, they were an unstoppable force.

"Come on. They'll stay with us," Mara said as she pulled a flashlight from the glove box.

The four of them picked their way over rocks and the occasional culvert until they reached a low stone wall just behind the ruins of the home.

"Work with me," Mara said as she called upon her water element. "Fog."

Shock gave Caitlin a second of pause. Mara was smart, capable, and almost completely unafraid. "How'd you know...?"

"I live in Seattle. We get plenty of fog." Mara cracked a weak smile, and Caitlin sent a feeble air charm towards the water elemental.

The wolves jumped over the wall with ease. Mara and Caitlin

were slower, but once they landed on the other side, the base-ment doors were only a few feet away.

She remembered those doors. The sound they made as Fergus slammed them shut, sealing her inside. The way the air would grow staler and staler until she could barely breathe. Until she'd just lie on the old, thin mattress, waiting to die, praying for it.

The dark stairway descended into an earthen maw, the steps worn by wind and rain and time. Cade descended with a low growl, charging ahead with his head lowered. Farren followed, and Caitlin stayed as close to Mara as she could.

Fergus had loved this room, and she shuddered as she passed under the house's rotting foundation.

The small basement was no more than twenty feet square, and Mara swept the beam of light over everything. "Oh, God. Someone...slept down here?"

Nothing had changed. The remains of the rotting mattress still lay in the corner opposite a toilet and a metal pipe dripping water.

"I did," Caitlin whispered. "He'd lock me down here when he needed to teach me a *lesson*. Every time he found me and dragged me back from wherever I'd managed to run to. He'd keep me here a week or two. The doors—the ones that used to be there—were sealed with resin. No air in or out. I can't...I can't stay."

She fled back up the stairs, and when she reached the surface, she fell to her knees and sucked in great lungfuls of air, trying to remind herself that Fergus wasn't here. That he didn't have the same power over her that he once did—even if he could still try to compel her.

Mara and Cade joined her a moment later. "Farren's nosing around down there, just in case," Mara said while Cade sat next to her, his warm, lupine body a solid weight against her side.

Caitlin wished she felt comfortable enough to hold on to him.

She didn't want Cade's wolf. She wanted Liam's. Shite. She loved Liam and she'd never even touched his wolf.

"He came here," Caitlin rasped. "I don't know when. But sometime in the past week. I can feel him. His element. And a hint of magic. But Liam was never here."

Cade's low sound—not exactly a bark, not a growl—confused her, and she looked to Mara. "He agrees with you."

"How do you do that? Understand him?" Caitlin got to her feet, and Cade padded over to Mara, sitting up tall so she could rub his head.

"You'll learn. You just have to listen. Every wolf is different. The few times I've been around Liam's wolf...it's almost like his wolf has an accent too." Mara's eyes unfocused for a brief moment, and she leaned harder against Cade.

"Mara?"

"I'm okay. Using both elements at Diedre's...the exhaustion finally hit."

Cade whined, nudging her palm and sniffing all along her wrist before a low growl rumbled through him.

"I'm *fine*, shaggy man. Calm down."

Farren padded up the stairs and shook her massive head. Nothing. Caitlin wasn't surprised.

"Is there anywhere else he might have taken Liam?" Mara asked. "What about that castle? The one where the dead elemental was found. You said he used to bring you there when he wanted to take someone's element. We passed it earlier. It's close, right?"

Farren barked and jerked her head north. Cade's response confused Caitlin, but Mara offered her an encouraging smile. "That means 'let's go.'"

Despite her desperate need to find and save Liam, worry slid up Caitlin's spine on the way back to the car. Cade and Farren— still in wolf form—jumped into the back seat, while Mara handed Caitlin the keys.

"You know where we're going more than I do. Plus, you've actually driven on this side of the road before."

Not to mention, I don't look like I'm about to pass out.

Caitlin paused with the key in the ignition. "What are we goin' to do if he *is* there? We don't have a plan..." Cade and Farren growled in tandem, and Caitlin didn't need Mara to translate this time. "We don't even know if killin' him is going to make a difference. Or maybe...it'll make things worse. What if the Thirteen come after us? They'll know if he dies. The brand they gave him—they'll feel it."

"He's power-hungry and desperate. Just like my sister was." Mara rubbed the spot between her breasts where the fragment of Katerina's crystal was still embedded in her skin. "So tell me this. Would Katerina have ever expected Cade and his pack to come after me at the hotel?"

She didn't have to think about it for more than a second. "No. She was positive they'd do exactly what she said. Because she held all the cards. You."

"Exactly." Mara glanced back at Cade and Farren. "We have two alpha wolves with us and three elements." Her mate growled, and she shot him a look. "I won't use my fire unless I have no other choice. I promise."

Caitlin turned the key, equal parts terrified, determined, and angry. Fergus had taken so much from her. He didn't get to take Liam too. "All right. The castle's not far. If he's there, ya' have to stay back, Mara. He wants ya' now, and ya' haven't had as much experience fightin' him as I have."

"I'll stay with Cade the whole time," she said, her green eyes almost glowing as she spun water droplets from palm to palm, raising the humidity inside the car and filling it with her unique scent.

Please, be there, Liam. And please be alive. I'm coming for you, luv. I promise.

FIVE STORIES TALL, with gaping, empty windows that let the wind howl through the spires, the old castle rose from the mists, illuminated only by the last vestiges of dusk and the headlights of the rental car.

The gate wasn't locked, and the four of them hurried inside, two by two. Caitlin couldn't sense Fergus, and told them so, but that didn't mean he wasn't using magic to hide his presence.

The wolves bounded to the top of the main tower, snarls and rough vocalizations carrying down the crumbling steps. Caitlin and Mara took a more cautious route, needing flashlights to guard against the uneven ground. At the top, they spilled out into an empty cavernous room.

In the eastern corner, a large, blackened circle marked the spot where the last elemental had died, and Farren sniffed all around it, pawing at some of the soot, until she uncovered a bit of gold, melted, with a ruby in the center. With a yip, she called to Mara, and the water elemental knelt next to her. "You want me to take this with us?"

Farren nodded, then made a small, mournful sound neither of the two women understood.

"He hasn't been here in days," Caitlin said and sagged against the wall next to one of the largest windows. The glass had broken decades ago, long before she and Fergus had found the place and claimed this room as their own. Memories of youthful charms— her bouncing rocks upon the air, him rippling the ground below like a ribbon—brought the melody of laughter to her ears. They'd been happy then, free and full of dreams.

If only he'd never left to go to Scotland. Maybe they'd still be happy. Maybe she and Liam would have mated long ago.

She gazed out over the sloping hillside. From here, she could see all the way down to the water. An unearthly glow shimmered at the edge of the horizon. The wolves scrambled through the rest of the structure, their toenails scraping against the weathered stone all around her and into the other, barely-accessible spires that Caitlin knew had to be empty.

A luminous, yellow moon rose, peaceful and calm along the barrier between sea and sky. Mesmerized, Caitlin tracked the movement from a sliver to a wedge, and finally, glorious fullness, illuminating the lands for miles. A blazing arc of light stretched over the water, and behind them, the two wolves howled mournfully.

Deep in her core, a yearning she'd never known twisted and stabbed, and she braced her hands on the edge of the stone and screamed into the night, "Liam!"

CHAPTER TWENTY-FOUR

Liam

*T*he scent of dirt filled his nose, along with the harsh, metallic scent of his blood. Lying on his side, his broken leg bent underneath him, every breath sent pure, unending agony shooting through him.

The wound to his side throbbed, but the last time he'd tried to shift before Fergus had pulled him out of the car's boot, he'd at least come close to stopping the bleeding.

He had to find a way out of here so he could get to his Caitlin. To stop that bastard from using him to force her hand. He knew her—knew himself too—and knew if their positions were reversed, there was no way he'd let her suffer for a single minute if he had the means to save her.

Rolling onto his back sent him into oblivion again, and he had no idea how much time had passed when he came to with a whimper. Reaching for his wolf, he fought against the magic holding the beast captive. He'd been born an alpha for fuck's sake. One of the strongest wolves in all of Ireland, his da' used to say. He could find a way to break free.

His fingers twitched and burned with the need to shift, but before the bones could break, an invisible weight slammed into his chest, and he couldn't breathe.

The beast faded into the shadows, angry as fuck but hobbled just the same.

Still, he tried again and again, until exhaustion turned him into a shivering, shaking mess. "Caitlin." The single word scraped over his raw throat, but it brought him a measure of comfort.

Until he felt the rise of the moon.

The searing pain of loss fractured his thoughts, and his wolf slammed against the chains that bound him, the desperate need to claim his mate giving him strength that took him by surprise.

"Move," he whispered to no one. "Get the fuck up and move."

Liam pushed up to one knee, and after the room stopped spinning, he felt all around him until his hand hit a cold stone wall.

Ignore the pain. You break bones all the time.

He'd just managed to force his broken leg straight and fought off another wave of dizziness from the motion when the earth started to shake all around him. Fergus. Fuck. He wasn't strong enough yet. He needed more time.

Unable to remain upright, he fell over with a stifled moan as the door slammed open.

Blinding light seared his eyes, and he turned his head away. Until rough hands grabbed him by the arms and shoved him against the wall.

"Ya' touched my Caitie. Turned her against me." Fergus shook him hard enough for his head to slam into the rough stones more than once, and blood trickled down his neck. The elemental's eyes were wild, and his words almost slurred as he raged.

"Ya' did that all yerself, fucker."

The small bit of satisfaction Liam drew from taunting the

man died as he sailed across the room, hitting the other wall with a sickening pop to his shoulder. Though his arm started to tingle, no longer completely numb.

The idiot had managed to *fix* his dislocated shoulder.

"She belongs to me. I hold her element. We're closer than any lovers could ever be." Spit flew from his thin lips as he bit off the words, and Liam shoved himself up onto an elbow. "Ya' thought ya' could come between us? That ya' could steal her away? Mate with her? I'm in control. Not some pathetic wolf who can't even shift."

Liam studied him, pacing back and forth in the dimly lit space. Fergus's hands clenched and unclenched, his fingers shaking with rage—and maybe something else. His eyes weren't simply wild. They were bloodshot too. The man looked positively green, and his entire body was wracked with tremors.

"Ye're sick, Fergus. When was the last time ya' had yer meds?" Liam managed to prop himself against the wall, his broken leg throbbing with every breath, but his vision had cleared enough to see how bad off the arse was.

"I don't need them," Fergus snarled, and Liam had to wipe his cheek with the back of his hand. "They stop me from usin' my air."

Liam was too far from the door. He'd never make it out of here with his leg as bad off as it was. But if he could distract Fergus long enough to start inching closer...

"It's not yer air, ya' daft bastard. It's Caitlin's."

With a roar, Fergus grabbed his ankle and yanked him halfway across the room. Liam's scream echoed against the stone walls, and spots floated in his vision.

Focus. Stay awake. Find a way to get to him.

"Did ya' take her from me eleven years ago? Did ya'?" Fergus kicked Liam in the ribs, and the resulting crack made each breath feel like he was being stabbed.

"No," he gasped. "Ye're hurtin' her, Fergus. Can't ya' see that?

Caitlin cares for ya'. Even now. She told me she does." The moon tugged hard on his soul, demanding he get to his mate, demanding he shift, but though he tried, reaching for his wolf again despite the pain, he couldn't manage to do more than roll onto his back with a groan.

Fergus stopped his frantic pacing and pressed his hands against his temples. "Caitie," he wailed. "I need ya'! It hurts too much!"

"What hurts? I can help, mate. Just let me shift, and I'll help." Fergus stood between him and the door, and he tried to sit up again, failed, and hissed out a breath. "She won't come, Fergus. Not while ye're like this. Ya' can feel the mania, yeah?"

"They won't let me go!" He yanked up his shirt and tried to claw at the dark red brand on his skin. It almost glowed with power, and Liam turned onto his side. One more inch close to the door. "I need my Caitie so we can finish what we started! She never would have left me if it hadn't been for ya'. I know that now."

"Caitlin left ya' because ya' hurt her. Because ya' took her air. Give it back. Let me shift and I'll go to her. We'll help ya'. I promise."

Fergus's voice softened, turning almost child-like. "Yeah?"

"I've no beef with ya'. Not if ya' let her go." He didn't care if he was lying through his teeth. Anything to get Fergus to listen to him. "Where are the meds ya' take?"

Fergus retreated into his own little world of sorrow. His broad shoulders collapsed inward, and he hunched, his lower lip jutting out slightly. Reaching into his pocket, he pulled out a prescription bottle, and the pills inside rattled as his hand shook.

"That's right, mate. Ya' need one of those pills."

His fingers fumbled with the cap, and he shook two of them into his hand, then stared at them for so long, Liam risked closing the distance between him and the door by another couple of inches.

"I'll never be free," Fergus said as he choked back a sob. The pills fell to the ground, and the desperate, needy boy disappeared before Liam's eyes. His hand flew, sending the ground rolling and bucking under Liam.

Can't breathe!

The charm pulled all the air into a tornado swirling around the earth elemental, and Liam made a desperate, feral sound as he tried to suck in even half a breath.

"Fer...gus," he rasped. "Please..."

His vision faded almost to nothing, and then, the pressure banding around his chest eased, the ground stopped shaking, and the air stilled. Fergus stood over him, his eyes dark. "I need my Caitie." He ripped Liam's shirt open, pulled his phone from his pocket, and snapped a picture of the still-bleeding deep cuts to Liam's chest. "She'll come back to me when she sees what I can do to ya'."

Liam fought to even lift his head. "No. She won't. If ya' kill me, she'll never be yers again. Ya' keep hurtin' her. That's why she threw herself off the cliffs in the first place. Because ya' hurt her. Take yer meds. Let me go. And we'll help ya' however we can."

Disgust twisted his expression, and he started to chant. Liam struggled to understand the Gaelic words, and rocks worked their way up from the ground underneath him. At first small, then larger and larger until Fergus had buried him almost to his chest.

The pressure threatened to crush him, and when Fergus snatched up a rock the size of a baseball and slammed it into Liam's skull, he stopped fighting. He was going to die, and now, he wouldn't even see Caitlin one last time.

"I need her," Fergus whispered. "Ya' have to bring her back to me."

Caitlin

The moon shimmered over the low stone wall surrounding Farren's estate and Caitlin couldn't stop staring at it. She lay on a plush mattress in the bedroom she and Liam had claimed as theirs, watching two wolves—Tierney and Ewan, she thought—playing tag at the edge of the property.

The absurdity of the game brought an inappropriate laugh bubbling up until her tears spilled over.

She'd spent over three hours with the book, ignoring Mara and Cade's urges to eat, looking up each rune, and scouring the internet for the various sigils—all but four of which she'd never seen before.

Eventually, her eyes had started to cross, and she'd trudged up the stairs, the book and Farren's laptop tucked under her arm, and collapsed on the bed wrapped in Liam's leather jacket.

"Caitlin?" Farren asked from the threshold.

Hastily swiping at her cheeks, Caitlin turned around. "I'm okay."

"No, ye're not. But I wouldn't expect ya' to be." Farren combed her fingers through her silver locks and eased herself down onto the edge of the bed. "Rest is what ya' need right now. We'll start searchin' again at first light."

"It's been six hours," Caitlin said with a sniffle. "It'll be a miracle if he's still alive."

Farren shifted closer and wrapped her arms around Caitlin. The touching gesture was unexpected, but not entirely unwelcome. "Liam's the strongest wolf I've ever met. And he loves ya'. That's a powerful motivator to survive, yeah?"

"It wasn't powerful enough for me. I loved him eleven years ago. And I still tried to end it all." She turned away, pulling out of Farren's embrace to sit up and stare out the window again. "What if I can't figure out that damn book? I know what the runes stand for, but that doesn't help me decipher what they mean. And the sigils? It's almost impossible to figure out another practitioner's sigils. They're...personal. Every time I think I might have found something, it turns out to be gibberish. Worse than Paddy's ramblings."

"Ah, Paddy. That man is lucky no one's murdered him for bein' so cryptic and daft." Farren scooted so her back was against the headboard, stretched her legs out, and yawned. "My wolf wants to run, and I'm goin' to let her in a few. But first, a story. Lie down and try to relax, yeah?"

"I can't take the time to sleep," Caitlin protested.

"Ya' will or ya' won't do him a damn bit of good. Someone will wake ya' in just a few hours. Now listen up, and don't be as stubborn as yer mate."

The alpha wolf's presence helped calm her, as did her imposing personality. She wasn't as confrontational as Cade. Nor as angry. Not even after everything she'd been through. No, she projected a confidence that Caitlin couldn't ignore. Sliding down, she wrapped her arms around one of the pillows and pretended Liam was with her.

Farren intertwined her fingers behind her head and stared up at the ceiling. "I met Liam when we were just pups. Six, I think. Our parents' packs were close. Lived only a few kilometers away from one another. We spent a lot of time together tryin' to listen in when our parents met to discuss pack business. My mum worked for the Garda." Farren's voice swelled with pride. "A detective. She could tell any time a suspect lied to her. There's a scent, yeah? Like fear. Ya' sweat more when ya' lie."

Caitlin almost laughed. "That couldn't have been pleasant."

"Not to hear her tell it." Farren patted Caitlin's shoulder. "Liam and I went to school together. And a fair bit of trouble we got into—almost had our parents convinced to separate us permanently. When we were fifteen, his mum and da' moved their pack to Kilkenny, but Liam had two more years of school in Dublin, so he moved in with us part time."

There was so much about Liam she still needed to learn. So many stories he'd never had the chance to tell her. Would he ever?

"We decided we'd go to this rock concert in the worst part of Dublin. Knife fights, killin's, drugs—there was a reason our parents had always forbidden us from goin'. But we were young and stupid. Sure enough, we no sooner get there and the whole place is raided. Some feckin' drug ring usin' the pub as a home base."

"Oh shite. What happened? Were ya' arrested?" Caitlin peered up at Farren, and the alpha wolf had a faraway look in her gray eyes.

"Liam and I end up runnin' for our lives with some of the lower level thugs from the drug ring. Once we were far enough away to be safe, they turned on us. Wanted all our cash, my class ring..." She shook her head and huffed out what might be a laugh. "We refused, and one of them drew a switchblade. We weren't afraid of a wee knife. We were wolves. But so was the ringleader. Told us if we even tried to shift, he'd gut us from neck to navel. But Liam...bein' the overconfident arse he is—started chatting the arse up about how we were the worst choice to kill because of some ridiculous connection his da' had to the Irish mafia, and if they let us go, we'd be willin' to overlook their mistake."

"They didn't believe ya', did they?"

Farren grinned, her delicate features softening in amusement. "Aye, they did. That boy could spin a tale like no one else. And he never quit—even when we were backed into a corner, he kept going until they listened."

Sadness settled deep in her core. "I've never seen that side of him."

"Ya' will. I know it. He's tougher than he looks, and not just because he's got a thick pelt—and a hard head. He's pure stubbornness and steel, that one. Don't underestimate him. He'll survive this. No matter where he is, his wolf's feelin' the pull of the moon. And the matin'. That'll keep him goin'. If ya' can find Fergus, we'll beat the bastard and get Liam back."

Caitlin closed her eyes and shuddered. "I didn't want to kill him. He's a victim too, ya' know? The Thirteen bound him every bit as much as he bound me. But now...after seein' him at Diedre's, I don't know that there's anything left of him worth savin'."

"Then we kill him."

Tears burned Caitlin's eyes, and she ducked her head as she tried to dash them away without Farren seeing. "I wish it were that simple. Diedre implied the book could help us save Mara. That it could break the Thirteen's hold over Fergus even. That is had all the answers we needed. Fergus is a monster—of that I have no doubt. He has Liam, and I know he's hurtin' him." A sob choked her, and Farren reached over to rub her back. "But can we really kill him when there's a chance we could save him?"

Farren hugged herself tightly, her brow furrowed in contemplation. "Cade told me a bit about ya'. About what happened to ya' with Mara's sister."

Caitlin squeezed her eyes shut, unsure she could handle seeing any judgement on Farren's face.

"Ya' carry a terrible lot of guilt for what happened, even though ya' had little choice. But Fergus had a choice. I faced him down, Caitlin. And for a few minutes here and there, he was sane. He listened to me. Even expressed a wee bit of remorse. But even when he was poppin' those pills, there was still a side of him that didn't want to listen. There's evil in him, luv. Evil that almost killed me."

Farren's tone softened. "I understand ya' want to be compassionate, and that ya' can even contemplate it? Speaks to yer character. I'm not that forgivin'. But if there is any good left in the bloke, could he live, knowin' what he'd done? If there's even a part of the man ya' say he was left, he'd wish himself dead to escape the reality of who he's become."

Caitlin's eyes burned with unshed tears. For the Fergus who might have been. For Liam, whose only crime was loving her. For her own sorrow as she relived everything she'd done under his control.

Farren gave her shoulder one final squeeze. "Killin' isn't always an act of retribution, luv. Sometimes, it's an act of mercy. Ya' need to remember that, because ye're not on yer own anymore. Ya' chose Liam. Chose to love him and everythin' that comes with him. We're all yer family now. We'll stand with ya'. And we'll face the consequences of all of our actions, together."

CHAPTER TWENTY-FIVE

Caitlin

*D*ark dreams haunted her sleep, and after two hours, Caitlin gave up. Her muscles ached, and her head throbbed. Farren was right. She was no used to anyone like this. Perhaps a bath would help. At the very least, it would wash Fergus's scent off her.

After fiddling with the brass knobs of the claw-foot tub, she stripped and pulled off the leather pouch with the red jasper. Almost immediately, Fergus's tether to her strengthened, and she braced herself against the counter.

Her mother had believed in the power of healing stones. So had Katerina.

And the smoky quartz had worked for Mara. Caitlin pulled the stone from the bag and clutched it in her hand until she steadied. Could this one piece of jasper really hold enough power to help her escape Fergus?

She sunk into the steaming water, unfurling her fingers to

stare at the stone. After everything that had happened, she'd need to cleanse it—and soon. Mara's quartz too.

If nothing else, the process would distract her from all the disturbing images her imagination was conjuring of Liam. Bleeding. Broken. Dying.

The hot water soothed her muscles, but she couldn't linger. Not with so much at stake. She braided her hair, then, needing to feel closer to Liam, rummaged in the suitcase for one of his flannel shirts to wear over her black leggings and boots.

A small box the size of her palm fell out of the pocket and popped open. "Oh, my God." Inside, a thin, braided leather necklace rested on a bed of tissue paper, and hanging from the leather, an amber pendant.

A small card was tucked into the lid, as she read her mate's words, tears burned her eyes.

My dearest Caitlin,

When I knew you back in Dublin, you always wore an amber pendant. After you gave Mara your quartz, I knew I had to find something to replace it. I love you, Caitlin. I always will.

Liam

Now, more than ever, she needed the healing, balance, and self-confidence amber could provide. And she needed Liam. Swiping away her tears, she put on the necklace, gathered the white sage smudge stick, the red jasper, and the rest of the quartz before heading downstairs.

Only a few lights remained blazing in the main room. A wolf curled up on one of the couches—Tierney by the color of his fur, and she heard the occasional snore from the back of the house.

Farren, her silver pelt shining in the moonlight, paced just outside the back door. When Caitlin took a seat at a small table on the stone patio, the wolf padded over and gave her an inquisitive yip.

"I'm going to cleanse my jasper and the extra quartz I picked up in Dublin. Crystals absorb negative energy. Or, at least that's what my mum believed. This...maybe it'll help change our luck."

Farren lay down next to her, and Caitlin reached down to stroke her fur. "I didn't expect you to be...soft."

The soft vocalization almost sounded like a laugh, and her tail thumped on the stone.

"You like that?" A nod, and Caitlin sobered. "All right. When I light the sage, focus your thoughts and intentions on finding Liam."

White smoke swirled around her, calming her frayed nerves. Drawing a sigil in the air over the stones, she offered up her intention.

For Liam. For Mara. For me. Protect us all, and lead me back to my mate.

Cleansing took so much out of her. The intense focus she sent into the task always left her feeling like she'd lost a part of herself, but under the light of the full moon, the process energized her.

After sealing the cleansing by drawing a sigil over her heart, she retrieved the book and laptop and curled up under a blanket on a chaise lounge.

Farren returned to her human form, and joined Caitlin after lighting a fire pit a few feet away. "How can I help?"

"See if any of the runes I've identified make any sense?"

Caitlin passed her a notebook where she'd copied the names of the runes down in precise order, and went back to researching sigils. After an hour, the door to the house clicked, and Tierney joined them with three mugs of coffee. "I thought ya' might be chilled," he said, his deep voice and accent reminiscent of Liam's.

"Do either of you speak Gaelic?" Caitlin asked.

"Aye. We both speak a little." Tierney pulled up a chair, and Caitlin averted her gaze from his bare chest. She knew wolves didn't care much about being naked in front of one another, but the only man she ached to see that way was her mate.

"Sigils are different from runes," she explained. "Runes are very much like the alphabet. Each symbol has a specific meaning. They don't change. So, this symbol—" she pointed to an X, "—is the rune *Geofu*. It means a promise has been made. This other one that looks a little like a *P* is *Thorn,* and it warns us to take caution because there are hazards ahead."

"And the sigils?" Tierney asked. "They have a lot more lines."

Caitlin took a sip of the strong coffee as she toyed with the amber pendant around her neck. "Sigils are made. Created by any practitioner—or even one without magic—for a basic intent." She sketched the symbol that had been carved into Colin's back—the same one the practitioners had used to brand Fergus.

"This one is for control. Ya' can see how the two vertical lines and the circle represent a person, yeah?" She waited for them to nod before continuing. "The half circle underneath the person is the magic that controls them. They're helpless to it. The magic is too big, too vast to escape. But that's the Thirteen's sigil. You won't find it used by many others. It's not in this book at all."

"So how do ya' figure out what all these sigils are then?" Farren asked.

"There are two types in this book. The first is like the sigil of control. Those...ya' need to interpret based on what ya' see in them. But the others...there's a second way ya' can make a sigil. First, ya' write down yer intention. Say, 'I want to find Liam.' Then, cross out all of the vowels. W-N-T-T-F-N-D-L-M. Now take all of those letters and make a symbol out of them." She sketched each letter in turn, spinning the paper as she went, until she had an intricate design that almost looked...pretty. "The power is in the creation—and the intention. The symbol alone holds none if ya' don't believe in it. Unless, of course, it's backed by the world's most powerful practitioners."

Tierney focused on one of the more complicated sigils. "It's like a word scramble, then. Without vowels."

"Somethin' like that, yeah." Caitlin tore a few pages out of the notebook with the sigils she thought had been made from words alone and handed them to the young wolf. "Have at it."

SUNRISE WAS STILL two hours away when her phone buzzed on the table, making all six of them flinch. Mara, Cade, and Ewan had joined them only minutes before, and with a fresh pot of coffee, and two additional notebooks, Caitlin thought they might finally be getting somewhere.

"No!" Caitlin cried when she saw the message waiting for her. *Time for your lesson, Caitie.*

A video of Liam played on a loop. Her wolf was half-buried by rocks and dirt, the scene lit only by a dim light from behind Fergus. Blood oozed from a deep gash on his temple, and on his chest... No. The same sigil the Thirteen had used to brand Fergus. He shuddered, fighting for each shallow breath.

"Fucking asshole," Cade growled.

"I...I can't." Caitlin's hands were shaking too much to reply, so she thrust the phone at Farren. "T-tell him...Liam's innocent. He has nothing to do with this. Tell him I'll give myself up—I'll come back—if he'll just let Liam go."

"Like hell you will." Cade snatched the phone away, and Caitlin shoved the chair back and got in the alpha wolf's face.

"Do ya' think I want to? I'd do anythin' to never see that man again. To stop him so he couldn't hurt another person, another wolf, another elemental! But he has my mate."

The two faced off until Mara rose and linked her arm with Cade's. "You told me what happened when Katerina took me. How you fought with Liam and the rest. What you were prepared to do. Can you really blame Caitlin for being willing to do the same?"

"She's not alpha of this pack."

"No. She's not. But she's Liam's mate." Mara gently turned Cade towards her and held his gaze. "I'm not suggesting we just let her go without a plan or backup. We're family, and we're with her until the end. But don't scream at the poor woman."

Cade scowled, but his entire demeanor shifted in that moment. "Fine. But you're not just going to him alone."

"Right now," Caitlin said, hugging herself tightly to try to stop shaking, "I just need him to stop torturing Liam."

Farren held out her hand for the phone, and started typing.

Liam's an innocent, Fergus. Can't you see what you're doing to him? He did nothing to you, and you're killing him. Let him go and I'll come back to you.

Nothing happened for several minutes, and Caitlin paced, Farren hovering close by, while Cade stalked to the edge of the large grassy area behind the house, grabbed a couple of large rocks, and threw them at nearby trees. Each one hit with finality, accompanied by deep, rough sounds of frustration, until he'd apparently calmed enough to rejoin the rest of them.

"He's playing with us," Farren said, frowning. "Or he's lost it again."

Caitlin couldn't focus on anything besides the video of Liam. She traced the outlines of his face, and she could almost feel his stubble rasp over her fingers.

When the phone vibrated again, her heart sank.

I'll consider letting him live. But you have to bring me the other elemental. The one with fire and water. Do that, and I'll let him go.

THEY'D BEEN ARGUING for an hour. Cade, Mara, Peter, and Farren. There was no way Cade would let Mara go anywhere near Fergus. Mara kept insisting she had to, because Liam would do it for her. Peter and Farren tried to be voices of reason, but with all the shouting from outside the French doors, it didn't appear they were having much luck.

Caitlin, Tierney, and Ewan had moved inside to the pack's large dining room table, still hoping the runes and sigils could provide answers. Some way to keep Mara safe, to take back Caitlin's air, and to bind Fergus's magic long enough to overpower him or kill him.

"Maybe it's exhaustion, but this is startin' to make some sense," Caitlin said, almost to herself.

"How?" Tierney sat up a little straighter. "Ya' want to talk it out?"

"The order's reversed. Right to left across the page, bottom to top. I think. At least, that's the only way I can see it working. Because if I read the runes that way, I come up with this."

She traced her finger along the symbols as she explained. "We're facin' what seems like an insurmountable obstacle. That's Ur reversed. Followed by a reversed Thorn. We have to be careful or we'll lose everything. Then there's Hagall—a sudden and unexpected change. After that, the next line has Eolh, the protection rune, on either side of six copies of Tir. That's the warrior rune. There are seven of us total. If I'm battling Fergus, it could mean the six of you: Farren, Cade, Mara, Peter, Ewan, and you. You're with me."

"Well, that's a given," Tierney said with a huff. "We're not lettin' ya' go alone."

"This next bit, I didn't understand until just now." Caitlin tapped four symbols, all of which looked like some version of a triangle. "These aren't sigils or runes. They're alchemical symbols for Earth, Air, Fire, and Water."

"Just how daft are these practitioners, anyway?" Ewan asked. "They couldn't have stuck to a single language?"

Caitlin huffed out a laugh. "Would have been a mite easier. But look at this. They're arranged in pairs. Earth and Air, Fire and Water. Logical, yeah?"

The two wolves nodded.

"Except in the center, you have the rune Gefu. It's a promise. There's no reverse of it, so this line doesn't tell us whether the promise is kept or broken. Diedre—the practitioner—she said something I didn't understand at the time. 'In the end, only if ye're willin' to sacrifice everythin' will ya' succeed. Ya' can only take what is freely given.' When Fergus took my element, the words he used...he said, 'Ya' give me this gift freely.' So what if this is part of the spell? The promise. The willin' promise."

"I don't understand. Even if it is, how does that help?" Tierney headed for the kitchen and came back with the coffee pot, refilling all of their mugs. "We need the spell to break yer elements apart, not bind them together."

Despite her worry for Liam, despite seeing his bloodied and battered body every time she closed her eyes, a hint of excitement started to flow through her veins. Maybe she'd learned more from Katerina than she'd thought over the years.

"Well, if I'm interpreting this right, I think the reason the spell never worked after Fergus used it on me is that no one else was ever *willing* to give up their element."

"How do ya' figure?" Tierney asked.

"Because of these two runes together. Ned and Lagu. An upright Lagu warns ya' not to try to force an outcome. And Ned usually means somethin' ya' can't just fight yer way through."

The two wolves still looked confused, and Caitlin had to admit, she was reaching for the smallest bit of hope. "Somethin' Paddy said. 'Storms rage on, here and there, ne're calmed by earth nor air.' Then, 'two become three but three can't do.' I think we need all four elements for me to take back my air. Which means—"

"You need me there." Mara stood just inside the French doors with Cade at her side. "What are you going to try to do?"

"I'm goin' to use these runes against him. If I can convince him ye're the center of everythin', that he'll never be successful, but that he can release my air and then give his earth to ya', we might have just enough time to stop him."

Cade's eyes churned, amber and silver streaks blending with the arctic blue. "You can't give Mara all four elements. I won't let you."

"No, I can't. Even if I could, I'd never do that to her. Not after everythin' the two of ya' have done for me. Which is why we're goin' to have to be quick about it. As soon as Fergus releases my air, the rest of ya' have to stop him."

Liam

He couldn't stop shaking. Not that it did him much good. The pressure of the rocks all around his legs, his hips, and halfway up his chest held him so tightly, he could barely breathe.

When he'd come to, alone, he'd been shocked Fergus hadn't just killed him. Why half-bury him and leave him to suffer?

The mark on his chest burned with a fire he'd never known, and with his one free arm, he yanked and pulled until his shirt ripped. It was dark, again, and even though he could see and hear better than a human whether he was in wolf form or not, nothing could penetrate this total and complete darkness.

But he ran his fingers over the wound. He hadn't managed to *see* it, but from what he could feel, it was the same fuckin' mark that the daft bastard had given Colin and tried to give Farren.

If he could destroy the mark, could he shift and find a way out of here? He didn't have to search the pile of dirt and rocks for more than a few seconds before he found a sharp stone.

This...would hurt.

He had to stop every three or four times he dragged the stone over the cuts. Either because the pain sent him into fits or because the full moon twisted his emotions into knots and he could do nothing but let out a hoarse scream and pray that some-where, Caitlin was still safe.

His memories both comforted and shattered him. Her scent, her kiss, her fingers in his hair. That breathy moan she made when he slipped inside her.

Fight, luv. I don't know if I'll survive this, but ya' have to fight.

Heavy footsteps thudded from behind the door, and he barely had time to drop the rock and try to arrange his shirt to cover the wounds before the door opened with a loud metallic screech.

Fergus's bulk blocked most of the light, and a hint of the sea wafted over Liam. He couldn't be far from the water. Not if he could smell it. Still in Doolin? Lahinch?

The earth elemental took two steps into the room. Just enough for Liam to be able to see his eyes. They were calmer now. His hands weren't shaking so much, and his voice carried a hint of remorse. "I'll turn ya' over to yer pack. A peace offerin' in exchange for my Caitie and the other one."

"The other one?" he managed. It took all of his focus to draw in enough air to speak. "What...other one?"

"The red-haired one with water and fire." Fergus hung his head for a moment, then met Liam's gaze. "I've no choice, ya' see. If I don't do this, they'll make me suffer too. Ya' understand, yeah?"

Liam's thoughts muddled from the pain, but he couldn't imagine any scenario in which Cade would let Mara risk her life. Not even for him.

Fergus pulled something from his pocket, and Liam blinked hard. A phone. "She won't trust me. Not unless ya' talk to her. Tell her ye're alive. After I have her and the other one, I'll tell yer pack where ya' are."

"No." The word was something between a whisper and a growl. Though he was desperate to talk to Caitlin, to tell her he loved her one last time, he wouldn't be a part in any plan that brought her closer to Fergus.

With a snarl, Fergus lunged forward and pressed his hand to the mark on Liam's chest. His voice lowered, and a gentle brush of air tickled Liam's cheeks. "I control ya', wolf. I can stop yer heart if I want. Break yer bones." The earth rumbled all around Liam, and another rib cracked, forcing an agonized whimper from his lips. "Ya' *want* to tell Caitie to bring me fire and water. And ya' will."

His skin started to burn, and he ached to talk to Caitlin. To tell her that she needed to do what Fergus asked.

No. You can't. Don't listen to him.

He knew it was wrong. Knew it was the last thing he truly wanted to do, but when Fergus dialed her number, he couldn't remember why.

CHAPTER TWENTY-SIX

Caitlin

*S*he paced between Farren's kitchen and dining room, her phone clutched in her hand. They'd come up with a plan—sort of—and now, they just needed Fergus to agree to it.

She'd texted him half an hour ago with a simple message.

Tell me where to meet you, and I'll try to get Mara away from her mate. But I need to talk to Liam first.

If he'd killed Liam already, she'd know. Wouldn't she?

Her phone rang just as she'd poured herself a fresh mug of coffee, and Caitlin yelped. She'd had so much in the past few hours, she was vibrating.

"I want to talk to Liam," she said before Fergus could speak. "Better yet, turn on video. Let me see him."

"If I do, will ya' come back to me? And bring Mara with ya'?"

"I will. I promise." Caitlin waved Mara and Cade over, but kept them out of the view of the incoming video call.

It was so dark, the video was grainy, and she could only see Liam's head and shoulders. But his eyes were open.

"Liam?"

"Ya' need to do...what he says, honey," Liam managed, his voice hoarse and so tired. "I won't last much...longer...without...meds."

"Liam, I love ya'. Ya' have to know... Tell me ya' know!"

"I know. But...Fergus...needs ya' more than I do. I'll never forget the week we spent...by the sea. Ya' smelled like it. Remember? When ya' first met my wolf?" Each word seemed to take more out of him than the last, and he closed his eyes, his head lolling to one side.

Caitlin choked back a sob. "Fergus, please. Ya' have to get him to a hospital."

The earth elemental's face shifted in and out of focus on screen. "Help me, Caitie. Everythin' hurts. All the time. Ya' can make it better. Ya' bring me Mara, and we'll go see the Thirteen, and they'll have to see...they'll let us live forever."

"I will. But Liam has to survive. I know what we have to do, Fergus. Diedre's book. Remember her? The practitioner from yesterday? She figured out how to reverse the spell. And how ya' can give the Thirteen what they want after ya' give me back my air."

"No!" he snarled. "We do this my way, Caitie. Ya' bring Mara and that damn book to the Cliffs of Moher in thirty minutes. Not a second longer. Once we're somewhere no one can find us, ya' can tell me who to ring with yer wolf's location."

He ended the call, and Caitlin slumped against the counter. She couldn't muster the energy to cry. Liam's eyes had been dull, his voice listless and almost monotone. He was dying, and if she couldn't figure out where he was...even if she did defeat Fergus at the Cliffs, even if she took back her air, she might not be able to find him.

Cade, with Mara held against his side, stepped in front of her. "Caitlin, look at me. Now."

She did it, because even though she and Liam hadn't formally mated, the man was an alpha to his very core.

"Did you hear what Liam said?"

"Of course, I did. Fergus did somethin' to him. Charmed him. Made him say those things. That wasn't my Liam talkin'." Did Cade really think she was that daft? Liam would never ask her to give herself up.

"He called you 'honey.' And said you spent a week by the sea. That you *smelled* like the sea."

"So?"

"You smell like fig blossoms," Mara said with a smile. "Liam told me that after...well, after I killed Katerina. And he calls you 'luv.' Cade calls me 'honey.' Plus, he didn't say he needed a doctor. Or that he needed to shift. He said he needed *meds.*"

"What are ya' on about?" Caitlin asked, too exhausted and terrified to think straight.

"Fergus is still self-medicating. And Liam was fighting whatever Fergus did to him. He's somewhere near the sea. He can smell it." Cade arched a brow. "If Fergus wants you to meet him at the Cliffs in thirty minutes, he can't be that far away. Neither can Liam."

Caitlin closed her eyes and replayed the video in her head. Liam had fought off her air charm. But that had been out of love.

Tears burned her eyes as she realized anything he was doing now was out of love as well. "So, what do we do now? Besides try to knock Fergus on his arse?"

FIVE MINUTES LATER, Farren, Cade, and Mara stood in front of the fire talking in whispered tones. Diedre's book sat open on the table in front of them, and Caitlin sketched one of the sigils in her notebook.

Between Tierney's word scramble skills and what she'd

learned from Katerina, she thought her plan might be daft enough to work.

Caitlin cradled the book to her chest. "Farren, do ya' have a safe?"

"Of course. What self-respectin' alpha doesn't?" she replied.

Cade flinched. "I don't."

"Well, get one, ya' bugger."

"We have banks. Safe deposit boxes."

Caitlin shook her head. "Can we debate this some other time? Liam's life is at stake here, and we only have a little more than twenty minutes to get to the Cliffs of Moher."

Everyone quieted down, thank God, and Caitlin joined the two alphas and Mara in front of the fireplace.

"The spell Fergus used to take my air required me to be a willing participant. That's why he could never take another element after mine. Because he tried to do it by force. And I think I might be able to reverse the spell if he lets me." She pulled the bottle of Clozapine from her pocket and shook it gently. "If we can get him to take these—or whatever else he's takin'—long enough to quell the mania for just a bit, I can try. But there's a chance I won't succeed, and if I don't..." She shook her head, unwilling to even consider what would happen to Liam if she failed.

"Ya' have to keep the book safe," she said, meeting Farren's gaze. "For Mara. We've only managed to figure out one page so far, and I don't even know if we're right. The few sigils—and Paddy's words—earth dampens fire, fire scorches earth...they're riddles. Nothin' but riddles. Still, that doesn't mean they're nonsense. If I can't get Fergus to listen to me, someone has to keep workin' on translatin' the book so we can protect Mara."

The water elemental took Caitlin's hands. "We're not losing you."

"You might not have a choice. I have to get close to him to even try, and he's not goin' to just give me a hug and a peck on the cheek and tell me all's forgiven. I can do this alone. It'll keep the rest of ya' safe. At least for a while."

"No fucking way," Cade spat.

Farren nodded. "Liam's my best friend. And ye're his mate. We're all family here. And that bastard is goin' to pay for hurtin' Liam if it's my last act in this world." The female wolf's fierce grin offered more bloodlust than mirth. "Either way, he's not leavin' the cliffs alive."

Despite everything he'd done, Caitlin still wished she could save Liam, Mara, and herself without killing the boy she'd once known. But deep down, she knew there was likely no other way.

Her chest burned. Both from the missing piece of her heart— Liam—and from the loss of her element. But where years ago, she'd fallen into tiny pieces from the pain, now...she'd fight. For Liam. For this new family she desperately wanted to save. And for herself.

Straightening her shoulders, she checked her pockets. The quartz she'd inscribed with a sigil of her own was a comforting, cool weight next to the bottle of pills and the leather pouch containing the red jasper.

"Everyone out to the cars," she said, her voice clear and true. "I'll tell you the rest of the plan on the way."

Liam

The bastard had left him alone again, and by the amount of blood coating his chest, he thought he might have done enough damage to that fucking mark to fight the man's control over his wolf.

Except there was no way his wolf could shift trapped under the weight of the rocks and soil that held him down.

He dropped the sharp piece of stone he'd been using to score his skin and started digging. Not easy with only one hand, but he had to believe that Cade, Farren, Peter, and anyone else who was still alive wouldn't let Caitlin face Fergus alone.

He knew the earth elemental would use him against Caitlin. Taunt her, tell her he'd kill Liam if she didn't do exactly what he commanded. If he could get free, he could take away Fergus's one advantage.

But he didn't have long. Before Fergus had left him alone in the dark again, he'd slipped up.

"She's comin'," he said, a gleeful smile curving his lips. "My Caitie will be here soon. I have to get up to the top of the cliffs to meet her. If she's been good, yer pack might find ya' before the rocks crush ya' to death."

This underground bunker, whatever it had once been, was within a few minutes at most of the clifftop. All he had to do was get free and get out that door, and he'd find Caitlin.

His fingers ached and bled, but he kept digging. After a few minutes, he was able to free his other arm. It had gone numb, but he slapped it all the way from his swollen shoulder down to his wrist until the skin started to tingle.

Fight. Don't let him win. Caitlin needs you.

If he escaped, if he got to hold her again, he'd never let her go. He'd tell her...everything he should have said eleven years ago. Mate with her. Get down on one knee and propose. Spend the rest of his life giving her anything she wanted, needed. And never once taking a moment with her for granted.

Every breath was more painful than the last. The darkness swirled around him as wave after wave of dizziness hit him. But he reached his hip. Then his thigh. Then his knee.

As the stuffy, dank air hit his broken leg, he let out a howl. The bone had torn right through the skin when Fergus had buried him. Fuck. Even if he shifted, he might not have the strength to walk. But he'd crawl if he had to. Anything to get to Caitlin.

Caitlin

From the front seat, Caitlin watched as the sun started to peek over the horizon. Winds raced up the hill behind them, sending tumbling stones skittering over the pavement.

Peter and Tierney bounded across the fields in wolf form. They'd chosen to run rather than drive, since Farren's home was only a few kilometers from the cliffs.

When the four of them emerged from the car, Caitlin curled her fingers around the amber pendant.

I'm coming, Liam. I'll find you.

"Ready to manufacture some fog again?" Mara asked, a hint of excitement flaring in her emerald eyes. "It's so much easier when you help me."

She and Caitlin held hands, and within two minutes, a blanket of white settled over the top of the cliffs.

"He'll be close to the edge," Caitlin said. "If ya' get within a hundred feet of him, he could send ya' into the sea—with my air, with another earthquake, or with magic. So keep yer distance.

"Mara, stay close to Cade. Ye're stronger together. Plus, he can stop ya' if Fergus tries to compel ya' again."

"I won't let anything happen to her," Cade said as he stripped off his shirt.

Caitlin reached into her cross-body bag and pulled out a book she'd stolen from Farren's library. It hadn't looked anywhere near as old as the one the practitioner had given them, but she didn't think Fergus had gotten too close a look at it. One more potential distraction that might buy them some time. "I hope this isn't too important to ya'."

Farren snorted. "*Tales of the Would-Be King*? It's a piece of utter shite that Tierney insists is classic literature. The boy's got heart, but his taste in books? Questionable."

Tierney, who'd just joined them, growled softly, then immediately looked down in submission.

"I'll buy ya' a new one," Farren said as she ruffled his ears.

"I'm goin' to try to distract him with this long enough for the rest of ya' to surround him." Caitlin shoved the book into her bag and shrugged. "Beyond that...ya' all know what to do."

"We do." Mara's skin practically glowed with the power of her element and she pulled Caitlin in for a swift embrace. "We'll get Liam back. I promise."

She couldn't guarantee that, and Caitlin knew it. But still, the woman's confidence was almost contagious. One way or another, in the next few hours, she'd be dead, or she'd be free.

Cade and Farren stripped and shifted. The moon was still full and wouldn't set for another six hours, and the difference in their coats, their demeanors, and even their eyes from the day before shocked her.

Both appeared larger, meaner, and a hell of a lot more powerful.

Peter, the last to join them, made some odd vocalizations, and the rest of the wolves joined in.

Mara touched Caitlin's arm. "I'm not sure, but I think Peter just saw Fergus."

Cade barked, a sound even Caitlin now recognized as a yes, and Peter and Tierney headed off together.

"I'll go first, and I'll protect ya' as long as I can," she told Mara. "Don't underestimate him, whatever ya' do." Kneeling, she stroked a hand over Cade's shoulder. "Please, let me try to save Fergus. If I'm right, he's still in there somewhere. The boy who just wanted to be strong. But if I fail, tear him apart."

Cade nudged her hip with an aggressive growl. Deep sadness, anger, and something she hadn't anticipated filled the sound. Respect. For her.

Weak sunlight sliced through the fog, and a cold, biting wind pulled strand after strand of hair free from her braid.

She could feel Fergus now. The tether between them drawing her closer to the top of the cliffs. Closer to the spot where she'd once tried to end it all.

"Fergus!" she shouted into the wind. "I'm here."

His hold over her strengthened, the cord pulled so tight, for a moment, she panicked, unsure she could take another breath. But she touched the amber—Liam's amber—and calmed enough to call a bit of her element swirling around her.

He stood at the very edge of the cliffs. The stone barrier meant to keep tourists safe and away from the precipice had been flattened for yards by his "earthquake."

The grasses around him lay almost horizontal from the gale, and his dark eyes narrowed as he turned to face her. "Caitie."

The single word was so soothing. Had he already worked a charm? Or was this merely a hint of the boy she'd once known? He appeared calm. Almost in control.

Spots of gray shadowed his temples, and lines dug in around his eyes. A hint of the boy remained in those eyes, but everything he'd endured—and all the chaos he'd caused—had overwhelmed so much of the good she'd once seen there.

"I did what ya' asked. And I brought ya' another gift too." Withdrawing the book from her bag, she held it aloft. "We took this from the practitioner's house. I think...Fergus if ya' want to be free from the Thirteen, I think there's a way to do it."

Shock played across his features, but in the next instant, it was replaced by anger, greed, and desperation. "I don't *want* to be free! I want what they promised me. Where's the elemental? Mara?"

His hands shook as he patted his pockets, and she called on a hint of her air, carrying the sound of rattling pills towards her. He had his meds on him. If she could get him to take them...

"Ya' look good, luv. It's been a long time."

Ignoring her, he raised his arms and swept the fog back, then swore. "Ya' weren't supposed to bring anyone with ya' but Mara!"

"You try telling an alpha wolf to leave his mate. I'm not that strong." She took a step closer, still holding the book in her hand, and trying to place herself between Fergus and Mara. "They can't stop us. No elemental or werewolf can best us when we're together. I've missed ya', Fergus."

The words tasted bitter on her tongue, but she forced warmth into her tone. "Ya' were right. Ye're the only one for me. I never should have left ya' all those years ago. I made a mistake."

A mask of confusion slid over his face. "Then why didn't ya' come back, Caitie? Ya' knew how much it hurt when I failed them. Every time. But without ya'...there was no way I could succeed."

Tears made his eyes glisten, and he pulled up his sweater. The brand the Thirteen had given him glowed bright red against the skin, and next to it, a second sigil, one she didn't recognize, and a third.

"Oh, shite. Fergus." She didn't have to fake concern or care. They'd so obviously made his life hell. Punished him for what she'd done. More to weigh on her conscience. Even though she'd had no choice.

"Why?" he asked again.

"I had to." Her words caught in her throat. "I met another elemental who compelled me until I forgot who I was. She had magic in her, just like them, and she used it against me. I was with her this whole time."

"I thought ya' were dead. When I felt ya' again..." He ran a hand through his black hair, and she could feel him. His emotions. How much he'd suffered. "It's time to go now. Bring me fire and water. Do away with the wolf."

The ground under their feet trembled, and Caitlin fought to remain upright.

"This is yer last warnin', Caitie. We've work to do, and I'm not lettin' ya get away from me again."

He flung his hand towards her, and a plume of air curled

around her, pressing her arms to her sides, tightening like endless coils of rope and urging her to give in.

Every cell in her body fought him, but he snarled and strengthened the charm. The slimy, foul stench of magic invaded her nose, and her thoughts muddled.

One step. Then another. She approached him, so close now she caught a hint of loamy earth and his cologne. She hated it, always had—even when she'd been with Katerina and another man had worn the same scent, she'd hated it, though she'd never known why.

It sickened her, being this close to him. And yet, there was a part of her that longed for his touch. For him to hold her and tell her it would all be okay.

No! That's his air and the Thirteen's magic. Not you. Fight him. Fight him for Liam.

Liam. Her mate. She could smell him too. And his blood. Tipping her face upwards to meet Fergus's dark-eyed gaze, his compulsion whispered into her mind.

"Tell me ya' love me, Caitie."

"I..." No. She loved a man with eyes as green as moss, with long, reddish hair, a strong jaw. With hands that soothed and supported. Not ones that caused her so much pain. She loved Liam, and always would.

This was her chance. She had to convince Fergus to trust her or their plan would never work.

"I love ya', Fergus. Now loosen the charm so I can hug ya' properly."

CHAPTER TWENTY-SEVEN

Caitlin

*T*he charm eased, but the magic still held tight. At least she could move now Caitlin swallowed hard and forced herself to wrap her arms around Fergus, though the magic pulsing within him made her want to throw up.

With slow purpose, she drew him closer, his big body both foreign and familiar. Slipping her hands down to his waist, she dropped the inscribed piece of quartz into his left pocket.

Her sigil had been hastily made, but she'd set her intention clearly and sealed it with sage, and she hoped it would be enough. If she could convince him to trust her, they might all survive this.

Fergus smelled like soil freshly churned for springtime, but soon, the scent turned cloying, and she eased herself from his hold.

"I came back to ya', so now we can be whole," she said. "I won't leave ya' again, but I need ya' to do somethin' for me. Will ya'? It'll make gettin' to Mara easier." She forced a smile, hoping the light sweetness to her voice would help convince him. If she called on her air now, he'd sense it, so she had to be careful.

"What do ya' need, Caitie?" he asked. His fingers shook as he touched her cheek, as if he couldn't quite believe she were real.

"I need ya' to take yer pills. And release my air so I can compel Mara."

Electricity crackled around them, and she sent all of her focus into the amber hanging from the leather cord around her neck. It was hidden under Liam's flannel shirt, but the weight of it helped center her.

Fergus pulled a small bottle out of his right pocket, and relief flooded her. Several pills tumbled into his palm, and he stared at them. "They make me feel better," he said, almost to himself, but then met her gaze. "But I don't need them now that ye're here."

He tossed them away, and as he turned, movement in their periphery pulled a wild snarl from his lips. "Ya' bitch!"

Caitlin flinched, panic flooding her as his sudden, over-whelming rage hit her square in the chest.

Flinging his arms wide, Fergus shook the ground with his power, sending a gale straight for the two wolves creeping up on their left. Peter and Tierney.

Yelps and whines accompanied their tumbling back down the hill, and he grabbed her arm, his fingers digging in so hard she'd have bruises.

"I'll make ya' sorry, Caitie. I will. Yer wolf...he'll die where I left him." Shoving her down, he kicked her in the stomach, and she retched, unable to draw even a single breath as he pulled even more of her element to him. "How many more?" he roared. "Show yerselves!" Turning around in a circle, he called a tornado to aid him, the gusts swirling and picking up dirt and rocks and bits of grass.

From her left, Cade growled and leapt, and when Fergus sent

him flying, Farren attacked. Her sharp teeth sank into his side, close to his mark, but he batted her away like she weighed nothing at all.

Caitlin crawled, her fingers digging into the muddy, mossy soil, needing to get to Mara—and put at least a few feet between her and Fergus—but he grabbed her by the ankle.

"Ye're not goin' anywhere, ya' whore."

All the air around her vanished in the space of a single heartbeat, and she clutched at her throat, at her chest. Black spots swam in her vision, then turned red.

Red?

She couldn't understand anything. Until with a great *whoosh*, she could breathe again, and saw flames licking up Fergus's hip.

Mara. Mara's fire. Shite. That wasn't part of the plan. If Mara lost control, she could kill them all. Or alert the Thirteen.

"Fergus!" Mara shouted from just outside the whirlwind still spinning all around them. "Let Caitlin go, right now, or I'll burn you alive."

The voice both was and wasn't Mara's. Deeper now, with a hint of Katerina's sing-song. More flames arced over the storm, this time hitting him right where the Thirteen had branded him.

Fergus screamed, then dropped and rolled to smother the flames. Before Caitlin could get up, he wrapped his fist around her braid and pulled her back to him.

The shaking all around them intensified, and bits of the cliffside sheared off and crashed into the sea below. Mara collapsed, but her hands still glowed, and Cade bounded to her side, howling.

Caitlin, on her knees as Fergus stood over her, struggled, clawing at his hand and trying to loosen his hold.

"Ya' betrayed me, Caitie. I'm goin' to have to teach ya' a lesson." His voice sent chills down her spine, and tears burned her eyes as Fergus sent a rock hurtling towards Mara and Cade.

The wolf jumped up, absorbing the impact and yelping before crumpling into a heap in front of Mara.

A second boulder gathered speed as it raced down the hill towards Farren, but the silver wolf managed to leap out of the way just in time.

No. He's going to kill them all. My family.

Her tears flowed freely, but they were fueled by anger now instead of fear. "I will not let ya' keep usin' my air, ya' piece of shite! It's *mine*, and so are they!" She bucked against his hold, twisting and fighting, but he was too strong, had her at too awkward of an angle.

Desperate, she pulled the sage stick from under her shirt and held it just out of his reach. "Mara! Fire!"

The water elemental staggered to her feet. Her eyes glowed silver, then amber. One hand held a churning ball of fire, and the other, a sphere of water the size of a baseball. Cade's lupine body spasmed on the ground, his fur rippling as he tried to shift enough to heal his broken bones.

Mara took a step forward, her hair now shining in sun. Sending first the fire, then the water hurtling towards Caitlin, she collapsed from the effort, and Cade nosed at her, desperately whining as he tried to get her to move.

The flames hit the edge of the sage, and thick white smoke surrounded them as the water drenched Caitlin's hair.

Fergus started to cough, and between the smoke and the water, Caitlin was able to wrench her braid from his grasp. Struggling to her feet, she traced runes in the air before him. Ing for a positive outcome, Eolh for protection, and Gefu to seal her promise to him. Then, she called on all of her air, every ounce of her power she could muster, and sent it flowing into him.

Fergus wheezed, the infusion of so much of her element shocking him, and he clutched at his chest. "What are ya' doin', Caitie?" he gasped.

"Takin' back what's mine."

Fergus threw off her charm, sending it back to her twice as strong, and she hit the ground hard enough to force all the air from her lungs. "I have magic on my side," he taunted as he stood over her.

Growls—Cade and Farren, if she had to guess—sounded from somewhere close by, and Fergus clenched his fists and opened up a great crack in the earth between them and the wolves. She rolled onto her side and watched, helplessly as the gaping maw grew. Two feet. Three. Five. Ten.

She wouldn't last much longer. Not without a miracle. With the last of her strength, she lurched up and drove the sage stick directly into his side, right over the Thirteen's mark.

He screamed in pain, and the shaking intensified. Caitlin lost her balance and the sage tumbled from her hand and rolled into the crevasse. When the smoke cleared, her stomach lurched. She and Fergus were trapped on a spire maybe twenty feet across and easily that far from the rest of the cliffside.

"I won't let ya' go," he said, advancing on her until her feet were only inches from the edge. "Ya' defied me for the final time." His hand shot out and grabbed her by the throat, and he held her body over the edge as she clung desperately to his arm.

"Please," she rasped. "Just...tell me...where Liam is." She craned her neck to see the rocks and the violently churning water far below. She wouldn't survive the fall.

"The wolf? The one ya' fucked instead of me? He's close by. Close enough that one good tremor will end him. I was goin' to let him go, but now, I think his death will be on yer head."

No!

The boy she'd once cared for held out his free hand, whispered a few words in Gaelic, and then twisted his fingers.

A kilometer away, maybe two, the rumble was so loud, it obliterated everything except her own heartbeat pounding in her ears.

The entire northwest peak of the cliffs imploded, and Caitlin screamed, a mournful, agonizing wail that stripped her bare and left her unable to feel...anything but rage.

Her toes were still balanced on the edge of the cliff, and she craned her head, desperately trying to see Mara.

She'd failed. Failed Liam. But she could still save Mara. The water elemental was crawling towards the far edge of the cliff, her mate on one side, Farren on the other, each bracing her so she wouldn't fall.

Stretching one arm in Mara's general direction, she started chanting, her words so low, she could barely hear them.

"Two become three, but three can't do. Two become three, but three can't do."

Fire hit her palm first, followed immediately by water, and Caitlin pulled them into her. *"Earth is his, but air is mine, and now I use it as a bind."*

Fergus's hold weakened, and she flung herself forward, sending both of them to the ground as fire, water, and air all battled for dominance within her.

The effort left her too weak to do more than roll off of him, until a howl from the distance made her turn her head.

A red wolf. Staggering towards Cade and Mara. Bloody. Dirty. One of his back legs dragging behind him. Looking like he was about to fall over. But very much alive and very, *very* angry.

Liam's wolf struggled for every step, until Peter and Tierney raced to his side and helped keep him upright. He let out a growl full of rage, and all of the other wolves joined in.

Caitlin smiled. It didn't matter now...whether she lived or died. Because Liam was safe. All she had to do was stop Fergus and she could let go.

"What...did ya' do...?" Fergus pinned her down, his bulk crushing her as he wrapped his hands around her throat, not cutting off her air, not yet. Anguish and betrayal churned in his eyes, and for a moment, she could almost feel sorry for him.

If not for the three elements battling for control within her, and the fourth, his, so close she could taste it. The power called to her. A siren song she didn't want to ignore. But then, she heard her wolf again, and though she couldn't be sure, his howl almost seemed to be calling her name.

"You can't have me!" she cried, both to the foreign elements and to Fergus. Her world exploded into light and sound and sensation. Flames blackened the grass all around them, and Fergus flew back ten feet before he started screaming, his hands pressed to his temples.

Rising, Caitlin twisted the three elements into a complex symphony, an endless, swirling living *thing* that almost overwhelmed her, before using the maelstrom pull some of Fergus's earth to join the three that couldn't do by themselves.

For a single moment, the world went quiet and still. Fergus stared at her, his mouth agape, his eyes bloodshot and weary, and he was the young boy she'd known once more. Ashamed. Terrified. And so very sad. "End it," he whispered. "End my suffering. Ye're the only one who can..."

Caitlin released her hold, and the quartz in Fergus's pocket served as a conduit, channeling more than just air, earth, fire, and water, but a whisper of spirit as well.

The explosion was like nothing she'd ever felt. Its power carried her up, higher and higher, air rushing all around her. *Can you suffocate on too much air?* she wondered as she tumbled, fell, and rose again.

Flames burst in a column a hundred feet high, surrounded by water, then air, then earth, with Fergus in the center. He was utterly silent as he burned. No longer struggling. Almost at peace.

When the firestorm reached his torso, a burst of green sparks consumed him. The brands. The Thirteen's marks. Magic scented the air, but even that was quickly overwhelmed by the four elements, and Caitlin hit the ground.

She couldn't move. Could only stare up at the clear blue sky as the last of Fergus Tharp turned to ash and scattered over the water and the rocks below.

SOMETHING NUDGED HER ARM. A weak whimper had her forcing her eyes open, and then a warm, solid weight fell against her.

Fur. Matted. Bloodied. Soft.

The scent she knew so well, pine with a hint of the ocean brought her back, and she rolled onto her side, staring into the eyes of Liam's wolf.

"How?" she whispered, and he nuzzled her neck, then whined. So much pain in that single sound. She pushed up onto an elbow, waited for the world to stop spinning, and stroked her hand down his side.

Her fingers came away stained with blood. "Oh, God. Liam. Ya' have to shift back."

"It's the moon." Cade's voice startled her, and she looked up to see him with his arm around Mara's waist. He was naked again, and she averted her eyes, returning her focus to Liam. "It's harder to shift back during the full moon. Usually, the human form is easier. But today...right now... He's in pain. I don't know if he can."

The alpha wolf sank to his knees and rested a hand on Liam's shoulder.

"If you don't do it, Liam, it's going to hurt a lot more later. That leg needs tending before the injuries set, and I'm pretty sure Caitlin would feel a lot better if she could hear your voice."

The wolf whined, fear in his eyes, and shook his head weakly. Caitlin wrapped her arms around him and buried her face against his neck. "Please, luv. Ya' have to try. I can give ya' some of my air, and...wait. I know what will help."

She almost fell over from the effort of merely sitting up, but managed to pull the red jasper pouch out of her pocket. The cord was long enough she could slide it over his muzzle and pressed it to his chest.

"Take some of my strength. This is a warrior's talisman, and it'll give you what you need if you just ask." Drawing a sigil over Liam's heart—or at least the general area of his torso where she thought a wolf's heart would be—she called upon her air, letting it wrap them both in a gentle embrace.

Her wolf relaxed as his pain eased, and closed his eyes. A mournful howl started low in his throat, and his fur rippled and bones broke, his entire body shaking as his dark reddish pelt turned back into pale, dirty, and bloody skin.

When he lay panting on his back, he looked so much worse. His left shoulder, where Fergus had carved the Thirteen's mark into his skin, was nothing but a mass of scars now. Criss-crossing scrapes, some so deep they'd formed thick scars over a hint of the lines and curves the blade had caused.

His right thigh was nothing but one massive dark purple bruise, and as he curled on his side and drew his legs up, he hissed in pain.

"What is it?" she asked with a gentle touch to his shoulder. "I thought shifting healed you."

"Too weak to do more," he managed.

Caitlin rested her hand over the red jasper, sending as much of her own power into the stone as she could. Liam sucked in a breath and his eyes opened, still pained, but clearer now.

"Ye're really here."

"I lost ya' once." She leaned closer and brushed her lips to his. "Never doin' it again."

He tried to reach for her, but fell back with a grunt, and tears burned her eyes, worry tightening a vise around her heart. "I don't think he can walk," she said as she looked to Cade.

"I can carry him. You help Mara. She's exhausted."

Farren strode up to their small group, her white hair flowing in the gentle breezes. "All that shakin' and fire drew some attention." Jerking her head towards the visitor center parking lot, she waited for a beat. "Listen."

Sirens. Getting closer.

"I'm afraid we'll all have some explainin' to do if we're still here when they arrive. Tierney, Ewan, and Peter all headed back to the house already." Farren wrapped her hand around Caitlin's arm and helped her to her feet. "Ya' steady enough now?"

"I think so. Mara?" Caitlin turned to the water elemental, who looked a bit like she'd just run a marathon. Her shoulders slumped, and her normally bright eyes had dulled slightly, but her skin still glowed and her hair gleamed in the sunlight. "How do ya' feel?"

"Like I want to throw up. Again."

"Again?" Caitlin held on to Mara as Cade pulled Liam's arm over his shoulders and straightened, lifting the man like he weighed nothing at all.

"She's vomited twice since she gave you her water and fire," Cade said. "When we get back to Farren's, I'm not letting you out of bed for two days, honey."

"Cade. I'm fine. Using the fire just...makes me nauseous, I guess. I need to brush my teeth and take a nap. That's all."

The look Cade shot her was anything but fine. And when they started walking, the alpha wolf groaned. "Shit, man. You weigh a ton. You're damn lucky the moon is full or you'd be crawling back to the car."

Liam managed a hoarse laugh. "Shut it. Ye're not much lighter. Everyone's okay, yeah?"

"Yeah. We are. Now that we have you back."

Caitlin had so many questions. How had Liam escaped wherever Fergus had him? How had she held on to all four elements for so long without losing herself to the storm she'd created? Most importantly...what happened next? Certainly the Thirteen would have sensed the power she'd loosed on the world. Would they come after her? After Mara?

But none of those questions were as important as having Liam in her arms. Once they were in the car and she held him close, letting him drift off to sleep with his head on her shoulder, she let herself cry silent tears.

For the life she'd ended. For the lives she'd saved. And most of all, for the love she shared with her mate.

CHAPTER TWENTY-EIGHT

Liam

$\mathcal{H}$e didn't remember the trip back to Farren's. Or have any idea how he'd ended up in bed. But he knew his mate was pressed to his side.

His leg ached, as did his chest where he'd destroyed Fergus's mark. When he'd finally freed himself enough from the suffocating mound of dirt and rocks to shift, he hadn't been able to walk, and for endless minutes, he'd wondered if he'd suffered all that pain only to die as his wolf, alone and in the dark.

And then the ground had started to rumble. The animal—so much a creature of instinct—had found a burst of adrenaline, and thrown himself at the metal door again and again until the earth all around had shifted enough to knock the damn thing right out of its frame.

Seeing his Caitlin trapped with Fergus's hand around her throat had almost killed him, and his wolf had called out to her, desperate to reach her even though he could barely walk. And then, she'd lit up like a Christmas tree. All fire and air and water. So bright he'd had to look away.

He didn't understand what she'd done or how, but he'd watched the earth elemental burn, and didn't feel a single second of remorse. Only relief that his mate could finally be free.

Caitlin stirred in his arms. "Liam?"

"Come closer, luv," he whispered, but when she rested her cheek against his, he sighed. "I shouldn't have asked. I reek."

She pressed her face against his neck to stifle her laughter, then quickly drew back. "Oh, God. Ye're right." Still, her smile warmed him from the inside. "If ya' think ya' can make it to the bath..."

"Only if ya' join me."

"I'm not leaving yer side for quite a while," she said. "Besides, I'm not convinced ya' wouldn't drown without me."

His leg was weak and stiff, too many hours spent without being able to heal himself, and he leaned on her for every step until she braced him against the counter and turned on the water.

He was already naked, but his Caitlin had on one of his shirts, and as he helped her undo the buttons, he froze. "Ya' found the necklace."

A blush bloomed on her cheeks. "It fell out of the shirt. I'm sorry. I can take it off." She fumbled for the clasp, but he reached up with a wince and stilled her hands.

"No, luv. I wanted to give it to ya' in Dublin. Hell, even before we left Seattle. But every time I tried, somethin' got in the way." He slid his fingers into her hair and kissed her, enjoying the way she melted against him, her soft moan, and her hand cupping his arse.

They only broke apart when the first curls of steam wafted up from the tub. His mate helped him wash his hair, massaged the knots from his shoulders, and held him as he told her how he'd escaped, and a little of what Fergus had done to him.

He kept as much from her as he thought he could, not wishing to cause her more pain. For all the man's faults, she'd cared for Fergus once, and he could feel her sorrow at having to end him.

By the time the water started to cool, he was steady again. Or close to it, and when she wrapped a towel around his waist, he dipped his head and trailed kisses along the curve of her neck. "I'll understand if ya' want to wait," he said when she helped him back to the bed. "But the moon... It's still full, but not for much longer."

"We're not waiting another minute."

Desperate kisses followed, and she straddled him, careful of his leg. His dick ached for her, but he wouldn't let himself take her until he gave as good as he hoped to get.

Fingers teasing her center, he let her ride his hand, and when she threw her head back and whimpered his name, his wolf howled inside right along with her.

"Are ya' certain, luv?" he said when she'd calmed enough to meet his gaze. "Ya' have to be sure. I know I said I claimed ya' long ago, but this...comin' together on the full moon, this is it for me."

Fuck. He didn't know what he'd do if she hesitated.

"I'm sure. I love ya', Liam. With everythin' I am. Claim me."

Liam slid down and guided her on top of him. Her nipples scraped against his chest and he nudged her entrance. "The moon's about to set. I don't know that I'll last."

"We have the rest of our lives to take things slow."

He plunged deep in one quick motion, and he'd never felt anything so perfect as his mate tensing around him. One hand on her waist, he slid the other between them, finding the spot that would send her flying.

"Kiss me, luv."

She obliged, slanting her mouth over his. And then stars obscured his sight, and his heartbeat roared in his ears. He filled her with a shout, and as they came down together, he and his wolf were finally at peace.

"CAITLIN."

Liam trailed his hand up her stomach to cup her breast. The peaceful blanket of night surrounded them, broken only by crickets and the breeze creaking a tree branch or rustling leaves outside their window.

"Feeling better?" she asked and then mewled when he pinched her nipple and bit her lightly just below her ear. They'd slept almost twelve hours.

He dotted her shoulder with kisses. "Luv, I need to run a bit. I can shift now and heal some more. But I don't want to leave ya'."

The moon had risen a few hours ago, and though no longer full, it was close enough to strengthen him.

Caitlin rolled over in his arms and pressed a gentle kiss to his lips. "How long?"

"An hour at most. I'm still tired." He smoothed a hand over her hair. "Tell me not to go."

"No. We're safe here. You should run." She cocked her head, listening. "Mara's sitting outside by the fire pit. Pretty sure I hear Cade's wolf. I'll go be with her, see if she needs me. We'll be waiting when you're done."

OUT ON THE PATIO, Caitlin and Mara sat wrapped in blankets, cups of steaming tea in their hands. Mara still looked a little green around the edges, but she assured them she just needed rest.

Liam crouched next to his mate, naked, and reached for his wolf. The animal roared as his bones cracked, his skin rippled, and fur covered his body. The thrill of the shift raced through him, the adrenaline making the pain fade away as he let the beast take over.

Tossing his head back, he howled—so much relief and joy in that single sound. And then his mate's fingers skimmed along the top of his head, down his neck, his back. He sat up tall and stared at her, still not quite believing they'd survived.

"You're magnificent," she said, and pride had him chuffing loudly. Until Cade's wolf called for him, then Farren's.

With quick swipe of his nose along her neck, he joined his pack, and though his leg still ached and his gait wasn't completely steady, he relished in the power he took from the moon—and from his Caitlin's love.

EPILOGUE

Caitlin

*T*wo days after she'd ended Fergus's life on the top of the cliffs, Caitlin and Liam curled together on one of the couches in Farren's living room with a fire roaring in the hearth.

Her mate was still weak, and he'd carry a limp for the rest of his life. But he claimed not to care. At least the sigil carved on his chest had been obscured by the mass of scar tissue he'd given himself. When he'd told her he'd used a rock to destroy the mark over painstaking hours alone, trapped by dirt and rocks and powerful magic, she'd buried her face in the curve of his neck so he wouldn't see her tears.

The practitioner's book was open on the low table in front of them, Caitlin's notebooks spread out on either side. She'd spent every waking moment she and Liam weren't naked pouring over the runes, hoping to find some way to protect Farren's home. To protect Mara.

Farren had gone off to find Paddy, hoping the man could give her some idea how they could protect themselves from the Thirteen they came after Caitlin or Mara after the battle on the cliffs.

"I'm *fine*, Cade. You don't need to hover like I'm going to shatter any second," Mara said from the staircase.

He growled something unintelligible in response, and Mara laughed. "Come on, then, shaggy man. I want to tell Caitlin."

She and Liam sat up a little straighter, exchanging glances. Liam shrugged.

"What is it?" Caitlin asked as the two joined them, Cade's expression somewhere between pride and terror.

Mara smiled. "I'm pregnant."

"Oh, my God. Mara!" Caitlin leapt up and wrapped her arms around the water elemental. "How long have ya' known?"

"Peter went to the store this morning and bought me a test."

"Ya' didn't..." Liam said as he slapped Cade on the back, then pulled him in for a quick hug.

"The poor man looked like he wanted to dig a hole in the backyard and hide for the rest of his life," Mara said. "But he did it."

"Do ya' know how far along ya' are?" Caitlin asked.

The two exchanged glances, and Mara's cheeks reddened. "At least six weeks. We think...maybe it's why the fire started to affect me more."

Her mind started racing, and she grabbed the book and flipped through page after page. "There was something in here. Something about transferring power. It was in Latin, and translating it has been...confusing."

Mara's stomach rumbled, and Cade pressed a kiss to her cheek. "I'll make you a sandwich, honey. You need to eat."

"Extra mayo!" she called after him.

"Here." She flipped through one of the notebooks for the translation. "It basically says that the 'source of power' can also be 'corrupted' by it or 'healed' by it. I didn't understand what it meant, but here in the margin, there's a drawing of the triple goddess." Caitlin pointed to a drawing of the moon with a waxing crescent on the left and a waning crescent on the right. "It's a Celtic symbol that can have a couple of different meanings, but one of them is for three Fates: the Maiden, the Mother, and the Crone."

"I don't understand. Are you saying the baby is making me lose time?" Mara's whole demeanor shifted, and she pressed her hands to her belly, fear lending a tremble to her voice.

"No, no, no." Caitlin reached over and rested her hand on Mara's knee. "I'm saying the baby might help save you."

A sharp knock sounded on the front door, and Caitlin and Mara flinched. Tierney thudded down the stairs and headed straight for the door, while Liam called for him to wait.

"Don't be openin' that door!" he shouted and limped awkwardly for the foyer. "We don't know who's out there."

Caitlin's charm wafted down the entryway, slipped under the massive slab of wood, and came back to her. "Shite. Liam...it's Diedre."

She hurried to her mate's side as he pulled the door open and snarled at the elderly practitioner. "Ya' abandoned us, witch. Ya' better have a damn good explanation."

"There's no time." The practitioner batted at him with her cane, and Liam stumbled back enough for her to enter the house and slam the door. "If ya' want to stay safe here, ye're goin' to shut yer mouth and let me ward this place. The Thirteen know their elemental slave is dead, and it won't be long before they come lookin' for who ended him."

THANK you for reading *A Shift in the Air*. This book was a labor of love for me. I published a different version of the story a few years ago, but I was simply never happy with it.

There were reasons...most of which came down to listening to advice I didn't agree with. But...sometimes, as authors, we make mistakes.

Well, I made a mistake.

But as authors, we also get to *fix* our mistakes. I hope you enjoyed *A Shift in the Air*, and I very much hope you'll go on to read *A Shift in the Earth* and *A Shift in Fire* as well.

Love,

Patricia

ABOUT THE AUTHOR

I've always made up stories. Sometimes I even acted them out. I probably shouldn't admit that my childhood best friend and I used to run around the backyard pretending to fly in our Invisible Jet and rescue Steve Trevor. Oops.

Now that I'm too old to spin around in circles with felt magic bracelets on my wrists, I put "pen to paper" instead. Figuratively, at least. Fingers to keyboard is more accurate.

Outside of my writing, I'm a professional editor, a software geek, a singer (in the shower only), and a runner. I love red wine, scotch (neat, please), and cider. Seattle is my home, and I share an old house with my husband and cats.

I'm on my fourth—fifth?—rewatching of the modern *Doctor Who*, and I think one particular quote from that show sums up my entire life.

"We're all stories, in the end. Make it a good one, eh?" — *The Eleventh Doctor, Doctor Who*

I hope your story is brilliant.

You can reach me all over the web...
patriciadeddy.com
patricia@patriciadeddy.com

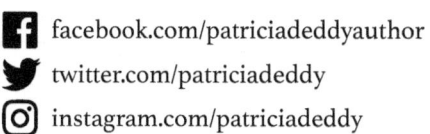

facebook.com/patriciadeddyauthor
twitter.com/patriciadeddy
instagram.com/patriciadeddy

ALSO BY PATRICIA D. EDDY

Away From Keyboard

Dive into a steamy mix of geekery and military prowess with the men and women of Hidden Agenda and Second Sight.

Breaking His Code

In Her Sights

On His Six

Second Sight

By Lethal Force

Fighting For Valor

Finding Their Forevers (a holiday short story)

Call Sign: Redemption

Braving His Past

Gone Rogue (an Away From Keyboard spinoff series)

Rogue Protector

Rogue Officer

Dark PNR

These novellas will take you into the darker side of the paranormal with vampires, witches, angels, demons, and more.

Forever Kept

Immortal Hunter

Wicked Omens

Storm of Sin

By the Fates

Check out the COMPLETE By the Fates series if you love dark and steamy tales of witches, devils, and an epic battle between good and evil.

By the Fates, Freed

Destined: A By the Fates Story

By the Fates, Fought

By the Fates, Fulfilled

In Blood

If you love hot Italian vampires and and a human who can hold her own against beings far stronger, then the In Blood series is for you.

Secrets in Blood

Revelations in Blood

Holidays and Heroes

Beauty isn't only skin deep and not all scars heal. Come swoon over sexy vets and the men and women who love them.

Mistletoe and Mochas

Love and Libations

Restrained

Do you like to be tied up? Or read about characters who do? Enjoy a fresh COMPLETE BDSM series that will leave you begging for more.

In His Silks

Christmas Silks

All Tied Up For New Year's

In His Collar

www.ingramcontent.com/pod-product-compliance
Lightning Source LLC
Chambersburg PA
CBHW070051030726
47506CB00002B/430